OF MICE AND MURDER

A BETTY SNICKERDOODLE MYSTERY (#6)

PEPPER FROST

WORKING STRATEGY

OF MICE AND MURDER

Paperback ISBN-13: 978-1-970044-13-3

Hardcover ISBN-13: 978-1-970044-16-4

Large print paperback ISBN-13: 978-1-970044-19-5

CHAPTER 1

"Look, Angie," Bea Sickles said way too loudly, even considering the noise of the storm outside. "Stand up and turn around! Look at who's waiting in line. It's the cash cows!"

Bea punctuated her announcement with an equally inappropriate cackle. "It's just like I told you. Those divas would never let a little rain ruin their moment in the sun."

Nearly eighty years old, Bea stood in the second row of chairs near the ballroom stage in her charming, Christmas-themed inn, Betty Snickerdoodle's Christmas Inn & Ranch. In her small, bony hand, she was holding her cane by its middle and waving it energetically at the ball-room's hallway doors. She had to make absolutely sure her young friend and business partner, Angela Garcia, noticed the new arrivals.

Bea and Angela and a small crowd of local luminaries were settling in for a performance of *The Ratcatcher* on the ballroom stage. The ballroom itself had been hurriedly transformed—more or less—into a community theater for the occasion. Five rows of eight chairs, with an aisle in the middle, had been set in front of the stage.

Outside, the biggest January storm to hit the wine country in decades had been raging all day, with no sign of letting up.

Winds howled, lightning flashed, thunder cracked, and rain lashed the huge French doors of the ballroom. At times, the rain pelted the roof so hard, it sounded like ping-pong balls dropping from the sky! And while long velvet drapes covered the French doors, the transom windows on top were bare, allowing occasional bolts of lightning to illuminate the entire room.

"A *little* rain?" Angela cried. "I bet half the roads in Napa Valley are flooded!"

Despite the truly terrible weather, Bea was at least partly right: VIP guests of the theater company had begun to arrive (some of them, anyway) and find their seats. The play's theme had inspired a few of them—horse people themselves—to turn up in hunting garb, perhaps figuring their tall, expensive riding boots were equally sensible for navigating foot-deep puddles. Most of the others dressed as one would expect of dames of the social register.

Some looked happy. Some looked skeptically curious. All looked glad to be out of the rain and wind.

"C'mon, get up, Angie. Look, by the door. And while you're at it, check out my special outfit." Bea had her hand on the zipper of her velour track suit—her all-purpose solution for whenever she needed to call herself "dressed."

Angela's own outfit suited the occasion: dark slacks and a white top, her chestnut hair tied up in a loose, pretty bun. She girded herself for what might be under Bea's jacket.

"OK. Unzip. And please tell me you're not trying to offend everybody."

"Ha! It's nothing but an homage to the murder mystery genre."

Bea opened her jacket to reveal a baggy t-shirt with an image of an old poster for Agatha Christie's *A Murder Is Announced*.

Angela looked pleased—not because she considered the t-shirt suitable attire for the event, which was intended to honor the donors who were keeping the community theater afloat. She was just remembering Bea's other recent t-shirt choices. By comparison, this one was a relief.

"Oh, wait! What's on the back?" Angela said. Her expression suggested she wasn't planning on getting tricked by Bea again.

Bea snorted. "Nothing, girlie. Trust me." Bea shrugged her jacket off her shoulders to confirm that she spoke the truth.

"Hmm. I liked *A Murder Is Announced*, but as far as Christie's plays go, why didn't you choose *The Mousetrap?* You know… ratcatcher… mousetrap."

"Good point, Angie. Bowditch stole half the plot of *The Ratcatcher* from each of Christie's excellent works. Unfortunately, the whole of *The Ratcatcher* is a lot less than the sum of its pilfered parts! Now stand up, will ya? Look who's arriving!"

Angela dutifully stood up, turned around, and spotted the theater company's two most generous benefactors at the check-in table, where her friend Connie was taking tickets. Bijou, Connie's copper-colored miniature dachshund, was sitting quietly under the table. Angela acknowledged her mother, Maria, who was helping Connie, with a little wave. They'd been through a lot in the past few days. Angela now saw Maria in a different light and with deeper gratitude.

The two arriving donors looked the part of socialites, though perhaps more like socialites of a few decades past. They both wore heavy pearl necklaces and earrings. One was in her sixties and the other in her late twenties.

The older, more slender woman fussed with her perfect wheat-colored chignon as she walked toward the rows of seats. Her shiny red fingernails flicked stray raindrops off her hair and her shoulders as she moved. Walking a half-step behind her, the younger, taller woman had dark brown hair in a plain, chin-length cut parted in the center.

Bea gestured wildly to the women.

"Yoohoo! Fancy gals! We've got your special seats all warmed up for ya!"

The younger of the VIPs looked to her left and right and over her shoulder.

Bea snickered and yelled again. "I'm talking to your friend! Over here, Vicky! Front row!"

Angela cringed. "I thought she preferred Victoria."

"What's the other one's name again?"

"Bea, you know that's Tibby. They were just here a couple of days ago."

"Oh, right. I guess she looks plumper in that peach dress. She looks like a juicy peach!"

"She's obviously not at all 'plump,' Bea. You might want to keep that opinion to yourself."

Bea unleashed another of her signature cackles. Several seated guests winced and scanned the room for the source of the noise.

"That's the whole point, girlie! Those golden geese are begging to be wound up. You can't expect me not to do the job."

Angela shook her head. "Can you at least be nice to Tibby? You know she's more easily upset—"

"C'mon, Angie. We don't have to suck up to these snobs—let alone feel sorry for them. We already gave them the best seats," Bea said with fake indignation, waving her hand over the backs of the front row seats. "Just kidding. I've seen *The Ratcatcher* before. I don't care if the richies take the best seats."

"You know you're pretty rich yourself—"

Bea ignored her. "I hope the littler one sits in front of me so I can see better. You know I'm vertically challenged. Oops! I hope it's OK with the chief of the politeness police if I say that about *myself*," Bea said, glaring at Angela melodramatically. "Then again, anything or anyone could fall off the stage of this rinky-dink production. Maybe I'd be safer with the stout one in front of me—"

"Bea! That wouldn't be appropriate even if Tibby were, you know, stout. And anyone can see she is not—not the least bit."

"For Pete's sake, what's wrong with a little fun?" Bea said, plopping back down in her chair as the two expensively dressed women arrived at their seats. "Welcome, ladies!"

Leaning toward them, Bea turned her nose up and sniffed dramatically. "Is there a wet dog in the house? Sorry, Vickster—must be that jacket of yours!"

Victoria looked down at her tailored lavender jacket and sniffed. "It can't be me," she said patiently, turning in her seat to look at Bea. "Everyone knows boiled wool is waterproof."

"Must be you then, Tubby—I mean, Tibby," Bea said. Tibby's eyes widened, then narrowed as she stifled a pout.

"Bea!" Angela said, wondering how many more times that one-word interjection would leave her lips tonight.

"Sorry, Tibby. All in good fun. You're not as fashionably underfed as Vicky, but she's had a couple more decades to diet. You hungry, Vicks? You look it." Bea reached under her seat and pulled out a grease-stained paper bag full of popcorn. "Here, help yourself."

Tibby's mouth fell open as she cocked her head to stare at Bea.

"Sorry, Tubs—I mean, Tibs. You want some?" Bea dove into the bag for a choice kernel and tossed it into Tibby's mouth. "There you go!"

Tibby coughed in surprise and spit the popcorn out into her hand, then held her hand out in front of herself and stared at it. Angela quickly extended her own hand between Victoria and Tibby to catch the kernel.

"Don't worry, Tibby. I'll take care of that for you," Angela said, sitting back down. Bea smirked, her shoulders shaking with suppressed laughter.

Tibby looked up at the stage lights, her hand involuntarily moving to her throat. A mix of spotlights and smaller lanterns was hanging from an aluminum scaffold that stood on the floor in front of the stage, just a few feet from the first row. The apparatus stretched almost the width of the ballroom and reached more than halfway to the ballroom's soaring ceiling.

"The lights are so close," Tibby said. "And so *big*."

"That's because they're professional grade,"

Angela said. "So is the structure. It's perfectly safe."

"Ignore the dings. They rent out the older stuff at a discount," Bea said. "Still works fine!"

The sky lit up again just as Todd, the show's stage manager, hustled over to the empty seat next to Victoria and Tibby. Todd had a full head of dark brown hair, a very thick beard, and a disproportionately large belly.

Angela wanted to like Todd, yet even after two weeks of his presence at the inn, she still wasn't sure she trusted him. She was inclined to give him the benefit of the doubt, partly because it was her nature, but mainly because Connie had developed a crush on him while volunteering for the theater.

Todd greeted the socialites warmly, then looked behind them toward Bea.

"Oh look, Angie! It's Humpty—"

"Hi, Todd!" Angela shouted, gently elbowing Bea on her shoulder.

"Owww," Bea blurted, but her whine dissolved into one of her ear-splitting laughs.

"I'm glad you ladies are having so much fun," Todd said. "Bea, would you believe Connie and I could hear you laughing from the entrance?" A tolerant smile was frozen on his face. "I hope I can ask you to keep quiet during the performance. It's time to get started."

"Sure! I know this is your big rehearsal," said Bea.

"It's not a rehearsal," Todd said. "It's—"

"I know. It's a 'special VIP preview,'" Bea said dismissively, making unnecessary quote signs with her bony fingers. "But it's the same thing, right? Since you haven't had any rehearsals, I mean."

"We've been rehearsing all week," Todd said.

"But not with the sets," Bea said. "Those stairs still weren't even finished as of yesterday. That reminds me—Vicky, Tibby, you two better watch for falling debris."

Tibby blanched and stared up at the spotlights again. Angela reached for Tibby's shoulder and touched it reassuringly. "She's joking, Tibby. Honestly."

Todd sighed and stood up to leave. "Excuse me, ladies. Time for the traditional *Ratcatcher* speech—"

"Where you tell us never to reveal the big twist? I'll never forget it. That was the best part when I saw the play," Bea roared again. "And don't you worry, any mystery writer worth her salt knows not to spoil the ending."

Bea had made her millions as the unlikely queen of treacly holiday romances under her Betty Snickerdoodle pen name, but she'd recently added mystery writing to her repertoire. She was enjoying it so much, she'd even started referring to herself as "the Jessica Fletcher of Napa Valley." This new nickname hadn't caught on yet with anyone but Bea herself.

"Don't worry, everyone," Bea said loudly, to anyone who might hear her. Then she made a dramatic impression of zipping her lips, looking around to be sure no one missed it.

Todd stood in front of the stage and called for the audience's attention. Just over half the chairs set out for the performance were occupied. Not a bad turnout, considering the horrible weather.

Todd began by thanking the cast, the crew—everyone involved in pulling the production together.

"He's not here, but I'd like to thank my new boss," Todd continued. "If he hadn't let me skip new-hire orientation, we couldn't have pulled this off."

Bea nudged Angela. "Gee, Angie, *shocker!* We know Todd's new employer wouldn't want competency to take root accidentally!" Then she let loose a cackle and half the audience stared in her direction. "Oops!" she cried, quickly "rezipping" her mouth shut.

Next, Todd called out Victoria and Tibby as the "diamond donors." When he asked them to take a bow, they looked especially pleased.

"Lastly, an important request. Traditionally, the stage manager asks the audience of every performance of *The Ratcatcher* to keep the show's twist ending a secret. I now ask you to protect the secret that has helped make Clara Bowditch's work the longest running American play in history."

The audience clapped politely, but their applause was drowned out by a gust of wind that shook the French doors, followed by another bolt of lightning. Tibby gasped audibly.

"Perfect timing," laughed Todd. "As you know, the storm has knocked out cell service, but please turn your phones off anyway, so they won't interrupt the show if service is restored. And remember, no video or photos.

"Without further ado, ladies and gentlemen, Clara Bowditch's *The Ratcatcher*."

As the lights went down, eerie, whistled strains of "A-Hunting We Will Go" began to play in the background. The curtain opened to a dilapidated

New England mansion, the scene lit only by blue footlights.

As the tune faded out, the crackling sound of a transistor radio replaced it. The announcer of a 1960s human interest program said, "Everyone connected with the operation ended up dead. And so ends the fascinating story—"

The stage lights slowly came up, revealing the details of the dated sitting room and library of an aging country mansion. A young woman in a gingham dress walked in and turned off the wooden radio, which sat on an end table next to the faded sofa.

"That character's Ellen, the naïve and earnest new owner of the mansion," Bea said, not bothering to whisper. "If I didn't know Lorelei was playing her, I'd say she reminds me of you, Angie!"

Angela frowned and shushed softly.

"What? I mean because you'll inherit *this* inn business someday!"

"Shh!"

The storm outside intruded again with lightning that illuminated the room. Members of the audience gasped and murmured.

"I told you we should have insisted they cancel the show," Angela murmured in Bea's ear.

Then the thunder arrived with a boom, but on

stage, Ellen took it in stride. She fussed over the sofa and glanced at the front door of the mansion, as if setting things just right for someone who would soon arrive.

"Pay close attention, ladies. Don't let the storm distract you," Bea croaked as she poked her head between Victoria and Tibby. "There's no pause and rewind with a murder mystery play. You only get one chance to pick up the clues!"

By midway through the first act, Bea had abandoned her lukewarm efforts at politeness and was laughing out loud at the latest in a string of distractions on stage.

Victoria turned around and looked at her with strained patience. "Bea, this play is not a comedy. Haven't you noticed you're the only one laughing?"

"Haven't you noticed they've barely gotten a single detail right? At least the old sofa's holding up!"

"You probably didn't need to yell out 'watch out for the bum leg,'" Angela sighed.

"Of course I did. Safety first!"

Tibby turned in her seat and looked pleadingly

at Bea. "Miss Sickles, you know I have a special—a personal—interest in this production."

Looking distressed, Tibby leaned toward Victoria and whispered something that neither Bea nor Angela heard.

Tibby turned to Bea again. "I'm sure you can understand, I'd like to see if my money was invested as promised."

Bea nodded, her shoulders shaking as she stopped laughing and got herself under control. "Sorry, Tibby. It's just that that sofa really could be dangerous. I've seen it close up. There's a nail—"

A sound of groaning metal came from above.

The audience gasped as a spotlight broke free from the truss. The clamp that had held it slanted toward the stage was dangling half-open from the rod, and the light now swung heavily on its safety cable, which looked much too delicate to hold it.

"It's starting to go faster!" Tibby squeaked.

"That… can't… be," Angela said. "It has to slow down."

Though it seemed impossible, the lamp appeared to gain momentum as it sailed first over the foot of the stage, then back toward the front row.

Another terrifying creak came from the scaffold just as a bolt of lightning once more lit up the room. Everyone saw the massive spotlight drop another foot as it lurched away from the stage and barreled toward the audience—straight toward Tibby.

Tibby dove to the floor with a yelp. Then all the lights of the ballroom flickered and went dark.

CHAPTER 2

The lights flickered back on after a beat.

Victoria looked warily at the swinging spotlight. It was wobbling and still moving far too fast for comfort, but its cable kept it firmly at a safe distance.

Tibby was cowering on the floor and weeping softly, half under her chair, mumbling incoherently about whether this was her punishment for not responding to the crew's requests for more money and whether someone had rigged the light to fall.

"Oh, Victoria, should we have—" Tibby started to say.

"Tibby, I know the cable looks thin, but it's

made of steel," Angela pleaded. "You're safe. Please don't worry."

"Yeah, Angie, but what about the hook?" Bea said. "You know how the old plot goes—maybe later we'll find someone softened the hook up with a file."

The light sailed by again, its momentum finally waning. "Was that another creak I heard? Hold on, little hook. You can do it!" Bea implored, then snorted with laughter.

"I'm just kidding," Bea said, still laughing. Tibby only cried harder.

"For heaven's sake, Tibby," Victoria hissed. "Just come over here and out of the way!"

Tibby looked sheepish as she stood up and hurried toward Victoria, who stood a couple of feet out of the path of the light.

"I'm sorry. It's just those... those demands I've been getting. Those threats from the crew—"

"We don't know they were from the crew, Tibby."

"That's what they said. Who else could it have been?"

Victoria started to respond, then pursed her lips and stayed quiet.

The actors gathered near the foot of the stage

and looked bleakly at the audience. Todd hustled down the aisle to stand in front of the first row.

"Don't worry, folks!" he said. He tried to grab the swaying lamp, but it was just out of reach. "See? It's not even close enough to hurt anyone. The clamp must not have been fully closed. A mistake, but no harm done—that's what the safety cable's for. It did its job perfectly. We'll reset the lights and check all the clamps and we can start back up."

Todd leaned to his right and cupped his hand by his ear. "Do I hear corks popping? Look, down by the fireplace—our sponsors are at the ready with champagne and tempting snacks. Please enjoy an early intermission and refreshments while we fix the light."

Angela touched Victoria's damp wool sleeve. "Would you and Tibby join me for a glass of bubbly, Victoria?"

"You seemed awfully frightened there, Tibs," Bea said a few minutes later. The four of them were standing next to the champagne table. Tibby had quickly downed a flute and was grabbing a second from the table.

"The stage light drop—that's a classic murder mystery technique. But trust me, it always involves an actor getting offed, never anyone in the audience. Right, Angie?"

Tibby's face crumpled again, and she quickly slugged half of her fresh glass of champagne.

"Tibby, please," Victoria said impatiently, "No one's out to get you—certainly no one on the crew, anyway. In our position, of course we have enemies, but it simply makes no sense that someone from the play wants to hurt you."

"You haven't received the threats. One of the housekeepers read one to me that came in the mail. She thought it was a scam at first—"

"It most certainly was a scam," Victoria said. "Who ever heard of a theater crew pressuring the biggest donors? By mail, no less? I suspect it was a two-bit phishing expedition. Some criminal probably bought, or stole, a list of charitable donors. They've no doubt moved on to another mark. But in the unlikely event Roberta put her underpaid stagehands up to guilting us, that's a scam, too. Either way, no one's going to threaten to kill you for a little more money. Much less actually *do* it."

"She's right, Tibs," Bea said. "They can't get more money out of you unless you're alive."

"The crew aren't just underpaid. They're *volunteers*," Angela added. "And very shorthanded. When would they even have time to harass you?"

"But that's what they said every time they asked for more money," Tibby replied. "I'm sure it wasn't random scammers. They knew all about *The Ratcatcher.* They even mentioned the play moving to the inn—"

"Tibby, even if it actually was the crew, you can't take the bait." Victoria paused and softened her voice. "You can't let people know they can bully you."

"Easy for you to say, Victoria," Tibby said. Her voice cracked and she started to tear up again. "You're not in my situation!"

"I know," Victoria said, her voice more soothing. She grabbed Tibby by the arm and eased her away from Bea and Angela. They could see Tibby growing more agitated, but they couldn't hear what Tibby and Victoria were saying. Angela frowned as Bea stepped to the side and craned her neck toward Victoria.

"'You can't let fear get the better of you,'" Bea said. "That's what Victoria's saying. 'You'll become a favorite target, Tibby.' She's right! Now she's telling Tibby, 'We—you—have nothing to feel guilty about.'"

"Bea, at least turn toward me. They can see you trying to eavesdrop."

Victoria took a delicately embroidered handkerchief out of her pocket and handed it to Tibby, who dabbed at her eyes and nodded as the two of them walked back to Bea and Angela.

"I think the more important question is, what happened to all the money Roberta raised?" Victoria said. "Not just from us. These sponsors must have paid handsomely for these tables."

"Todd barely spent anything on lumber," Bea added. "And it shows."

"And with volunteers, there are no labor costs," Angela said. "Unless… is Grayson Gates volunteering? He must command a high salary."

"I should hope he's donating his time," Victoria said. "But if Roberta was determined to hire a show pony director from New York City, she should've spent her own money."

"Roberta? Her own money?" Angela said, confused. "Why do you say that?"

But before Victoria could answer, the lights flashed softly on and off. Victoria and Tibby turned away and started walking back toward the front of the room. Xylophone chimes floated through the ballroom.

Angela turned around and saw Todd weaving deftly through the crowd, encouraging people to take their seats.

"Humpty moves well for a big guy," Bea said to

Angela as Todd strode past them. "He's like a thoroughbred."

"Legs like strong, slender pistons?"

"With a big, round barrel on top. Maybe he's more like a pregnant thoroughbred."

Angela clucked her tongue and sighed.

Despite the hints from the lights and the xylophone, some guests seemed to enjoy the champagne too much to leave it behind. Todd approached small groups of people, smiling broadly and making a scooping motion with his arms as if guiding livestock into a pen.

"Quickly take your seats, everyone," he said. "We're ready to pick up where we left off. We've got another twenty minutes of Act One and you are *not* going to want to miss a moment!"

"Can you believe there was sheer panic in here thirty minutes ago?" Angela said, sitting down next to Bea.

"A medicinal nip or two and a few snacks and everyone's happy as clams again," Bea chortled.

"I think the bad luck's behind the crew. I predict the rest of the performance will go without a hitch," Angela said brightly.

"Um, girlie, have you kept count of all the 'bad luck' they've already had?" Bea said. "Not just that flyaway spotlight. I've run out of fingers and toes counting all the on-stage gaffes. Way too many even for a rehearsal."

"For the hundredth time, it's a *preview performance*," Angela said, remembering the reviewer she'd secretly arranged for. She scanned the room, wondering if the journalist had braved the storm.

More lightning brightened the ballroom. Bea looked around. "Hey, Angie, where are Tibby and Victoria? Shouldn't they have beaten us back here?"

"Maybe they changed seats. Tibby said during the break that she wanted to move away from the lights."

Bea let out another hoarse laugh. "I could say I'm surprised that Tibby's such a fraidy-cat, but that would be a lie."

"The safety chain did its job. But who could blame her for being nervous?" Angela said. "Especially with those threats she's been receiving. I'm not sure Victoria's managed to convince her the crew couldn't be behind them."

Bea scanned the room. Almost everyone had returned to their seats. The few lingerers at the back had finally been coaxed into leaving the refreshments behind.

"Angie, could Tibby and Victoria have left without saying goodbye?"

"Tibby might have wanted to, but they made such an effort to get here—why head back out into the storm without seeing the play? Besides, they're the guests of honor. They probably just went to the ladies' room."

The ballroom lights went down again and a spotlight focused on Todd, who was back in front of the stage.

"Aren't we all feeling better now?" Todd announced. "There's almost nothing a little champagne can't cure, right?"

A few guests laughed nervously.

"Rest assured, we've triple-checked everything. No danger whatsoever," he said. He looked up at the lights and made an exaggerated praying gesture, then chuckled. "Please settle back in as we pick up where we left off in Act One. In case anyone's a little tipsy, I'll recap what we've seen so far.

"It's the late 1960s in woodsy, old-money New England. Our young marrieds, Ellen and William, have inherited a country house from Ellen's distant great aunt. Once-majestic Helliwell Hall isn't just in disrepair, though. It's encumbered by unpaid property taxes. The mansion has hosted the Oakleigh Hunt Club for decades, but its well-heeled members' fees haven't been sufficient to stave off financial ruin.

"Despite its problems, Ellen has fallen in love with the old place. So she's got a plan: The horsey set will keep using Helliwell Hall as their home base while Ellen and her husband launch a new line of business, inviting paying guests to stay in the mansion's many bedrooms.

"'*Town & Country* says B&Bs are all the rage in Britain,' Ellen reasons. 'Surely they'll be popular here soon. Anglophiles will love the foxhunting theme. We won't even have to renovate!' Will worries it's risky, but can't help but hope his pretty wife is right.

"Adding to the drama: Ellen just discovered a dark secret in her great aunt's diary: Honora realized—too late—that the foxhunters had been swindling her for years…. That raises the stakes, doesn't it?

"As we resume our performance, most of the equestrians have enjoyed their post-hunt tea and departed, but the few remaining riders, tongues loosened by liquor, have revealed they already resent the tourists—the B&B's first guests. As huntmaster Frederic sneered, 'We're reduced to a country sideshow for the… *middle classes.*'

"Without further ado, ladies and gentlemen, the continuation of Act One of Clara Bowditch's classic play, *The Ratcatcher.*"

Todd slipped into the wings. The lights dimmed, then shined on center stage as the curtain opened.

Angela leaned over to Bea and whispered, "Todd's an impressive speaker. You have to admit he's full of surprises."

"I agree. Some of them even pleasant. So why is this show such a festival of incompetence?"

"Angie, that's the third blown line since they restarted the show," Bea chuckled. "Too bad bungled lines won't terrify anybody. I could use another snack break."

"No one would notice the mistakes if you didn't keep talking and laughing at all the wrong times," Angela whispered, index finger on her lips. She reached under her seat for Bea's popcorn and passed it to her.

"Always worrying about appearances," Bea said. "Now that Tibby and Vicky aren't here, nobody cares if we talk."

A patron two seats down spun in her chair and glared at Bea.

"My bad," Bea said, shrugging and shoving a fistful of kernels into her mouth. "Don't worry," she said, chomping loudly. "We're *finally* getting to the big finish of the first act."

Angela closed her eyes and tipped her head back.

A broad-shouldered woman with a booming voice was alone on stage. Her character was Edie Doyle, a sharp-tongued snob who'd had way too many cocktails at tea.

Though well into her sixties, the actress passed easily for the mid-fifties age of her character. She looked trim in beige breeches, tall boots, and a pale pink shirt with a tie that wrapped twice around the collar. Her velvet riding cap completed the look. The brim was tilted downward, shielding her eyes and covering her hair.

Edie gripped a pewter cup in one hand. As she lumbered unsteadily around the room, the cup waved about wildly, its tawny contents splashing onto the stage floor.

"Is it just me, or is her acting improving?" Bea said. "Tonight's Edie looks genuinely drunk."

"Something about her seems... off," Angela said. "I wish we could get a clear look at her face. The riding hat's in the way."

Bijou trotted on stage, dragging her leash. She sniffed the puddles and turned up her nose, then looked up at Edie expectantly.

A white-haired man in his early seventies, wearing a scarlet jacket and white breeches smudged with dirt, strode in and reached down for the dog's leash, looking slightly confused as he ad-libbed a line.

"I...I... couldn't resist bringing Rudy out from the kennel. Great run today, wouldn't you say, Edie?"

"That's Bijou!" Angela giggled. "Is she supposed to be on stage?"

"I don't recall any live animals when I saw this thing before. And a dachshund's a little small for foxhunting."

"Frederic, I just shlipped in here for a lil' privacy," Edie slurred. "Nobody's wish you—I mean, nobody following you?"

Frederic turned around. "I don't think so. Let me take care of that for you," he said, gently taking the cup.

"I'm awwight," she protested, yanking the cup back, spilling half its contents onto the stage. She wobbled away from Frederic and stepped on Bijou's toe. The dog let out a yowl and scurried backwards. "Sowwy, doggie," Edie said.

"Poor Bijou!" Angela blurted.

"I think she's OK, Angie," Bea whispered, pointing on stage. Bijou was happily sniffing around Frederic's feet. "But can we say the same for Edie? Doesn't this drunken act seem a little too good?"

Two inn guests, a man and a woman in their late twenties, appeared stage left at the sitting-room door, laughing boisterously. They wore youthful, clean-cut Sixties fashions—plaid Capri pants for her, corduroys and an argyle sweater for him.

"Look, honey," the woman squealed, pointing at the equestrians. "They're still in their riding clothes. He's all dirty from the hunt. Oh, I want a candid shot!"

The woman crouched in the corner and aimed her Instamatic at Frederic and Edie. She clicked the shutter and the film and the flash cube noisily advanced.

"Just one more," she said in their general direction. "Mister, do you have your jacket and hat handy, by chance? Oooh, your riding crop would really make the shot."

Edie slammed the pewter cup onto the end table, splashing more liquid over its sides. Then she drew her arm back for a punch and lunged drunkenly at the young woman.

As she dodged Edie's clumsy swing, the guest stumbled backward. Her male companion rushed first to steady her, then defend her, seemingly socking Edie right in the face. Bright magenta "blood" gushed from the neighborhood of Edie's nose as she staggered backwards.

"Not a bad fight scene. That blood, though," Bea snorted. "Isn't that the raspberry jam from the breakfast room? And why's it pouring down her cheek instead of from her nose?"

Angela giggled. "Shouldn't we just be glad it's on the right face?"

Ellen and Will rushed in, looking believably alarmed. Will hurried the young couple out of the room while Ellen led Edie to the tattered sofa. Edie sat down with Ellen on one side of her, Frederic on the other.

"Stay here," Ellen said. "I'll get a towel. Sit back and hold your chin up. I don't think your nose is broken. Pinch it. The bleeding should stop."

"I'm fine!" said Edie, seeming slightly sobered up by the scuffle. "I'd shust like to… be alone." She leaned back and brushed the back of her hand against her forehead melodramatically. Her eyes closed as if she were about to nod off. "Please."

Ellen and the huntmaster nodded at each other and walked out of the room, Ellen dimming the lights before she slipped out the door.

Edie snored operatically. A pale, orange glow

could barely be seen in the corner of the partially draped library window, as if dawn were breaking.

Looking every bit a bewildered, rudely awakened drunk, Edie rose clumsily from the couch. She shook her head and looked around.

"Who's there?" she yelled toward the library's far entrance—offstage, to her left. "Oh, it's—it's just you! This is a surprise—"

A gloved hand reached from the wings and flipped a light switch on the library wall. Then the stage—and the ballroom—went completely dark.

"Wait—what are you doing?" Edie shouted. "Stop! You're hurting me! Why?!" A loud scuffle was heard, then a crash on the stage floor.

The soft security and exit lights of the ballroom came back on. On stage, the dawn glow in the library window reappeared, brighter now. Ellen walked purposefully into the scene and pulled the drapes wide open. Then she spotted Edie's lifeless body on the floor and let out a warbly scream. The stage lights dimmed again, and the curtain whipped to a close.

The lights in the ballroom came up and the audience murmured and halfheartedly applauded.

"Some scream. That's supposed to be the big dramatic moment of the whole play!" Bea laughed. "At least they had a few high points toward the end. The fight was pretty good. Best of all, we're halfway through the show."

Angela looked at Bea and shook her head disapprovingly, but then she, too, couldn't help but laugh. Others in the audience were stretching and turning in their seats, contemplating their options for their second intermission.

Then from behind the curtain came a bark from Bijou, followed by several more—and a bloodcurdling shriek.

"Now *that* was a realistic scream. Better late than never, Lorelei!" Bea roared.

Bijou began barking anxiously, and Lorelei screamed again, even louder.

"That wasn't realistic, Bea," Angela said. "That scream was *real!*"

Lorelei frantically drew one side of the curtain back. The cast crowded around the spot where Ellen had found Edie's body. The audience collectively inhaled as they realized Edie was still on the floor, unconscious. Those closest to the stage noticed a small puddle of blood near her head.

"I think she's… I think she's… she's really…." Lorelei babbled.

"Whoa. The blood looks real, too," Bea said. "Not like jam."

"She could have hit her head on that sofa leg as

she fell," Angela said, jumping to her feet and leaning forward. "Look—is that nail still sticking out of the sofa?"

From the stage, Lorelei shouted, "Todd! Help! She's really hurt!"

Todd was standing near one of the side doors, close to the wings. He bounded to the front of the room and called for everyone's attention. Several audience members stood up. The rumblings from the audience grew louder.

And in all this time, the actress lying on stage still hadn't moved.

"Stay in your seats and stay calm, everyone," Todd announced. "I'm in charge here."

"Hold on a minute, Todd," Angela interrupted. "You know I'm the manager of the inn."

Todd ignored her and continued. He placed his hands on his hips inside his open jacket for a moment.

Angela let out a loud squeak as she sucked in a lungful of air. She whispered urgently to Bea, "Did you see that?!"

"I was just about to ask you the same question!" Bea was chuckling, despite the palpably anxious mood in the room.

Angela stared at Todd. She noticed that he'd put his hands down. His jacket was covering his hips once more. She lowered her voice. "I thought I saw a gun. *Did you see a gun?*"

Bea clucked her tongue. "Yes, but that's not what I was going to ask you about. Fooey! You missed it."

Todd set his arms akimbo again inside his jacket and barked at everyone to calm down.

"Wait, there it is again. Look—look at his shirt!" Bea said.

Then Todd seemed to hear them. Or maybe it was the other voices in the room now nervously asking *was that a gun?* that grabbed his attention. He hurriedly lowered his hands and closed his blazer, but not before Angela finally spotted what Bea had seen.

"O... M... G.... What on earth?" Angela said.

"I know!" Bea said, laughing hysterically now, despite the shaky voices and growing feeling of chaos all around her.

"Wait—what's so funny? Do we even know what we saw? And Edie still hasn't moved, has she? Bea... no one seems to be helping her. What if she's... dead?"

"You're right, girlie. I'll behave," Bea said, collecting herself and speaking quietly. "But if she is dead, think about the silver lining. With this bunch of characters, my next murder mystery's gonna write itself!"

"Speaking of characters," Angela said nervously, "I don't see any sign of Tibby and Victoria, do you?"

CHAPTER 3

"Knock knock!" Angela said, as Bea cracked open the door to her suite.

"You're awfully cheerful for this late hour," Bea said.

"I guess it's 'cause I've got a special delivery. C'mon. You know you want it."

Angela had a drinks carrier in one hand. It was loaded up with two tall, milky iced coffees and paper plates and napkins. In the other hand she held a large pizza box. An irresistible aroma of pepperoni and cheese wafted from it as she walked into the room. "Double pep and cheese. Bonus: They even had decaf iced coffee."

Bea looked down at her threadbare nightie.

Even the sections without tears or holes were practically transparent.

Seeing Bea in her worst nightie would usually result in Angela politely trying, yet failing, to suppress a wince and avert her eyes. Yet tonight, Angela seemed unfazed. And Bea found herself feeling a little self-conscious—an odd sensation that put her off balance.

"I don't care what I've done to deserve this surprise visit," Bea said, shrugging. "I'll never reject a delectable nighttime snack. It'll be good fuel for my writing streak. Can you come back in twenty minutes? I'll finish the chapter I'm on and change into something more presentable."

"Don't be silly," Angela said, moving Bea's keyboard to make space for the pizza on her desk. "The pizza will get cold. Just throw on your robe if you're self-conscious," she added. "As if—right?"

Wheels started slowly turning in Bea's mind. She stared at Angela with her right eye half-closed, the brow above her left making a run for her hairline.

"Angie, it's nice that you brought some of my favorite treats, but don't you have a big day to prepare for? The guests are expecting a mighty-fine send-off after the good times of these past few days."

"I'm all ready," Angela said, flipping up the lid on the pizza box.

Tomorrow was the final day of the second-annual BettyCon conference, and Angela's schedule was packed to the max. There would be awards presentations to the "Bake It Like Betty" and ornament design contest winners, raffle drawings, and, most important, Angela's closing remarks. Bea assumed Angela had long since prepared a perfect speech, but that wouldn't normally stop her from polishing and rehearsing right up until she stood at the podium.

"In case you're wondering," Bea said, "I'm working on my new Christmas romance—the one about childhood pals reuniting and finding out they're more than just friends. I'm thinking of calling it *Candy Canes on Memory Lane*. I'm getting close to the end. Don't you want me to—"

"Nah. It's past nine o'clock. Time to clock out!" Angela said, loading up two plates with pizza.

"Angie, you know I like to work at night. If you don't need to prepare for tomorrow, why aren't you relaxing with your handsome prince?"

Angela carried the pizza plates to Bea's bed. She placed them in the middle of the holiday-themed bedspread and plopped down on the end, patting the spot next to her and nodding at Bea expectantly.

"Aseem's spending the night in Silicon Valley. He's got a breakfast meeting tomorrow. Enough about him."

Click-click-click, the pieces fell into place in Bea's mind. She turned away to hide her smirk and grab her robe off the hook in the bathroom.

"OK, spill the beans. Since when do you discourage me from finishing a new product? 'Fess up. Is something on your—"

"OK, enough already, Bea! You pried it out of me!" Angela blurted.

Bea stepped out of the bathroom and let loose a cackle.

"Girlie, your spy career's on hold. You're like a piglet fixin' to squeal. You haven't been this ready to burst since you got engaged and managed to keep it secret for a full fifteen seconds."

Angela frowned. "I guess—I do—I did—have something to tell you, but now I realize I'm being inappropriate. I shouldn't gossip."

"I see. I guess I should have said spill the *tea* instead of spill the beans," Bea snickered, plopping down on the end of the bed and grabbing her slice. "Gossiping's *not* inappropriate. In fact, it's essential to healthy information flow. Not to mention quality of life."

"No matter what you say, *I* know I shouldn't gossip. But it's not wrong if… if it's because I care about someone, is it?" Angela's expression suggested she wasn't waiting for an answer.

"Of coursh it ishnt," Bea mumbled through a mouthful of pizza.

"OK, good, because it's about Connie!" Angela squealed. "She's got a new man in her life. His name's Todd. She stopped by on her way home tonight just to tell me about him. She says they're just friends. But I can tell she really likes him."

Bea motioned toward the drink carrier and Angela passed her an iced coffee. "So what's the problem?"

"For one thing, you know she doesn't have the greatest track record in choosing men."

Connie Hollander had purchased the winery next door about a year ago. Since then, she'd thrown herself into building Heavenly West, a subsidiary of her family's famous Heavenly Mash Kentucky whiskey business. Like Angela, Connie had a passion for her work; it was the great glue of their friendship. But with her own love life on such a positive track, Angela secretly hoped Connie would also open herself up to new people.

The ugly memories of Connie's volatile former husband, though, always seemed to loom large.

"I want to be happy for her. But am I right that Billy Ray was the worst husband *ever*?"

"He's in the running, but he's got competition. You know, if we're including murderers and such. Aren't you getting a little ahead of yourself, though? Didn't Connie say she and Todd are just friends? Don't get me wrong—I'll take any excuse for late night gossip and my favorite pizza. But I'm not seeing the problem."

"It's just… with her famous family… couldn't she be a target for… scammers?"

"What are they like together? Is this Todd a professional Lothario? Has he bewitched Connie with stunning looks and hypnotic charm?"

"I haven't met him yet. But I'm guessing not. Connie met him volunteering for Pinot Playhouse Community Theater. They're putting on *The Rat-catcher*."

"*The Ratcatcher*! That old—"

"Yep. The Clara Bowditch classic."

"'Classic' is one word for it," Bea snorted. "I'm surprised anyone remembers it—I think I was about your age when it was a 'hit.'"

"Actually," Angela said, raising her index finger, "it's the longest running play in the country.

Off-off-Broadway, but still. Or is it off-off-off-Broadway?"

"Off-off-off-Broadway means New Hampshire, right? Or does it include high schools?" Bea guffawed, slapping her knee.

"I know you're a big fan of Mrs. Bowditch. You've read all of her mysteries—"

"It's true. I want to copy nearly every step of her career. But every writer has at least one dud to their name. *The Ratcatcher* is hers. That's the step I want to skip."

Bea eventually stopped laughing and collected herself. "Back to Todd. Let's assess the facts. He's hanging around with a bunch of unfulfilled divas and oddballs. Said oddballs dream of putting on a dusty whodunnit hardly anyone will want to see. And he's a do-gooder who does this for free—and for fun. Doesn't sound much like Billy Ray so far. And you say Connie seems really happy—and that she says they're just friends anyway."

"All true. Connie did say the theater group is 'like a bag of the nicest mixed nuts,'" Angela said, giggling and imitating Connie's sweet Kentucky drawl. "And she said that Todd's been volunteering full-time."

"If he can afford to volunteer full-time, maybe that proves he's not after her money."

"Maybe. Connie said that he moved here for a job," Angela sighed. "He arrived a couple months early to find a place to live. That's why he had time to help out Pinot Playhouse."

"Pinot Playhouse… that name rings a bell. Didn't their building burn to the ground last week?"

"It burned down? I heard about the fire, but I didn't know the place was destroyed."

Angela pulled her phone from her pocket for a quick internet search. "You're right. Looks like they won't be performing at that playhouse—at least, not for a long while. They're still working on something, though. Connie said she'd just left a crew meeting when she dropped by tonight."

"I hope they've found a way to put on their *Ratcatcher*. I'd kind of like to see it again. Maybe there's a reason that play's still going after all these years. Maybe I've got something to learn."

"Who knows? We might be able to turn one of your mystery books into a play someday. We could try for off-Broadway—or even the Great White Way."

"No way, girlie. I wanna learn how to do it right because Hollywood's gonna come calling first."

"Connie's going to bring Todd by tomorrow.

We can get the scoop about the show direct from the source."

"More important," Bea snickered, "We'll get our chance to size up Todd."

"BETTYCON 2 IS A WRAP!" Angela said from atop the ballroom stage. "Help yourselves to cocoa and cookies," she added, pointing to the overflowing tables by the fireplace at the back of the room. If you aren't rushing off to the airport, stay and mingle as long as you like."

Though the holidays had come and gone a few weeks before, the ballroom was decorated lavishly to match the inn's permanent yuletide theme. A massive wreath hung above the mantel, the streamers of its red velvet bow dangling several feet below the greenery. A fourteen-foot Christmas tree, decorated with Angela's abundant yet elegant style, stood in the corner, next to the French doors that led out to the expansive deck.

"If you've signed up for tonight's field trip to San Francisco, our dear friend Oliver has provided luxury shuttles to take you in safety and style," Angela said. She pointed to the back of the room, where Oliver stood next to the row of shiny urns full of cocoa. He looked neat as a pin in pressed chinos and a white button-down shirt, his sandy hair trimmed and tidy.

"Let the gals know who you are, Cutie Pie!" said Bea, who stood beside Angela onstage. Oliver had a mouthful of sugar cookie, but he blushed and complied with a shy wave. The large contingent of middle-aged women in the audience responded with a collective "Aww."

"Stop by the front desk to pick up your personal goodie bag," Angela continued. "If you're staying with us another night, you'll find yours in your room.

"Lastly, thank you so much for coming. Without you—Betty Snickerdoodle's most loyal fans—we couldn't have BettyCon. We love having you visit our little patch of Christmas here in the wine country. Bea and I will be here in the ballroom for a while, so find us and share any ideas you have to make next year's BettyCon even better than this one!"

"See ya next year, everybody!" shouted Bea.

While Bea lingered and took several bows, Angela didn't wait for the applause to die down before descending the center stairs to greet the fans.

"Mrs. Newberg, congratulations again on your second-place finish," Angela said warmly to one of the guests, a tall woman in her sixties with gray hair cropped in a close, practical style. The woman wore big round glasses on a thick chain, a nondescript wool cardigan, and plain slacks. Her sturdy brown Oxfords looked ancient but well cared-for. She'd pinned the red second-place ribbon through one of the buttonholes near the top of her sweater.

"The competition in the ornament contest was fierce this year," Angela added.

"Thank you," the woman replied. "And it's 'Ms. not Mrs.,' but please call me Roberta anyway. I haven't been called 'Ms. Newberg' since I retired. Hearing it makes me think I'll soon be monitoring a detention."

Angela giggled, but Roberta didn't crack a smile. Angela cleared her throat and sobered up her expression.

"Does that mean you were a principal, Ms. New—I mean, Roberta?"

"Until I retired a couple of years ago. Middle school principal for most of my career, though I started out as an English teacher."

"That's amazing," Angela said. "May I thank you? It might sound corny, but I'm grateful for all teachers, not just mine."

Roberta sniffed. "My career in education

began with a vision of nurturing young minds. Sadly, there is more room for soft-heartedness in the military than in a middle school. I wish I'd taught second or third graders instead. Indulging in crafting here at your conference reminded me of the innocent joy with which younger children approach art. At least you and Miss Sickles offered me the chance to stretch my creative muscles here at your convention."

"Our pleasure," Angela said. "Will you be joining the group heading to San Francisco? It's a lovely night to cross the Golden Gate Bridge—clear, with a bright moon. It's something to see, truly."

"I've crossed the bridge many times. I live here in Napa Valley."

"I'm sorry, I should have recognized your name—we don't have many locals attending BettyCon," Angela said. Out of the corner of her eye, she noticed Connie and a rather rotund, bearded man with thick dark hair at the entrance to the ballroom. "Would you excuse me a moment?"

Angela moved through the crowd to an open spot a few steps away and waved to catch Connie's attention. Connie grabbed the man's sleeve and they made their way through groups of chatting Betty fans toward the stage.

"See, Todd? I told you this ballroom is enormous," Angela heard Connie saying as she and Todd approached. "More than large enough, right?"

Todd didn't answer immediately. He was scanning the dimensions of the room and the stage as he walked behind her. "You're right, the room's large enough. Though the stage is not exactly—"

"Large enough for what?" Angela started to say. Behind her, Roberta overheard them and turned around, catching Connie by surprise.

"Roberta!" Connie said. "I didn't take you for a Betty Snickerdoodle fan."

"Nor I you," Roberta said.

"Actually, I'm—"

"Now Connie, I hope you're not going to say you're not a fan of mine," Bea cracked as she walked toward them from the stage.

"Bless your heart!" Connie said. "Of course not, I swear. I was just about to say that I'm actually your *neighbor.* Roberta, have you met Bea?"

"Not officially."

Bea extended her small, slender hand toward Roberta's more robust one. "Now it's official. Are you heading home tonight, Roberta?"

"As I explained to Angela, I live here in the Valley."

"That's right," Connie piped up. "I know Roberta from Pinot Playhouse, the community theater. That's where Todd and I met, too. Where are my manners? Todd Jameson, meet Bea Sickles and Angela Garcia."

Todd shook hands amiably with Bea and Angela.

"We heard there was a fire at the playhouse last week," Angela said.

"That's true, unfortunately," Roberta said evenly. "I suppose that the destruction of our playhouse has a silver lining of sorts, since it freed me up to attend your convention. I'd expected to be far too busy with our production of *The Ratcatcher*."

"So it's true—the building couldn't be saved?" Angela said.

Roberta sighed and nodded. "Apparently not. The insurance adjuster technically still has to rule on the matter. But it's clear we're out of commission for this season's production."

"That's why we're here," Connie said brightly. "Todd had an idea—"

Todd grabbed Connie's arm and pulled her toward him. The look on his face suggested he'd grabbed her more roughly than he intended.

"I was thinking just what Roberta was thinking. I didn't hear about the convention until it was too late, but I still wanted to see Betty Snicker-doodle's famous Christmas Inn & Ranch. With the play on hold, I had time. Betty's a household word —who doesn't love her?"

Connie looked up at Todd's face with a confused grin.

"Speaking of this lovely property, didn't you promise me a tour?" Todd said, looking at Connie. His smile looked forced and tinged with urgency.

Connie turned to Angela. "I shouldn't have *promised*—I was just hoping Angela might be willing to show us around. What do you think? Are you too tired from three days of BettyCon, honey?"

Angela scanned the room. A slow-but-steady line had formed near the hallway doors. Guests were making their way to Oliver's buses or heading for home. A few die-hards were chatting near the cookie tables.

"Sure! Let's do a short tour."

"I've got things covered here," Bea said. She turned to Roberta, who was looking at Todd and Connie with a puzzled expression. "Roberta, would you like to hang with me a while?"

Roberta scanned Todd's face for a beat, then turned to Bea and nodded.

"Great! Let's take the French doors to the deck and avoid the traffic jam," Angela said to Connie and Todd. "We'll get a nice view of your place from that direction, too, Connie—in case Todd hasn't seen it yet."

A peachy blush bloomed on Connie's cheeks and the three of them walked toward the deck.

Bea turned to Roberta. "Looks to me like Connie's got a crush on Todd."

"I hadn't noticed," Roberta said gruffly. "I barely know them."

Bea grinned crookedly. "Not even Todd? Doesn't he help run the place at your community theater?"

"My focus is always on the fundraising—and other strategic issues," Roberta sniffed. "Todd helps with the stage crews. Manages the various teams, I guess you'd say. He only just joined the company a few weeks ago, so he's still quite new."

"Sounds like that was a lucky break, getting a volunteer to fill such a big job on short notice."

"Todd would say as much. I think we'd have done perfectly well without him, but, thanks to the fire, I guess we'll never know. Anyway, as far as your friend's romantic prospects go, I've learned there's never a shortage of courtship melodrama at a community theater. I find it's mostly pain with no evident gain. Part of the artistic process, I suppose. But not the most life-enhancing part. Perhaps your friend Connie will fare better than most."

"Bless her heart," Bea said.

"Thanks for coming," Angela said, shutting the door of her suite behind Bea. Bea plopped down in the guest chair and Angela flopped back down on her bed face first, her cheek landing in the indentation she'd previously made in her pillow. "I'd have stopped by your suite, but I'm too tired to move. I'm glad I showed Todd around, even if it took my last drop of energy. I could tell it was important to Connie. What a week!"

"No wonder you're tired. Awesome job with BettyCon, Angie. As the owner of this place, I direct you to give yourself a big, fat bonus."

"I should remind you that you made me company president. I'm supposed to make those sorts of financial decisions. Lucky for us both, I'm too exhausted to argue," Angela said, her words partly muffled by her pillow. "Besides, I have to admit, BettyCon was pretty great. It helped a lot that you weren't doing jail time like last year. I think you got to talk to every fan who wanted to meet you."

"I try not to think about my time in Beef Jerky's bed-and-no-breakfast," Bea said with a chuckle.

"Beef Jerky" was the smart-alecky nickname Bea used for Sergeant McGregor, the cop who led the modest police outpost in their quiet little wine-country village. Though deliberately rude, it might have included a dollop of endearment—one could never be sure with Bea—but there was little doubt that McGregor perceived it as an insult. He'd tried responding in kind, calling Bea names like "Tater Tot." His needling skills were strictly amateur compared to Bea.

"Bea, we've made progress on our relationship with local law enforcement. Don't you want to keep it up?"

"Are you saying I can't call him Beef Jerky behind his back? If I have to be nice to him even when he's not here, I might burst into flames," Bea said with a croaky laugh, slapping her knee enthusiastically. "Listen, girlie, you asked me to come by to hear about the grand tour with Connie and her new crush, but can't it wait until tomorrow?"

"Sorry," Angela said, rolling over. With a soft groan she sat up with her back against the headboard. "I'll rally. I'm tired, but this can't wait."

Angela explained that Todd and Connie had come up with an idea to save their production of *The Ratcatcher:* They were hoping to present it at the inn.

"Todd said he was worried about the donors. Most of the funds have already been spent on things like making sets and costumes—and many of them were destroyed in the fire. They've spent money on advertising, too. There's nothing left to refund to the donors, most of whom are VIPs around here. Todd's asking us to donate the use of the ballroom stage in return for a sponsorship. He said they've sold quite a few tickets—"

"I was with you until you said they'd sold a lot of tickets to that old relic," Bea laughed.

"It's not hard to believe! People love live theater. People love supporting their community. And people love a mystery. Look what happened to you—your first mystery was a best-seller right out of the gate."

"I hope you're not saying that wasn't entirely due to my talent. But either way, you know my mysteries are modern. *The Ratcatcher*'s dated and dusty."

"Loads of people love historical mysteries, and they love re-visiting old ones, too. *The Ratcatcher*'s got a faded-glory mansion, rich people swindling each other, a suspicious death…. Who doesn't love that sort of thing? I know for a fact *you* do!"

"Are you trying to convince me or yourself? You know you can decide whatever you want. Why not just go for it, girlie?"

"I'm leaning that way. It's mostly the timing. I was actually looking forward to a rest after Betty-Con. Todd insists they won't need my help at all, but I doubt that's true."

"I'd like to see them try to do it without you," Bea snickered.

"That's a vote of confidence in my management skills, right? I'm sure you're not implying I'm a control freak. The biggest issue is the changes they'd need to make. The ballroom stage was never meant for anything but our awards presentations and business functions. For starters, we'd have to take down the stairs in the center. Hopefully, Aseem knows the best way to detach them. Then wings also have to be added somehow on the sides.

It's also much smaller than their current stage, so they'd have to figure out how to build new sets or adapt what survived the fire. There probably are other things we haven't thought of yet.

"And here's the real kicker: they want to have their first performance on schedule, which is not much more than two weeks away!

"OK, you've convinced me. Let's not do it," Bea chuckled.

"But then, Pinot Playhouse is a local non-profit. Shouldn't we help them out? And the sponsors are all local businesses and wealthy donors. It can't hurt to build ties with the wine country's wealthy influencers, right?"

"Um, remember when you thought it would be great to host the richie-rich charity poker tournament as our first event here at the inn?"

Angela frowned. "I know. It was *murder*."

"Literally. At least I made some nice bank in that tournament."

"But the poker people were strangers. These people are our neighbors."

A quizzical expression flashed across Bea's face. "Don't you wonder why Todd is behind this? Roberta says he only showed up and volunteered a few weeks ago. How'd he end up in the driver's seat? Roberta says her role is 'strategic,' and she does all the fundraising. Why isn't she leading the charge?"

"Todd said Roberta gave up without even trying. He says the fire was barely out when Roberta told the sponsors they were canceling. He called the most important ones himself to tell them he was looking for a solution."

"It sounds like you agree with Roberta. If there's not much chance all the work can be done in time, isn't it safer to just say no?"

"It would be, but Todd's very convincing. He says the volunteers are all really up for it, including—"

"Connie!" Bea said, laughing and slapping her forehead. "I get it now. You want to say yes for your pal."

"Is that so wrong? Todd seems like a nice guy, doesn't he? What if he and Connie have a real shot at a relationship?"

Bea paused for a moment, pondering Roberta's lukewarm assessment of Todd and Connie's chances. "You got a good feeling about Todd?"

"He seems like a nice guy. Not a Lothario type at all," Angela said, smiling. "But I'm sure you noticed that."

"Sounds like the show must go on. Besides, what's the worst that could happen?"

"Bea, what did I tell you about saying that? It's always bad luck."

"At least this time, Todd's doing most of the gambling."

"Yes, *most* of the gambling. If the show bombs, it might hurt our reputation, too. That's why I'm going to help the theater people pull this off—whether they like it or not."

"That's my girlie. You never met a job you didn't want to do. If that's settled, you should get some sleep. Aren't you and handsome shopping for engagement rings again tomorrow?"

"I guess it's settled," Angela said drowsily, sliding back down on her bed and lying on her side. "And yes—Aseem and I have ring shopping tomorrow. It's our first time, actually. Something has always come up when we've planned to before. There's no rush, right? I hope Aseem won't mind helping Todd with some work on the ballroom stage first. I told Todd that he and his team could get started with measurements and plans in the morning."

"Hmm... a murder mystery play here at the inn... the idea's starting to grow on me. Might even be a hoot to see the ol' *Ratcatcher* again. And even if it's as bad as I remember… what's the worst that could happen?"

"Bea!"

CHAPTER 5

The next morning, after ten hours of sleeping like a stone, Angela showered, dressed, tied her glossy hair into a high ponytail, and headed to the inn's breakfast room. Her fiancé was already. He'd brought lattes and pastries from Angela's favorite café.

"Just what I need," she said, grabbing a cup and a chocolate croissant from the two trays. "My hero. I could kiss you. In fact, I think I will." After a quick sip and nibble she put the coffee and the roll down and looped her arms around Aseem's neck. "I'm so glad to see you."

Aseem happily returned her kiss. "Good morning to you, too, Angel," he said after a few moments, his arms still around Angela's waist. "I ran into some inn guests as they were checking out. They were raving about BettyCon. They said it was even better than last year. But I want to hear all about it from you, of course. All the details."

"And I want to hear about your big week down in tech country," Angela said, sitting back down and taking a long sip of her coffee. "You go first."

Between bites of an iced cinnamon bun, Aseem told Angela about his presentations—the nerves, the tough questions, and how he eventually hit his stride and established a handful of key business partnerships.

"I never had any doubt," Angela said. Then she described the highlights of BettyCon as minimally as possible. Leaving out most of the details she'd normally meticulously include, she boiled her biggest annual project down to a few sentences.

Aseem laughed. "'Everyone loved BettyCon. The End.' That's all you got?"

"I can't help it. I've got more important news to share."

Then she launched into the story of Connie's new crush, the fire at the community theater where Connie and Todd had been volunteering, and Todd's idea to use the inn stage so the show could go on.

"And actually, there is a BettyCon connection. One of our guests—her name is Roberta—is involved with the theater company, too. Apparently, she handles all the fundraising. According to Todd, she didn't even try to relocate the show—just told the donors their money was gone."

"Interesting. I wonder how Roberta felt about Todd contradicting her. He must have made her look bad to those donors. They probably took her word for it that the show couldn't be moved until Todd told them otherwise."

"I hadn't even thought about that."

"And didn't you say Todd only signed up as a volunteer a few weeks ago? If Roberta's handling the fundraising—"

"She also told Bea she does the 'strategic' work. Whatever that means."

"Sounds like she's a paid employee. Either way, Roberta's got egg on her face. Todd went over her head, too. Nobody likes that."

"Roberta struck me as a little grumpy."

"Probably getting grumpier by the second with Todd," Aseem laughed. "OK, now that we're caffeinated and all caught up on the last week, are you *finally* ready for some serious ring shopping? I've done some homework. I've got a few ideas that I hope you'll like."

Angela's face crumpled into a worried frown. She opened her mouth to speak, but only managed an "um."

"Don't worry, Angel. You can feel free to reject any of my ideas. They're just a starting point for shopping. Besides, I didn't come up with them alone—I got expert help from Preeti." Preeti, Aseem's sister-in-law, had a sense of style that Angela admired. "But you can just ignore them if you want—"

"That's not it," Angela rushed to say. "I'm sure they're wonderful. I'm sorry, it's just… I kind of enlisted you to help Todd this morning. I hope you don't mind. He wants to get started on modifying the stage."

"Whatever you need. I should be there to make sure the stage isn't damaged. Besides, I'd like to meet this new love interest of Connie's. He needs the stamp of approval from both of us, right?"

Angela smiled. "Thank you. Some of the volunteers will be helping, too. Todd says they're super-motivated."

"With the task they're taking on, they'll have to be. And they better have skills. Retrofitting the stage and rebuilding the sets is a lot to get done in two weeks."

They held hands for the short walk to the

breakfast room. The inn was nearly empty, so they abandoned their normal caution about public displays of affection. Not that anyone could help but see the deep connection between them, even when they tried to conceal it. They were just so *cute* together!

They weren't doing it on purpose. They were just being themselves. But some people would always be peeved by the bubble of adorableness that floated around them whenever they were together.

Then there was the matter of Angela's job: she was a consummate professional, and Aseem still worked part-time for Betty Snickerdoodle, Inc. So they always tried their best to hide their feelings when they might be seen together, especially at the inn.

But this morning the hallway was empty, and they were delighted to be back in each other's company. So Angela didn't hesitate when her handsome fiancé reached for her left hand. Aseem held it up briefly, kissed it gently, and reminded her that, later, they'd at last be shopping for just the right ring for it.

They neared the door of the ballroom and found it propped ajar. From a few steps away, they heard a pair of raised voices.

"Let's listen a minute," Angela whispered, standing in front of Aseem just short of the door. The two of them pressed their backs against the wall to eavesdrop. "That woman's voice—that's Roberta! And she's talking to Todd."

"She doesn't sound pleased," Aseem said softly into Angela's ear.

"Do enlighten me, Todd. What were you thinking?" they heard Roberta snarl. "You think you're clever, promising the donors you'll somehow get this show assembled. Look at this stage! It's completely inappropriate. There's far too little time to adapt it before opening night—much less allow time to rehearse. You're just getting their hopes up. That will only make matters worse."

"Try not to be bitter, Roberta," Todd said. "It's not a good look at your age, especially in your position."

"In my position? I know what you're up to, currying favor with the wealthy donors. You think you're slick. Making me a scapegoat is just icing on your cake, but have you considered how it will look when the show fails? Your reputation will sink just as surely as mine."

"Why would I want to make you look bad? As you say, I'd only make myself look worse in the process. But aren't you at least happy you'll still get to perform? You've practiced Edie's lines with the grim repetition of a drill sergeant—and several other parts, too. You were ready for dress rehearsals before the director even picked the rest of the cast."

"Does that mean she's acting in the show?" Aseem whispered. Angela looked at him and shrugged.

"You had no business interfering with my relationships with the donors, Todd, much less entering into an agreement with Betty Snickerdoodle, Inc., on behalf of Pinot Playhouse," Roberta hissed.

"Why are you set against trying? We promised the donors a show in return for their donations."

"I'm aware. I'm also aware that when you're the stage manager, that means you *manage* the stage—not select it!" Roberta practically shouted. "I don't know what's worse—you acting as if you were in charge or that silly author and her babe-in-the-woods manager believing you were."

"The nerve!" Angela turned and whispered urgently to Aseem. "We're only trying to help—"

"Excuse me! Did someone call for a silly author?"

Aseem and Angela recognized Bea's voice. Angela leaned forward to sneak a peek through the door. She saw Bea turn around from the floor in front of the stage, where she'd been talking to a female volunteer.

Roberta began to stammer. "Miss Sickles… I'm sorry, I didn't see you—"

Bea let loose a piercing cackle. "I get that all the time," she announced, holding her arms out in an exaggerated flourish. She was wearing a bright orange track suit and neon teal sneakers. The ends of her gray bowl cut still sported the Christmassy red and green tips she'd added to celebrate Betty-Con. "There's no denying it, Roberta. I'm easy to miss. I *blend.*"

"I just meant that I didn't see you come in," Roberta said.

"That is because I, the silly author, own the place. I can cut through the kitchen any time I want. I was just speaking with young Lorelei from your fine crew." Bea waved up at the stage. A young woman wearing a utility belt and a fanny pack along with her jeans and a t-shirt waved back with a book she was holding.

"Lorelei emailed me to ask me to autograph one of her books, so I came right over to oblige. *Sweeter than Sugarplums.* It's one of my favorites. Have you read it? Just wondering—you know, since you told us yesterday at BettyCon that you were a big fan of Betty Snickerdoodle."

"Yes, of course it's true that I'm a fan of your work. And I didn't mean anything by 'silly author.' I'm just… caught off guard by this arrangement you worked out with Todd—"

"Actually, that was Angela's doing. Yo! Babe in the woods! I know you can hear us. Bring handsome, too."

Angela walked into the room with a shy smile on her face, Aseem at her side.

Roberta tilted her head as she appraised them.

"Do you two make a point of dressing alike?" she asked, a slight sneer in her tone.

Angela and Aseem looked down at the white hoodies and dark blue jeans they were wearing, then looked at each other and laughed.

"No, we didn't plan anything," Angela said. "A hoodie and jeans is pretty standard California fare."

Roberta said nothing but a barely audible, "Huh."

"Try to cope, Roberta. They're naturally adorable," Bea chuckled. "Anyway, as I was saying, Lorelei tells me she helps with costumes and props and even the sets. And she says that she's very happy the show's back on. Isn't that right, Lorelei?"

"Lori plays a guest in the show, too, and even shares the role of Ellen," Todd piped up from the back of the stage. "We're mighty multi-taskers, and the whole cast and crew—well, *most* of the cast—is excited to be back in business. Wouldn't you agree, Lori?"

"Um, Todd, it's *Lorelei*," Lorelei said.

"Sorry, hun,'" Todd said with a wink.

"But yes," Lorelei added, "I think we're all happy that there's a way for the show to go on. Ms. Newberg—Roberta—I don't think any of us realized you would be against the idea—" Lorelei continued tentatively.

Roberta stared at Lorelei, who unconsciously stepped backwards at the sight of the hard look on Roberta's face. The others looked surprised, too. Roberta hurriedly softened her expression.

"I'm just… I apologize. I'm just taken aback," Roberta said quickly. "There's just an awful lot to be done if we're to pull this off, but Todd has assured me you're all ready to do the hard work." Then she stormed out before Todd could reply.

"Bye, Roberta! Apology accepted! And you're welcome!" Bea yelled after her.

After an awkward pause, Aseem introduced

himself to Todd. "How about I show you what I know about the stage? I led the build-out for the ballroom."

Aseem joined Todd on stage and they began assessing and measuring its components. Todd seemed grateful for the help and began rattling off questions and ideas.

"Roberta is something," Angela said, half-watching Aseem from the ballroom floor, beaming at his resourcefulness.

"Be careful with all that smiling. I think she's allergic to cuteness. You and handsome might accidentally kill her," Bea chortled.

"Doesn't seem like the kind of thing that would bug a Treacle Town fan, does it?"

"True," Bea cackled. "Though I wasn't much for cute couples until I started writing about them. Speaking of couples, should we be worried about that wink between Todd and 'Lori'?"

"You noticed that, too, huh?" Angela frowned. "I hope it means nothing. Besides, didn't Lorelei seem a little annoyed? I don't think she liked Todd's nickname for her."

"Good point," Bea said, deciding not to remind Angela that many a meet-cute starts out with annoyance.

CHAPTER 6

The next morning, Bea and Angela headed down to the ballroom, to-go coffee cups in hand.

"Angie, I forgot to ask, why aren't you wearing your new ring? Did you decide on something custom? Or did they have to size it for you?"

"We didn't get to ring shopping after all," Angela said with a sigh. "Maybe today. Aseem really wants to."

"Don't you?"

"I do, I just… you know, the work Aseem helped Todd with yesterday was important. Besides, I don't see why Aseem's in such a hurry."

"Let's see… by my math, you've been engaged for a month and a half—"

"Exactly! What's the rush?"

Bea chuckled. "For once, I feel ya, girlie. But if you're gonna get engaged, isn't that when most people start wearing that ring?"

"I'm not most people," Angela said, opening the ballroom door.

"Indeed you're not. Well, here we go—time to sneak a peek at the work in progress," Bea said with a smirk. "If there is any progress."

"Time to be *supportive*," Angela said. "And look —Todd's not wasting any time."

Several volunteers—none of them young, but all seemingly new to carpentry—were attempting to build the side stairs and wings needed for the actors' entrances and exits. Todd had made a noticeable effort to dress right for the team's task. He wore a plaid shirt tucked into basic jeans, a tool-belt cinched tightly around his belly. The belt appeared to be about six inches too short.

"That looks painful. Todd could use one of those seat-belt extenders they use on airplanes," Bea said, pointing and guffawing.

"That's so rude, Bea! Thank God Connie's not here. Besides… you're not exactly the world's leading authority on fashion—"

"I beg your pardon!" Bea opened her mouth wide in an exaggerated display of offense, followed by a hearty laugh. "I'm not criticizing, Angie. I mean, that's gotta hurt. Should he be worried about organ damage? And is it just me, or does his belly look a lot bigger today? With those skinny legs and that belt, he looks like a head of cauliflower—except not as natural!"

Angela's face reddened. She shook her head and raised a finger to her lips. "Sound travels in here. They might be able to hear us, and I'm sure you don't want that. What if Connie overheard you? Just because you don't think Todd's attractive doesn't mean—"

Bea snickered again and shook her head no, but simultaneously whispered, "We all have our types. I guess Connie's is pasty and oddly shaped."

"Honestly, Bea! Of course Todd looks a little tired. Didn't you hear the volunteers leaving last night? It must have been at least eleven. And Todd stayed even later. I think he looks pretty good, considering."

While the crew worked together on one side of the stage, Todd sifted through a pile of mismatched planks and two-by-fours on the other. To avoid asking donors for more cash, he'd gone to local builders and lumber companies to ask for donations of goods. What he received was a mishmash of odd lots, leftovers from local development, and recycled lumber from demolished buildings.

The quality of the materials was only one challenge. The skill of the team was a bigger one.

"Ow!" wailed one of the volunteers, who was working with two others on building the left-side stairs. He dropped the end of a large plank with a loud clatter. "Nail!" he said, holding up a torn, bleeding finger.

"Gloves! I told you all before: Check for nails and wear gloves! That reclaimed wood was sent to us pre-inspection," Todd yelled.

"What if we don't have any gloves?" muttered a volunteer who was assisting from the floor in front of the stage. "Seems like the least this production could do is provide us with some."

"Phil, that gash looks bad," the man holding the other end of the plank said. He turned it over to inspect the nail, which was covered in rust. "Have you had a tetanus booster recently?"

Phil clumsily sat down on the end of the stage, holding up his injured hand. "I'm OK, Dave," Phil said unconvincingly. His face grew pale as he watched a growing stream of blood flow down his arm, staining the rolled-up sleeve of his shirt.

Angela dashed into the kitchen and jogged back into the ballroom toward the stage with a bright white towel. "Fresh out of the bleach wash," she said, gently wrapping the towel around Phil's injured hand. "Keep pressure on it, and keep it elevated. Todd, we've got a first aid kit—should I run and get it for you?"

"I... I think I'd better go to the emergency room," Phil said. "I'm sorry, Todd. I haven't had a tetanus shot in years, and I think I need stitches." A red stain was already blooming on the towel.

"OK. I understand," Todd sighed grumpily. "Dave, can you take him?"

Dave and Phil left for the hospital. Todd pulled a little notebook out of his pocket and paged through it. "Maybe there's something on my list that one person can work on alone."

The remaining volunteer looked at Todd with disbelief. "I'm not working with these materials unless you can provide gloves—"

"Todd, Aseem will be coming to help disassemble the center stairs this afternoon, right?" Angela interrupted. "I'll ask him if he can bring an extra pair or two of gloves. In the meantime, why don't the two of you grab some coffee? There's a fresh carafe in the breakfast room, and a box of doughnut holes, too."

"They're off to a good start," Bea cracked, once the theater crew had left the room. "Doesn't seem to be much danger of Todd overdoing the preparation."

"Well, they are on an unusually tight schedule."

"You know what they say, girlie. If you don't have time to do it right, how will you find the time to fix it when it's wrong?"

"Yes, I know *'they'* say that. You heard that expression from me, remember?"

"Thanks for the vote of confidence," Todd said, reappearing in the ballroom. "Sorry to interrupt. I have a question—"

"No, we're sorry, Todd," Angela said. "We're here to support you, not criticize."

"Speak for yourself," Bea chortled.

"Your question, Todd?" Angela said.

"Obviously, we've still got work to do on the stage, but the cast needs to start rehearsing."

Bea and Angela looked at each other, then back at Todd.

"This is the only large space we have. Couldn't they rehearse here on the floor while you and the volunteers work on the stage?" Angela said.

"Too loud and distracting. For them and for us," Todd said.

"What about the barn, Angie?" Bea said.

"We'd need a day to clear it out."

"Actually, the director and the actors would

prefer to be closer by," Todd said. "What about the deck?" Todd pointed outside to the expansive patio attached to the far side of the ballroom. "It's much larger than the stage, but we could tape it off to get the cast comfortable with the dimensions of the real thing."

"Well, we won't have any inn guests, so that's not a problem. We'd already planned on some downtime. And the weather's supposed to be dry for at least a week," Angela said. "I don't see a problem with it."

"Great," Todd said. "One other thing. The director's coming by any minute. I just thought I should warn you, he's a bit of a handful."

"A perfectionist?" Angela said. "Isn't that the stereotype?"

"That's part of it. But it's hard to be a perfectionist when you're not sure you're even willing to do your job," Todd said caustically.

"Slagging off the help again, Todd?" said a tall, broad-shouldered man in his early 50s as he strode into the ballroom. He wore an expertly tailored leather blazer over a neat black shirt and trousers. A belt with a prominent designer buckle emphasized his taut physique, and his perfectly shaved head showed off his smooth ebony skin. "Surely even you can understand that once a wise person's off the hook, they're cautious about jumping back on it."

"Good to see you, too, Grayson," Todd said. "And please—no one's asking you to jump onto any hooks. Surely even you can understand that we're just fulfilling our commitments, right?"

"Yes, community theater," Grayson said with a soft snort. "Meant to be fun, *right?*"

Without seeking permission, Grayson picked up Angela's hand and clasped it between both of his own. His sleeve slid up an inch, revealing a heavy, diamond-studded Swiss watch. "And who might this lovely creature be? I suppose it's too much to hope for that you're a last-minute addition to the cast."

Grayson gazed appreciatively at Angela's face, earning an awkward frown from her and a smirk from Bea.

First gently, then firmly, Angela regained control of her hand, turning it sideways and giving Grayson's right one a businesslike shake. "I'm Angela Garcia. I manage the inn. Nice to meet you."

"Grayson Gates."

The director kept Angela's hand in his a beat too long and flashed his eyebrows suggestively. Angela furrowed hers and finally slipped her hand out of his grip.

"Don't mind me. I'm Bea Sickles. I just own the place," Bea interrupted. "Grayson Gates. That name rings a bell. Should I know you from somewhere?"

"Only if you're a live theater devotee," Grayson said unctuously.

"Now, now, no need for excessive modesty, Grayson," Todd said. "Multiple Obie awards can't be wrong."

"Mostly retired now," Grayson said. "Except for opportunities to give back. Well-chosen opportunities—usually."

"You chose well here, even if you've forgotten that," Todd said. "Keep your mind open. We've already made progress adapting the stage, as you can see."

Todd pointed to the disheveled heaps of wood on either end of the stage, earning a doubting shake of Grayson's head.

"And to think Roberta had already told all the donors we were out of business," Grayson said, clucking his tongue. "We were just inches from a clean getaway. She maintains this is all your doing. Now instead of taking the requisite time to properly plan a new production—"

"We're living up to our commitment to our donors and the community," Todd said bullishly.

"You worry too much, Grayson. With your decades of success off-Broadway, I'm sure you'll figure out how to make the production work. Your actors couldn't be more dedicated—"

"Or less seasoned," Grayson said.

"Let me show you around," Todd said, his voice trailing as he led Grayson toward the French doors and out onto the deck.

"Goodbye, Miss Sickles," Grayson said. As he turned to follow Todd, he took a longer look in Angela's direction and added, "and I hope we'll say 'hello' again soon, Miss Garcia."

"That reminds me," Bea said. "When's your ring shopping?"

"I promised Aseem I'd find time later today," Angela sighed.

"Maybe if you'd been wearing a ring, Grayson would've backed off. Then again, some guys are so entitled, they don't let a little thing like a fiancé slow them down."

"Mr. Gates sure seems like he could be one of them."

CHAPTER 7

"Ready?" Aseem said. "Weather's perfect for a long run. I'm looking forward to it almost as much as ring shopping later."

He was standing at the door of Angela's suite, dressed suitably for a Northern California winter afternoon run: sleek pants, running shoes, long- and short-sleeved layered t-shirts. He pulled two pairs of gloves from the pockets of the windbreaker he had wrapped around his waist. "Brought these for Todd and his crew."

"Thanks!" Angela tossed the gloves onto her bed on her way out the door, but then changed her mind. "On second thought, let's stop at the ballroom on our way out," she said, squeezing the gloves into the pockets of her fleece vest. "I'm worried about the crew working without gloves."

As they made their way down the hall to the ballroom, Angela told Aseem about Todd's idea of using the deck as a rehearsal area—and about Phil's accident. "Wait 'til you see the materials they're working with. It's no wonder someone got hurt. I'm surprised Todd didn't think more about safety."

"It doesn't sound like he's taking time to think any of this through. Then again, the main thing they lack is time."

In the ballroom, Angela and Aseem found a lone volunteer on stage trying to assemble part of the new stairs all by himself. He was huffing loudly and looked ready to storm off. Angela looked at him, then turned away to avoid his eye.

Angela and Aseem moved closer to the French doors, stopping a few feet shy of them to watch the action on the deck. A group of actors, mostly new faces of varying ages, were collaborating in a taped-offed section that appeared to signify the stage, making elaborate gestures and practicing physical moves. Roberta was standing outside the taped lines with Grayson, under the corner eaves where the deck connected with the inn walls. Their conversation looked heated.

"That's the director with Roberta," Angela whispered.

"He doesn't look too happy."

"Neither does she. And look over there."

Angela elbowed Aseem and tilted her head toward the other end of the deck, where Todd and Lorelei were standing together. Todd's back was to the window, but they could see Lorelei smiling broadly. Angela and Aseem looked at each other uneasily and whispered together, "Connie."

"This will only take a minute," Angela sighed. She walked to the door closest to Todd. She opened it and stuck her head out.

"Just wanted to get these to you as quickly as possible," she said, handing the gloves to him. Todd hurriedly thanked her and asked if she'd like to meet the cast members.

"Maybe later. Aseem and I are off for a run, and we know how pressed for time you are."

"Wait—before you go," Todd said, "I've been meaning to ask another favor. You know I've already been keeping some long hours here. After the volunteers are done for the night, that's the only time I can revise our plans and do paperwork—"

"And hang out with Connie?" Angela said

hopefully. She blushed, regretting putting Todd on the spot.

"Well, yes—of course, when there's time," taking Angela's question in stride. "Which brings me to my favor. So far, I've been driving across town to another hotel here in the wine country. It's quite nice, but I'm just sleeping there, not really enjoying it. Do you think I could take a room here?"

"We don't have housekeeping service at the moment. The staff worked so much overtime during BettyCon, I gave them extra vacation."

"That's no problem. I can make my own bed."

"Well, if you were hoping for a donation, I'm sorry. We donated the use of the ballroom, but I can't—"

"No worries at all. I'm paying across town. I'm happy to pay your rack rates here. I was wondering if I could take one of those casitas behind the main building."

"Won't that be a lot of extra space? They're usually booked by families or at least couples."

"Sorry if I'm being bold. I was just thinking that I could come and go from the loading area behind the ballroom without disturbing anyone. And with the extra space, I could lay out all my diagrams."

"They're about twice as much as a regular room, but if you're fine with that—"

"Deal! Don't worry about the higher room rate. Can I move in tonight?"

"Move in?" Grayson said, moving briskly toward them from across the deck. "Angela, did I hear something about moving in?"

"None of your business, Grayson," Todd interrupted.

"Let's let the captivating Miss Garcia answer my question, Todd."

Grayson moved his arm presumptuously around Angela's shoulder, but she deftly eluded him. She glanced back through the big windows into the ballroom where Aseem was looking at her with a furrowed brow.

"Todd was just asking about booking one of our casitas. He'll be doing without housekeeping service—or any service at all—since we're technically closed until next week, but it will be more convenient for—"

"That sounds delightful. I'll take one of those casitas, too, Angela."

"But Grayson, don't you have a *house* here in the wine country?" Todd said. "Isn't that why you were willing to help Pinot Playhouse in the first place?"

"And surely that's none of *your* business," Grayson sneered. "Besides, Todd, shouldn't you be glad to have me close by—"

"Gentlemen, I'll leave you to your debate," Angela said. "I'll have keys for you tomorrow."

ANGELA AND ASEEM headed out of the main entrance at a jog toward the foothills and Connie's property, the first stage of a long, scenic loop they loved to run whenever they had time. They were quiet for the first mile, enjoying their peaceful surroundings and the soft rhythm of their breathing and the varying sounds of their footsteps first on pavement, then dirt paths. Twenty minutes later, as they circled back through the trail that ran alongside the dormant vines of Heavenly West and toward the inn, they'd settled into a pleasant groove and were sure no one could overhear them.

"Angel, I've been thinking about Todd and Connie and maybe Lorelei and—don't take this the wrong way—but it's not like Todd is male model material. I mean, I'm not implying that women are superficial. Maybe he's got a great personality. He is a volunteer, that must count for something—"

"I'm lucky you're the whole package," Angela laughed. "No one will ever know if I'm in love with your brains or your beauty. But if what you're trying to say is that Todd doesn't have the looks of a ladykiller, you know how mysterious attraction can be. Maybe it's all about charm. Some women just crave appreciation."

"Yeah, and in Connie's case, let's not forget her first husband was no prize."

"Right. Connie might be drawn to Todd because he's a do-gooder—"

"The exact opposite of Billy Ray."

"Todd just asked me for a room here at the inn, though. He said he wanted to be close by for work on the production. Is it odd that he isn't staying with Connie? She's got several empty guest rooms in that new house of hers."

"Nah. They hardly know each other. Plus, she's still got work during the week," Aseem said, jumping over a big stick on his side of the trail. "Whoa, watch out, Angel!"

"Thank you—the wind has blown all kinds of stuff around lately. I suppose you're right about Todd and Connie. We don't even know if Todd reciprocates her feelings. I only saw them together when I gave them a tour, and Todd was focused on whether the inn could fill in for the playhouse.

Speaking of body language, what did you make of Grayson and Roberta's?"

"Let's see. I'd say Grayson's an impressive-looking guy, but Roberta didn't look too impressed with him. He didn't look too impressed with her, either."

"We already know Roberta's a grump, so we have to factor that in—" Angela laughed.

"Everyone involved in this project seems grumpy. Grayson looked rather testy with Todd."

Angela hesitated. "When Grayson heard Todd was getting a room here, he asked for one, too." Angela kept her gaze straight ahead but tried to gauge Aseem's reaction out of the corner of her eye. She wasn't sure, but she thought she saw him flinch.

"Todd didn't like that," Angela continued lightly. "He asked Grayson why he wouldn't stay in his own house here in Napa."

"Multiple houses? Grayson seems like a big deal for community theater."

Angela tried to laugh it off. "Yes, just ask him. I believe he's got a bunch of off-Broadway awards, but he's retired now. Todd warned me he's kind of… difficult. Bea thinks he's the sort of man who's used to getting whatever he wants—"

"He seems young to be retired."

"I agree. And he seems… I don't know, disgruntled? If he doesn't like it, why even bother with this little community theater?" Angela said. "We're turning for home. How about a sprint?"

"Love it! The sooner we get back, the sooner we start our ring shopping."

Angela burst ahead, playfully brushing past Aseem, forcing him to take extra strides around a large rock.

"Oops, sorry!" she shouted gaily.

Moments later, they were racing around the back of the inn and heading toward the deck. As the deck came into focus, they saw a cluster of people standing beneath it.

"Is that Lorelei on the ground?" Angela cried.

They hurried closer and saw that Lorelei was trying to sit up. "I'm fine. Really. Just a little dazed." She tried to stand up but cried out in pain as she put weight on her left foot. "Must be just a bruise… or maybe a sprain."

"It could be broken," Todd yelled, running to her. "What happened?"

"I just… I fell off the stairs," Lorelei said meekly.

"Grayson—where are the safety protocols? Who's minding the store here?" Todd barked.

Grayson looked peeved. "Lorelei wasn't even

supposed to be on the stairs. If your actors can't even take basic direction—"

"We need to get you to the emergency room. I'll take you." Todd bent down and put his arm under Lorelei's and whisked her to her feet.

"Can we help?" Angela said, panting softly as she and Aseem reached the deck.

"All under control. Can you hobble, Lori?" Todd said. "See? Could be a fracture. We've got to get you to the ER as quickly as possible!" He scooped her up and carried her quickly around the inn entrance toward the parking lot. "We'll be back as soon as we can," he shouted.

"Good thing Phil wasn't here to see this," Angela whispered to Aseem. "When he got hurt, Todd didn't seem to care if he bled to death."

"Is it just me," Aseem whispered back, "or did Lorelei look a little embarrassed?"

"More like *a lot* embarrassed. No one likes to look like a klutz," Angela said, wiping a bead of sweat off her brow with the sleeve of her t-shirt.

Grayson caught Angela's eye. He strode across the deck and bounded down the stairs toward her. Roberta stayed behind, jaw slightly agape, her face rigid.

"Now it's Roberta who looks disgruntled," Aseem laughed. His expression changed as

Grayson brushed past him, apparently not even noticing he was there.

"Should we finish our run?" Aseem asked. Distracted by Grayson, Angela didn't respond.

"Beautiful Angela," Grayson said, picking up Angela's hand presumptuously. "Lorelei's unfortunate predicament may have left us without our pretty hotel guest for Act One. Is it too much to hope that acting is one of your many talents?"

Angela tried to once more gently extract her hand from Grayson's, but this time, he was ready. "Wasn't—isn't—Lorelei part of the stage crew, too?"

"Oh, yes. It's community theater, *beautiful*," Grayson purred. He enveloped Angela's hand with his free one, gently caressing her fingers and gazing into her eyes. "Many of the actors multitask. Even Roberta has a role and a job," he added, tipping his head in Roberta's direction. "Replacing Lorelei's crew contributions is Todd's problem, though, not mine."

Angela smiled wanly and turned away from Grayson's gaze. A blush spread hotly across her cheeks. She was glad to realize her skin was still warm and damp from running. Then, out of the corner of her eye, she saw Aseem's face. His eyes were wide. He'd leaned forward, as if intending to insert himself physically between Grayson and Angela.

Angela managed to yank her hand away. "Grayson, let me introduce you to my boyfriend, Aseem. Grayson, Aseem. Aseem, Grayson."

Grayson took a slow step backward, then smirked as he looked Aseem up and down. "Nice to meet you, *boyfriend*." He didn't offer a handshake, and neither did Aseem.

"Aseem and I were just out jogging. Honey, shouldn't we finish our run?"

"You mean like I said two minutes ago?" Aseem didn't wait for a reply, just started off toward the inn entrance at top speed.

"Sorry, Grayson—I'm no good at acting, and I don't have time for Lorelei's other duties. Good luck with the show," Angela said, sprinting after Aseem. As they approached the inn entrance, Angela was still short of catching him. Bea was walking toward the door from the parking lot.

"There you two go again, being all healthy and stuff," Bea yelled. "How 'bout you balance that virtue out with a little vice? 'Cuz I just saw something in the parking lot that was mighty interesting. Care to dish?"

Aseem blew past Bea into the inn without a word.

"Yeah, we know Todd took Lorelei to the emergency room," Angela said, barely pausing as she hurried after Aseem. "Todd thinks she broke her ankle."

"That's not what I saw," Bea yelled. "Don't you wanna hear?"

But Angela was focused on her fiancé, who was halfway down the hall. "Aseem, wait, please. Are you upset? Because you look upset!" She dashed through the inn lobby, trying to catch him.

Bea shook her head and chuckled to herself. "Ah, young love. A supposedly fun thing I'll never do again." Then she laughed heartily at her own joke and slapped her knee for good measure.

"My stars, are you talking to yourself again, Bea?" a sweet, Southern voice called from the parking lot.

It was Connie, coming out of her car and heading toward the inn entrance. She looked pretty and businesslike in a pink pantsuit and a gray turtleneck sweater. Her blond bob looked sleek and professional. She turned on her designer heels for an instant and clicked her remote, pausing for the beep and flash of her taillights before walking briskly up to Bea.

"I was just stopping by on my way home to see how Todd was doing with the show," Connie said brightly, removing her cellphone earpiece and tucking it into her pocket. "I mean, to see how everyone was doing with the show. Was that Angela and Aseem I just saw? What'd I miss?"

"Not much that I know of." Delivering a white lie was easy for a former professional bluffer. "Couple of minor accidents, but I guess that's to be expected."

"Oh, no! Todd wasn't hurt, was he?"

"Nope, but he was the first to help the ones that were. In fact, I thought I saw Todd take one of the crew to the emergency room just a while ago. You'll have to get the details from someone else, though. I didn't see what happened."

"Oh, well, that must have been Todd that I saw driving out—with a young lady in the front seat. They weren't in his truck, so I wasn't sure."

"Yes, that's probably right," Bea said brightly. "A young lady hurt her ankle. Must have been pretty bad. Todd had to carry—er, help her to the car."

"Was that Lorelei?" Connie said, a note of sadness dampening her Southern lilt. "In the front seat, I mean. She didn't look badly injured—at least, it seemed like she was laughing a lot."

"You know they say that a broken bone releases all kinds of adrenaline, and adrenaline makes you giddy. I researched it for my new mystery book."

Bea was being careful of Connie's feelings—a relatively new sensation for her. Back in her card-playing days, Bea would've blurted out the truth and let the chips fall where they may. Sometimes she missed her old self. Caring about other people's feelings was a lot of responsibility!

"I'm sure you're right, Bea," Connie said, squaring her shoulders. "They're adults, besides. It's no business of mine if they're having fun, is it?" Connie leaned in with a conspiratorial grin on her face. "Though if it was who I thought it was, she's awfully young—well, I mean, she looks more like a girl than a woman, doesn't she?"

"That she does," Bea said truthfully. "That she does."

"For a second, I swear, I saw another head pop up in the back seat. It was gone before they drove by me. Do I sound crazy?"

Bea looked cockeyed, but Connie didn't wait for her to reply before answering her own question with a sigh.

"Probably just wishful thinking," she said softly.

CHAPTER 8

Connie and Angela were sitting in a quiet booth in their favorite little wine bar on the cutest block of their village's charming main street. A server had just brought them two large glasses of chardonnay. The golden wine glinted under the wine bar's lighting.

"I've worked out a plan for entertaining the blue bloods," Connie said.

The day before, Todd had confessed to Angela that the biggest donors to the *Ratcatcher* production were insisting on visiting the inn to check on the show's progress. He'd turned to Angela for help—and Angela had turned to Connie, the one person she knew who understood what socialites expect.

"Cheers to that!" Angela said, clinking her glass against Connie's.

"Before I give you my pitch, how are you? We haven't talked in days!"

"Wouldn't you rather talk about Todd?"

"Not much to say. You're the one with a real love life. Tell me what's been happening with you and that sweet fiancé of yours and let me live vicariously," Connie said in her gentle, unhurried way.

A blush colored Angela's cheeks. "I think… did you see us fighting yesterday? I… I guess we still are fighting."

"I wasn't sure what I saw," Connie said, putting her hand softly on Angela's arm. "The truth is, I barely saw the backs of the two of you running into the inn. Bea told me she thought you two were—"

"It was a fight over nothing! Aseem got jealous—"

"A little jealousy can be kind of touching—in moderation, I mean."

"But he had nothing to be jealous *about*. It was just… I swear, it was harmless. It was the director, Grayson."

"Oh yes. He has a bit of a reputation."

"I wasn't encouraging him, I promise. I tried to

gently *discourage* him, but I have to be polite, don't I? But the worst part was, I made a mistake—it didn't mean anything, but Aseem overreacted."

Connie opened her mouth as if about to say something, but held back.

Angela blew out a sigh. "I introduced him as my… *boyfriend*."

Before she could control her reaction, Connie cringed slightly. "Not 'fiancé'?"

"I know, I know. It's just… it's still so new. And then Grayson kept sarcastically saying, 'the boyfriend' with Aseem right there."

Angela crossed her arms on the table and put her head down on them. "It was an innocent mistake. We've only been engaged a little while. Before I could correct myself or apologize, Aseem took off."

"I suppose you could say it hasn't been a very long time. What's it been… a month? Or two?" Connie looked at Angela's hands. "How's the ring shopping going?"

"Ugh!" Angela said, picking her head up from the table. "Not you, too? Why does everyone think I need to have a ring like, yesterday?"

"I'm sorry, honey," Connie said kindly. "I was just thinking it might have deterred Grayson's unwanted attention. But please know you'll get no pressure from me at all. You have to do what you think is right."

"I mean, I'm only doing this once," Angela cried. "We shouldn't rush should we?"

"I'm sorry for touching a nerve. Should we change the subject? I could tell you about my plan for the society queens."

"Please do," Angela said, taking a gulp of wine.

FOCUSING on work almost always brightened Angela's mood. Twenty minutes later, with a big smile, she pronounced Connie's plan "perfect."

"To recap," Angela said, taking another sip, "we start by scheduling the fancy ladies' visit in the evening. That way, they might notice we've got our Christmas trees and wreaths still lit up—"

"Exactly," Connie said. "Any distraction from the disarray on stage is a good thing. And the volunteers are working at night, so the ladies'll see a busy crew putting elbow grease behind their donations."

"Next, we serve them something special, but dainty."

"There's a reason it's a cliche that society ladies

can't be too rich or too thin," Connie laughed. "That's how they think. I'm sure they'll appreciate some sort of luxurious potent potable, though. I'll bring a couple of bottles from my barrel clients."

Connie's new business selling her family's prized whiskey casks had made her many friends among Napa's top winemakers. The vintners said the barrels contributed subtly yet distinctively to the flavor profiles of complex wines—and "bourbon-cask aging" on the label added a tidy profit margin to their highest-end bottles. The winemakers often thanked Connie with cases of the wines they were most proud of.

"I'll bring some of our best bourbon, too. We could whip up a custom cocktail. We could call it a Ratcatcher!"

"I love that. We could model our small plates on a hunt tea—like they have in the play."

"If you can find tiny scones the size of a fingerprint, they might even eat one."

Angela grinned. "Maybe I can track down some of that pretty antique china that features British foxhunting scenes. And we'll start the tour so it overlaps with rehearsals. Todd mentioned one of the donors has a relative in the cast. She probably wants a sneak peek."

"That's the plan," Connie said, raising her glass for another clink against Angela's. "Easy peasy, no? I might even have some of that china tucked away somewhere. I'll look for it—and I'll do some research on our donor guests. Just so we don't walk into any landmines."

"Landmines?"

"You know—delicate subjects. Those ladies probably have plenty of topics they never want to talk about."

"Oh yes, I'd say if we offend them, we've failed as hostesses," Angela laughed.

"Or worse," Connie said, smiling conspiratorially. "Would you believe there's a rumor that an heiress in our part of Kentucky actually had someone *murdered* over unsavory gossip? The charges never stuck, but we all definitely wondered about it. Let's just say we sure as heck stick to the weather when talking with her at parties— we don't even mention the Kentucky Derby, just in case her horse didn't win!"

"Need for landmine research duly noted. Now I've got a question for you. What should I wear? You already know my wardrobe's mostly jeans and a few dressy holiday party outfits. This sort of outfit is about all I have that's in between," Angela said, smoothing out the short denim skirt she was wearing over tights and boots.

"You look adorable, honey, but for this occasion, let me help. I have a few suitably ladylike suits that will fill the bill.

"And just so you know," Connie said with a giggle, "by ladylike I mean pastels, pearls, and above all, *boring*. You're a little smaller than I am around the waistline, but that's what a statement belt is for. I'll bring some choices by tomorrow, when we start turning the business center into the dressing area. Speaking of which, there's Martina."

Connie waved at the door and a pretty woman in her late thirties walked over to join them. She wore jeans, a flowing floral tunic, and a shorter, dark yellow jacket on top. As she walked, her small backpack and her chandelier earrings swayed and her flat boots clicked along the wood floor. Her long blond hair was braided artfully and her makeup was expertly applied, if a little heavy for Northern California. It accentuated her bold features, including her regal, aquiline nose.

"I'm Martina," she said, extending a hand to Angela. "Great to see you, Connie."

"Thanks for meeting us, sugar," Connie said, scooting over to make space in the booth. "Angela, why don't you fill Martina in?"

Angela explained that she'd offered Todd the business center as a space for costumes, hair, and makeup, and that she'd been delighted when Todd suggested that she and Connie team up on the project, together with Martina, who was handling hair and makeup for *The Ratcatcher.*

"Todd didn't know whether you'll need windows for natural light, special electrical outlets, or who knows what. So… that's why we're glad you're able to help us. What do you think, Martina?"

"No need to worry about windows or lights. Pinot Playhouse invested in makeup stations with lighting built in. If they fit the space, we'll be good to go. Just need enough juice for them and our hairstyling equipment. Oh, and Lorelei gave me some instructions, too. She's sewing costumes at home while her foot heals, but I'll be helping get the dressing area figured out. She mentioned we'll have clothes irons and steamers that will need electricity—they're fairly power hungry but not industrial-strength."

"Normally, we have a dozen PCs, a fax, and a bunch of other electricity hogs running in that room. I think our wiring can handle everything you listed."

"Don't forget, you've got that newfangled power plant now, too."

Martina looked confused.

"Just a big generator. In case the power goes out," Angela said. "You know that record rain we got last fall? We lost power three times. We had inn guests, too. So I said 'never again.'"

"You're so smart, my friend," Connie smiled. "Now you don't have to worry about that—and neither does the theater group."

"Do you think it would come to that?" Angela said. "If the weather's that bad, won't they just cancel the play?"

Connie looked at Martina, who said nothing, just raised her eyebrows slightly and pursed her lips.

"Todd seems pretty determined that the show must go on. Let's hope we won't have to worry about that, good Lord willing and the creek don't rise," Connie said. "Literally in this case. We're in luck, though. The weather looks good for the next week."

Martina smiled and changed the subject. "Why don't I come by the inn tomorrow and we'll figure out the layout together? Sometime after five? I'll bring some of the furniture. I've been driving around with most of it in my van. I'm glad it was saved from the fire at the playhouse, but I'd love to get it out of my way for a while."

"I've got a busy day tomorrow. Can we say six o'clock?" Connie said, pushing back her chair. "Speaking of work, I'm afraid I have to call it a night. I've got a bunch of proposals to write before I can turn in."

Angela stood up to give her friend a hug, then turned to Martina. "Can you stay? You didn't even get a drink. Let me buy you a glass of wine. I hardly get out for girl talk anymore. I'd love to hear more about the theater and how you got involved with it."

Martina shrugged and smiled. "I don't mind boring you with my story over a drink."

"Great! Let's get something to nibble on, too."

Over crab cakes and salad, Angela quizzed Martina about her work and how she got involved with Pinot Playhouse.

"Would it surprise you to know my mother dreamed I'd be an international tennis star?" Martina laughed. "She wanted a career of 'easy money' for me, I suppose. She gave that up when it turned out I had zero athletic ability. I disappointed her again when I chose makeup as a career. She adjusted. It helps that I make her look great for all her big occasions."

"You didn't get the drama bug from her?"

"Nope. That was just my stumble into marketing. When I first started out—with my brand new license—I was too shy to promote my business. I worked as a substitute high school teacher to pay the bills, up near Chico, where I grew up. I found out the drama club needed makeup help, so I volunteered. I'd never done drama when I was in high school, but I realized pretty fast that I'd missed out. Then when I found out the drama teacher was getting married, I offered to do her hair and makeup—and my mobile hair and makeup business was launched.

"That was ten years ago. Since then, I've always looked for volunteer opportunities in community theater. By volunteering, I contribute to the community and get free promotion for my business, like for hair and makeup for head shots and corporate events. Those gigs pay way better than weddings."

Martina stopped for a bite of salad and a swallow of wine.

"You mean for the actors—or the donors, too?"

"Mm-hmm," Martina said, wiping her mouth with a napkin. "The actors in this one aren't even semi-professional. I usually try to meet some of the patrons—society lady types, Junior League and all that. They often like custom makeup for the ballet or whatever. With the van, I bring the salon to them. They don't have to worry about mixing with the general public in a salon," she added with a laugh.

"Now that the show's back on, won't you have a chance?"

Martina took another sip. "I hope so. I don't have to tell you that the show's looking a little... well, you know... shaky." Her face reddened and she fanned herself lightly. "Sorry. No offense to your inn. Must be the wine talking. I know you're trying to help. It's just—some of the crew have been feeling a little frustrated. Maybe I shouldn't speak out of turn—"

"Nobody but us girls here. If you've got doubts, it would help me to know about them. That way, I can try to help Todd out. And you know, actually, you haven't mentioned how you found Pinot Playhouse. We're not very close to Chico, after all."

Martina grinned sheepishly and lifted her glass above her head. "What the heck. Still got wine left, so I guess we have to keep talking. My story with the playhouse is a short one—but then again, so's everybody's."

"How so?"

"As I understand it, Pinot Playhouse was basically dead until Roberta came along to rescue it. I don't think that was even a year ago now. *The Ratcatcher* was supposed to be the grand revival."

"Roberta rescued the community theater?"

"Yep. From what I heard, Roberta owns it."

"*Owns it?* That doesn't seem possible."

"I think Todd had that same question. At least, he hinted at it—not that I heard from him directly—"

Their friendly server stopped by their table and quickly apologized for interrupting. "I can see you're deep in conversation. Just wondered if you needed anything else. I can come back—"

"It's OK," Angela rushed to say. "Everything's been great, but we're definitely going to need two refills of wine."

AN HOUR LATER, still feeling the effects of her third glass of wine, Angela slid into the back seat of a rideshare headed back to the inn. She pulled her phone out of her pocket and plucked the phone number of Bea's suite from her call history.

Is it too late to call? Bea won't go to bed for another couple of hours. This is too important to discuss by phone, anyway.

She put the phone back in her pocket.

"Excuse me," she said to the driver. "Mind if we make a quick stop at that pizza place around the corner?"

CHAPTER 9

Angela knocked softly on the door of Bea's suite.

"Bea! You awake?" she whispered, her face close to where the door met the frame. She waited a moment, convinced she heard rustling behind the door. Holding the pizza in her left hand, she leaned her shoulder on the door, pressing her ear against it. She said Bea's name again, this time a little louder.

Shoot. It's late, but it's not late for Bea. Is she asleep already?

Angela pressed her ear closer to the door and tapped her fingernails on the wood. Before she realized what was happening, the door flew open. She let out a squeak and landed in a heap on the floor, on top of a big pile of plush pillows. As Angela fell, Bea deftly snatched the pizza box out of her hand.

It was a good thing that there were no guests in the inn. If there had been, they'd all have been awakened by jubilant cackling that was loud enough to raise the dead.

"You really think that's funny, Bea?" Angela whined, scrambling awkwardly up from the floor.

"You're right, it's not funny," Bea said. "It's hilarious!"

"And here I was being so nice, bringing you a treat."

"I do like me a treat, but how often do I get a set-up that perfect? I heard you leaning on the door, scratching and whispering, and could hardly keep from laughing. I deserve a reward for self-restraint. Anyway, you know we haven't had any crimes to solve or crooks to chase lately. If it weren't for our community theater clowns, I'd be completely starved for fun. And notice that I took precautions," Bea said, pointing at the pillows on the floor and slapping her knee. "See? I'm learning about safety from you."

"*'No crooks to chase?'* That's your excuse? We just solved a murder a month ago. Two of them, actually," Angela sighed. "We're all just pieces in your comedy chess game, aren't we?"

"Some chess pieces are more equal than others," Bea said, her shoulders still shaking under her fleece robe as she chortled. "You, Angie, are obviously the queen. Who else would get a cushioned landing? Finally, a good use for all those bed pillows you picked out. And I saved our snack, didn't I? That's what really matters.

Still chuckling, Bea put the pizza on the desk. She pulled paper plates from a drawer, then opened the box and selected her perfect slice. The familiar aroma of cheese and pepperoni wafted through the room. "OK, Angie, this is the second late-night snack you've brought me in a week. Either you're buttering me up for something or you've got more juicy gossip. Out with it!" Bea picked up a second plate and pointed at the pizza.

"No, thanks. No pizza for me." Angela picked pillows up off the floor and tossed them back onto Bea's bed, then plopped on it and put her feet up. "Well, maybe if there's a small piece. I've got a lot of things to discuss. This could take a while."

Bea handed Angela her slice and slid onto the bed, balancing her own plate. "OK, girlie, let 'er rip!"

"Just to prepare you, I'm not buttering you up,

and I wouldn't call what I'm about to say 'gossip.' I mean... it technically might be... let's just say I don't know what to make of it."

In between bites, Angela told Bea about meeting Connie and Martina at the wine bar and the plan to adapt the business center for the play.

"After Connie left, Martina and I stayed for another glass of wine—"

"I thought you must be a little tipsy with all that scratching at the door," Bea laughed. "Sorry. Continue."

Angela explained how she and Martina got to know each other a bit—and how she'd taken the opportunity to ask her about Pinot Playhouse and Todd.

"You know, I just wanted the inside scoop on the company—"

"Be honest. You wanted to find out if Todd's a good guy. And if he's interested in Connie."

"Partly, yes. But Martina mentioned something about Roberta that took the conversation in a completely different direction."

Angela paused to take a deep breath and a nibble of pizza. "Martina says she heard Roberta saved the Pinot Playhouse theater group by *buying* it. Doesn't that seem... odd?"

"You mean because Roberta's a humble retired

principal? That does seem weird to me. Can't imagine a theater company comes cheap. Especially up here in the wine country."

"Something else strikes me as much stranger. Can a person actually *own* a nonprofit? And if Roberta's employing all these people as volunteers—"

"Good point. If you own a business, I believe it's customary to pay your employees," Bea snickered. She pulled an ancient tissue from the pocket of her robe and wiped a dribble of tomato sauce off her face. "Cheating people out of their pay wouldn't be very principled of Madame Principal. Of course, working for Roberta might be so great, people gladly do it for free!"

Once Angela stopped laughing, she paused to finish her last bite of pizza crust. "And it's not just the unpaid help. What about the donors funding her operations? You can't 'donate' to a private business, can you?"

"Not if you're doing it for tax purposes."

"So does that mean that what Roberta's been doing is… illegal?"

"I'm not a lawyer, but I bet the IRS might think so. I've also got a load of questions, though. For starters, you just met Martina. How reliable is her word? Roberta seems to me to be the kind of person someone might start nasty rumors about."

"She seems honest—" Angela hesitated and frowned as she looked at Bea. "I know what you're thinking—that I'm not the best judge."

"I didn't say a word!" Bea said. Her lips were pursed but her eyes were grinning.

"Your opinion is well documented," Angela said dryly. "But listen, Martina's not as invested in the theater as the crew and the actors are. To her, it's just a little fun, plus free promotion for her hair and makeup business. She didn't strike me as someone who'd get involved in all the drama behind the drama. Plus, she's not at the theater all the time like the actors or the crew building the sets—at least not normally. She said she'll be around the inn a bit more for a while, to help out until Lorelei's back on her feet."

"But even if she's not deliberately stirring the pot, Martina might have gotten the rumor wrong. And if she's keeping her nose so clean, how'd she come across this tasty little tidbit?"

Angela sighed. "Luckily, Connie had already left when she told me—"

"Ah, lemme guess. She heard it from Todd?"

Angela sighed. "Sort of. She said after the playhouse burned down, some of the crew were talking about how there wasn't a board for Pinot Playhouse like a normal nonprofit, and wasn't that weird. Martina said people weren't sure who they heard it from first. Most people thought it was Todd, but some said Grayson. Nobody seemed certain."

"Grayson? I wonder if Mr. Unwanted Advances has something against Roberta."

"Me too. Actually, I wonder how he even got involved in this little community production. Why's he even tangling with Roberta?"

"It sounds like nobody spreading this rumor knows who started it or whether it's true! Like the journos say, some scoops are too good to check. Some rumors are too fun not to spread."

"But what if it really was Todd spreading the rumors—" Angela fumbled for the right words. "If he really thought Roberta was up to something illegal, why not just report her to the authorities?"

"Are you thinking he's got it in for Roberta and could have made the whole thing up?"

Angela nodded sadly.

"That would make him kind of a dirtbag—and low-quality boyfriend material for Connie."

"To say the least."

"That's only one possibility. He could actually be

a good guy who's watching out for the donors. You know me, I've always been the first to question any do-gooder behavior," Bea paused for a bark of laughter. "But thanks to you, I can see it's possible—even if the probability's next to nothing—that he's just interested in putting things right. The donors get nothing for their money if the show doesn't go on, right? And he's the one making that happen."

"Except a tax deduction. But then, if the theater isn't really a nonprofit, they don't even get that. All that money, straight down the drain."

"That's another point in the do-gooder column. And there's the fact that Todd's moving here, but his job hasn't started yet, so maybe he's got nothing else to do—"

"And maybe he wants to polish his reputation with the local movers and shakers, just like we do," Angela said, her face brightening. "Maybe Todd felt bad for the actors, too—"

"He seems to have a certain interest in one of them."

Angela blew out a sigh. "What's up with him calling Lorelei 'Lori'?"

"Could just be an oafish attempt at charm. Todd seems to lack an oaf-ometer," Bea laughed. "Angie, I know you hope he's the one for Connie.

Remember, though, we don't even know if he's interested."

"It's not that I hope he's 'the one.' I just don't want her to get hurt."

"Connie's a big girl. I'm not sure Lorelei's anything to worry about, either. When Todd carried her off to the ER, I was watching from my bench."

Months before, Angela had noticed how much Bea liked puttering around the grounds of the inn. She'd had a carpenter install a flip-down bench by Bea's own suite's window, so that she could enjoy the fresh air and endless wine-country views while pondering how best to murder someone in her next mystery novel.

"They didn't notice me, but I had a clear view of them," Bea continued. "Let's just say Todd looked sincerely worried and that girl looked like she might need a name change to Lori *Lies.*

"I saw Todd put her down by the passenger side. Todd opened the door and offered to help her into the car. Lorelei waved him off, balancing on one foot like a trouper. Then while he ran around to the driver's side and she tried to climb in by herself, she lost her balance—and landed hard on that bad foot without so much as a whimper. She might be a very brave individual... or it could be that Lorelei does her best acting off-stage."

"You sure?"

"Pretty sure. After you ran off after your handsome fiancé, Connie told me she saw Todd and Lorelei, too."

"Oh, no! What did she see?"

"Do we need to discuss the downside of matchmaking, girlie?" Bea snickered. "Connie can handle herself. And if she's going to be disappointed, now's the time, before anything happens—"

"I'm not matchmaking!"

"Call it meddling, then. Whatever you call it—"

"OK, OK. Maybe we'll get a read on what Todd thinks about Connie when the top donors come for their tour. Todd asked me and Connie to help entertain them—" Angela stopped herself, but the horse was out of the barn.

"The donors are coming? The senior snobs? When? I'll mark my calendar!" Bea was rubbing her hands together with fiendish anticipation.

"Well… um… we haven't set a day yet. But it's going to be very stuffy and very boring, Bea—not your kind of scene at all—"

"How thoughtful of you to consider my feelings, Angie," Bea said gravely. "But you know those hoity-toities will insist on meeting *the pro-prietress.*" Bea said "the proprietress" as if doing her impression of a British person with a very bad cold, then burst into a fit of guffaws. "Besides, if it's going to be boring, that's why you need me!" she added, throwing both hands into the air as if jumping out of a cake.

"I'll let you know once I know when they're coming." Angela paused briefly, then her face lit up as an idea popped into her head. "You know, Bea, we've already prepared the menu. Mostly caviar, endive—that kind of fancy stuff, and very little of it. No pizza or tacos or anything you'd like, I'm afraid."

"Thanks for the tip! I'll be sure to have a hearty snack before the upper crust arrive."

Angela sighed and changed the subject.

"Bea, there's one more thing I'm worried about. If Roberta's business is illegal, could that blow back on us? Maybe we should call McGregor."

"That would do more harm than good. He'd love to catch us involved in something illegal," Bea snorted. "Besides, if Roberta is breaking the law, it's probably more of a federal situation."

"FBI? Should I call Drew Faulkner?"

"Um, girlie, you just got engaged. Do you really

think it's a good idea to call your foxy old boyfriend? Especially when you and your fiancé are fighting?"

"Drew's not an old boyfriend and Aseem and I are not fighting," Angela pouted. "At least, I'm not fighting. Maybe he is."

"You worry about taking care of Aseem. I'll take care of the legal advice. It's time to call my old friend, Charlie."

CHAPTER 10

The next morning, Angela entered the ballroom expecting to find the crew building sets with Todd on stage and the actors rehearsing on the deck. Instead, she found Todd and Grayson fighting on the ballroom floor.

Grayson was wagging a finger in Todd's face and shouting invective inspired by Shakespeare. Todd was throwing back equally hostile but decidedly saltier insults. The crew was going through the motions of working but mostly keeping their eyes and ears focused on the argument. The actors on the deck had gathered near the French doors. They were peering through their hands for a better view, trying to read Grayson and Todd's lips.

"If you wake me up again tonight, Todd, you may not live long enough to regret it!" Grayson stormed. His face was just inches from Todd's.

"Unlike some people involved in this production, I have *work* to do, Grayson. Lots and lots of it. It goes until late at night. Isn't it better if my crew and I do this work? Or are your actors so talented they don't need scenery?"

"Perhaps instead of your absurd rhetoric you could stick to the point. Your contributions are greatly appreciated. However, it's unacceptable for you to shine your car lights into my bedroom at two in the morning!"

"Gentlemen!" Angela cried. Grayson and Todd hadn't even noticed her until she was right beside them—and even then, she had to shout to get their attention. "Let's take this someplace more private. Come with me." She led the way briskly out the door to the reception area.

"Of course," Grayson said ingratiatingly. "My apologies for the disturbance. Thank you for bringing us to our senses, dear Angela."

Todd made a gagging gesture. Grayson gave him a warning sneer and tried to push ahead of him, but Todd tipped his shoulder toward Grayson to block him from passing.

"Sit down," Angela said as they reached the

empty reception area, which was quiet and dimly lit, except for the Christmas lights on the tree in the corner. She pointed to two plush chairs on either side of the tree. "What's all this about?"

"I moved into my splendid casita last night—thank you very much," Grayson began. "The bed is exceedingly comfortable, but my peaceful slumber was interrupted by the boor next door," he said, tilting his head toward Todd.

"What's this about shining car lights into Grayson's windows?" Angela asked Todd.

"I was moving into my own casita. I suppose it was a bit late," Todd said.

"It was late enough that some people would call it early!" Grayson blurted, prompting a reproachful look from Angela. "Once more, I'd like to apologize to you, Angela."

"That's because I'd been *working*, Grayson. There was no bulb in the lamp over the door, and I needed the light to get inside," Todd said.

"You needed the light for half an hour?" Grayson railed. "Was that your first experience of opening a door?"

"More like half a minute," Todd replied.

"You turned it on again while you were milling around in the back yard for another half hour after that! Frankly, I'll be surprised if your car starts after all that battery draining. Shall we go test my theory?"

Angela exhaled loudly and the two men said "sorry" in unison.

"A missing bulb is odd. I'm sorry about that, Todd. I'll see that it's fixed. Could you be a bit more sensitive about noise when you're working late? Wasn't that the reason you gave me for wanting a casita in the first place—that you didn't want to disturb anyone?"

"You're right. I'm sorry, Angela. And sorry, Grayson."

"Shake?"

Todd made a show of wiping his right hand repeatedly on his jeans, then extended it to Grayson. Grayson sulked but eventually shook Todd's hand.

Grayson turned to Angela. "It pains me that you had to get involved in our little squabble." He picked up Angela's right hand with his left and raised it toward his lips, but Angela managed to slip it from his grasp.

"Grayson, let's be professional, shall we?" Angela said. "We've all got work to do—"

"Speaking of work, there is a group of actors on the deck in need of direction," Roberta said imperiously as she walked through the inn's front door. "A discussion is underway there about whether rehearsals are done for the day. Laughable considering how far behind schedule we are, don't you agree? Grayson, care to rejoin us?"

"I do. As quoth the Bard, my joy's soul lies in the doing. Thank you, Roberta. Let us restore order." He bowed melodramatically in Angela's direction before heading out the front door with Roberta.

"That's not something you see every day," Todd snickered to Angela. "Community theater understudy giving orders to a big-time director."

Angela saw an opportunity to test Todd. "Almost like she owns the place. That sense of ownership—that's what community theater is all about, isn't it?" Angela said. She paused for a moment, but Todd's expression revealed nothing.

"Thanks for solving our little dust-up, Angela," Todd said, standing up. "I'd better check on the stage crew, too."

"Better get a wiggle on, Todd," Bea said, marching toward them from the direction of the ballroom. "I'm hearing signs of a mutiny. Better get back in the ballroom before they prepare the plank."

"'A sense of ownership,' huh? Nice touch, Angie," Bea said, once Todd was gone and she and Angela were alone in the lobby.

"Too bad I didn't learn anything."

"Speaking of learning, the crew said they thought Todd and Grayson were about to come to blows," Bea said. "Too bad you broke them up. I would have paid good money to watch those two duke it out."

"Bea, are you serious about the crew being ready to quit?"

"They may love the theater, but they say the crazy schedule, crappy materials, and lack of appreciation have sucked the joy out of volunteering. Todd's lucky they spilled their guts to me, though. I just did him a big favor."

"Why am I suddenly feeling a little nervous?"

"I invited all three of them for poker lessons at the Valley Card Room the night after tomorrow. I'd already promised Phil I'd teach him, so I figured I'd invite the others and see if any actors want to come, too. It should be a real morale booster!"

"The night after tomorrow—are you sure Todd can spare them? The show's not even a week away now."

"He'll have to spare them altogether if they

quit! If they have a chance to blow off a little steam, maybe they'll stick around."

A little smile formed on Angela's face.

"Glad the idea's growing on you, Angie." It looked like wheels might be turning in Bea's head, too.

"The night after tomorrow you said, right?"

"That's right. That's the soonest they can do it. They've got stage light rentals coming in to-morrow night, and they didn't want to stick Todd with all that work. Kinda sweet, don't you think? They're thinking of storming off in a huff, but they feel guilty about it."

"Sounds like you've got it all worked out. Would you excuse me, Bea? I'm going to replace a light bulb at the casitas," Angela said, stepping into the closet behind the vacant reception desk.

"Sure thing, girlie," Bea said, heading down the hall to her suite. "I got planning to do! Pepperoni pizza, cheap beer—I'll spare no expense for this poker night!"

Still smiling, Angela retrieved a stepladder and the bulb she needed, then pulled her cell from her pocket. She found Connie's last text and typed out a quick reply.

· · ·

I FIGURED out perfect time 4 society ladies night! You free the night after tomorrow?

ANGELA PULLED on a fleece and headed to the business center to meet Connie and Martina. It was a bright, crisp evening, so she'd decided to walk outside, along the perimeter of the inn. Winter rains were due in a few days, but tonight the sky was clear. A silvery moon cast a misty, tranquil glow on the dormant vines of the neighboring wineries.

A faint smell of wood burning hung in the air. At first, Angela found it pleasant. Then she remembered the ruined playhouse, and the constant fear of fire everyone in the wine country felt during dry weather. She scanned the horizon for signs of fire and sighed with relief when she saw none, just a bit of wispy smoke from the chimney of a building a few miles away.

The business center was close to one of the back entrances to the inn. Angela approached it and silently scanned her key card. Inside, she heard Connie's voice coming from the business center, along with someone else's. When she recognized the second voice, she stopped short.

"I think both plans sound terrific," Todd said. "Angela was right. You are brilliant."

Connie giggled. "Entertaining heiresses—I suppose you could call it a skill."

"I was truly worried about pleasing those wealthy ladies. I should have realized you'd know just what to do—I just—I haven't thought of you as being from that world—"

"My donation was on the modest side. I'm so sorry—I'm embarrassed. I'm trying to make it on my own, without relying on my Hollander name or family money. Maybe it's nuttier than a fruitcake, but I've got something to prove."

"I meant it as a compliment. I just picture those society types as, you know, like that saying about thinking you hit a triple when you were born on third base. How many of those folks got their money because their ancestors cheated other people, and the more they get, the more they want! They'll stop at nothing!" Todd paused for a breath and chuckled at himself. "I guess you can tell, I don't like moneyed types. But you're nothing like that at all."

"In my family, we remember our roots. We enjoy mingling with the society set, but we never forget our humble beginnings. And as far as I know, nobody ever got cheated by my ancestors except maybe the government. Most people thought they deserved it back then." Connie laughed, then lowered her voice and turned her Southern accent up to eleven. "Our forefathers were bootleggers, dontcha know."

Todd chuckled. "For the record, your donation was generous, and you've given your time, too. All while trying to build your own business. That's why I've hesitated to ask you for more help, even though… even though I'd love to see more of you."

It was suddenly quiet in the business center. Angela leaned forward to try to hear what was happening. It was all she could do to resist peeking around the door.

"Hey, girlie!"

Angela gasped and spun around to find Martina and Bea. Angela hadn't even heard them walk up behind her.

"Everything OK, Angie?" Bea said. "Overheard any good convos lately?"

"Don't be silly, Bea. I just got here myself," Angela said. "I thought I heard Connie's voice. Maybe she's already here?"

"I met Martina here wandering the halls and thought I'd give her a personal escort," Bea said. "She tells me she's Pinot Playhouse's hair and makeup expert. Now that BettyCon's behind us,

I'm thinking of ditching the Christmas tips." Bea touched the ends of her gray bob. "Martina's going to hook me up with a new color. I'm thinking electric pink."

Connie and Todd walked slowly out of the business center together, all smiles, and Bea winked at Angela in an exaggerated fashion that was missed by no one. When Angela squinted at her and frowned, Bea winked again.

"I'd better go see how the crew is doing," Todd said.

"Good idea, Cap'n Bligh," Bea cackled. "I'll come with, just in case anyone suggests you take a long walk off a short board. I'll tell you all about the night out I've got planned for your crew."

"Wait—what—night out? It's crunch time—" Todd said.

"Don't you worry, I've got it all handled," Bea said. "Let's go. Bye, ladies!"

As they turned to walk down the hall, Bea stopped to look at Todd's stomach, which was protruding over his tightly cinched belt and over-hanging his chinos. "Todd, is it my imagination, or have you lost weight?"

Then she reached over and rubbed Todd's belly firmly, as if she were petting a very large, very friendly St. Bernard.

Angela caught a glimpse of Todd practically leaping backwards from Bea's touch. Angela's jaw dropped and she let out a little squeak. Bea stared at Todd with a wry smile.

"Angela, are you all right?" Connie called out.

Angela turned around and sighed with relief when she realized that Connie and Martina had seen none of Bea's unsolicited contact with Todd's midsection. They'd already stepped inside the business center.

"How 'bout I take notes, and you and Martina measure?" Connie said sweetly, peering around the door. She was holding a small leather-bound notebook.

"Sounds good," Angela said, pulling a tape measure from her pocket. Martina was already striding along the long side of the room and counting to herself. "I hope Aseem will have time to help us move everything, once we figure out where it all goes."

"Don't worry if your dreamboat fiancé is busy, sugar," Connie said with a little twinkle in her eye. "I'm sure I can persuade Todd to help us."

CHAPTER 11

"As soon as we're done with breakfast, I've got some time to help with your dressing room project," Aseem said. He and Angela were sitting at table in the inn's otherwise empty breakfast room. "Before I head down to the Peninsula, I mean."

"Thank you," Angela said, puzzled. She pulled a muffin from the bag on the table in front of them. "Thank you for breakfast, I mean, and for making time to help with the show. Here—Connie wrote down all the measurements." She passed him Connie's notebook. "You're going down to Silicon Valley today?"

"That look on your face says you forgot. I told you a few days ago that I have to spend the rest of this week in the office. I won't be back until Saturday." He pointed at his rolling suitcase, stowed underneath the table.

"I'm sorry, I remember now. But if you're gone all week, that means—"

"I know. No ring shopping until the weekend, at least."

"Yes… right, but I was going to say that you won't be here for the first performance of *The Ratcatcher*. I was hoping you'd be my date—"

"Like a 'boyfriend'?"

"As my *fiancé.* I want to show you off to everyone."

"You've got a funny way of showing it, refusing to even look at engagement rings."

"I'm not refusing. I'm looking forward to it. I just don't understand why you're in such a hurry. We just got engaged!"

"Angela, it's been over a month now. Nearly two, actually. And you've canceled ring shopping, what, four times now? Or is it five?"

"I've been busy! I thought you understood. I'm looking forward to choosing a ring once the show's behind us. I promise I am."

"Yeah. Once the show's over, there will probably be some other reason to put it off."

"I'm *not* dragging my feet. I promise you."

Angela reached across the table for his hand just as Aseem stood up and grabbed his suitcase and headed for the door.

"Not dragging your feet. Right," Aseem muttered. "Maybe they're just cold."

"What did you say?" Angela cried.

"Nothing. I'm going to put my suitcase in the car. I'll meet you at the business center in five minutes."

"THE CATERERS HAVE SET up in the ballroom. Your English china is perfect. And the food looks good, too, I think," Angela said.

She and Connie were standing by the inn entrance, facing the parking lot, waiting for their VIP guests to arrive. "Maybe more like 'good,'" Angela said, making air quotes with her fingers and giggling. "It's pretty. Artistic. Not sure how it will taste. The miniature scones look tasty, at least."

"Appearance is what matters," Connie smiled. "They probably won't eat the food, anyway. Speaking of appearances, what about the bartender? Is he set up? And most important—is he *handsome?*"

"Straight out of *GQ*."

"That's what I'm talkin' about, sugar. Shall we go over the ladies' mini-biographies one more time?"

Connie revisited the brief histories of the benefactors they'd invited. There was Dorothy Heaton, whose family railroad wealth was accumulated more than one hundred and fifty years ago.

"Dori's lovely, known for politeness and generosity," Connie said. "Her secretary wasn't certain if she'd be able to attend on short notice, though. I took that as a 'no.'"

Two other benefactresses were unlikely to show up: Eleanor Havenhurst, whose great-great-grandfather launched a media empire in the late nineteenth century, and Jane Landerson, of the famed banking family.

"We'd have a better turnout if we'd given more notice. I got the impression those three all wanted to do a site visit and expected it to be scheduled weeks ago, at the playhouse. But I don't believe Todd was concerned about those three, anyway," Connie said. "They're the donors charities dream about. They write checks and say nice things—or say nothing at all. It's the play's two biggest donors that he's worried about. Victoria McGiven—"

"Maiden name Victoria Hartman," Angela said. "Her family founded the "Hartland" organic grocery chain in the 1970s. She's convinced she doesn't get as much society-page love as other donors."

"Right. One might say she has a bit of a chip on her shoulder," Connie chuckled.

"Maybe the society page reporters have chips on their shoulders. I remember one story that said Hartland foods were double the prices of regular stores, and questioned whether the foods were actually organic. Maybe the journalists are mad they can't afford to shop there."

Connie laughed. "That's why some people call it 'Heartless Grocers.' Truly, Victoria gets plenty of society page ink. If she's hoping to change her image from 'Heartless' to kindhearted, though, she probably wants to be caught on camera doing good works as often as she can."

"Maybe that's why she wants to check on her donation. If Todd can't turn this show around, will it hurt her reputation more than help it?"

"It could, but sometimes backing a struggling charity can cultivate sympathy. Especially a community based one."

"And lastly, there's Elizabeth Velton," Angela said. "Otherwise known as Tibby Velton?"

"That's her. Her family founded Vel-Tone Value Laundromats and Dry Cleaners."

"I'm surprised the business hasn't disappeared. I never wear dry clean only clothing anymore. Do you?"

"Quite a bit more than you do, I expect," Connie laughed. "Dry cleaning may be getting less popular, but the Velton laundromat business keeps growing. But as I understand it, the clothes-cleaning business hasn't been their main source of wealth for years. They turned all those laundries into a billion-dollar real estate empire."

"Hardly seems possible. A billion-dollar property empire on the back of coin-operated laundries?" Angela paused, her face scrunched. "Then again, you always hear that the best business opportunities involve doing dirty jobs."

"Indeed. I should know," Connie laughed. "In Tibby's case, though, that soiled history seems to have affected her self-esteem. She's had trouble socially, especially with the heiresses around her age. She'll be joined at the hip with Victoria, who must be more than thirty years older than she is. Victoria is like her society page mentor."

"Even though Victoria feels she hasn't mastered the game herself?"

"Victoria and Tibby may be 'country bumpkins' compared to the San Francisco social set, but they are well-known socialites in Sacramento and Tahoe. I think the discrimination could be mostly in Victoria's imagination. Then again, people treat you how you expect to be treated, don't they?"

Angela pondered Connie's point from its various angles.

"Victoria and Tibby should be here by now, shouldn't they?"

"They're bound to be fashionably late. Speaking of *fashionable*, you look great."

Angela did a little twirl, showing off the ensemble Connie put together for her. The pale pink designer suit—cinched with a wide, elegant belt—was feminine yet staid. "All thanks to you. Do I look serious enough? I can't remember the last time I wore pumps and stockings."

"You look serious as a Junior League secretary. I think we look great together."

Connie wore an equally dignified outfit of a black wool skirt, black hose, and a cashmere sweater with a faux-fur collar. A white blouse with a delicate bow peeked out of the cardigan.

"What about my outfit?" The question came from behind them and was accompanied by a familiar cackle.

Connie and Angela spun around to find Bea standing just inches from them.

"Where did you come from?" Angela stammered.

Bea pointed one of her teal Velcro sneakers off to the side, pivoting and flexing her leg on the tip of her toe. She was mimicking a 1960s fashion model's pose, but in her light russet track suit, Bea's stance brought to mind an ornery roan pony about to kick.

"Answer my question first. How do you like the *look,* dahlings?" Bea reached up with her palm and gave her little cap of a haircut an upward push. "Lucky me. Martina was here again and I got her to switch up my color." Bea's green and red tips had been swapped for orange and pink running almost up to her roots.

Angela and Connie gaped at her wordlessly for a beat.

"I knew it! I should have broken out my fluffy winter boots instead of the sneaks."

"Don't worry, Bea," Angela said. "You'll be best dressed in the Valley Card Room tonight.

Speaking of 'sneaks,' why were you sneaking up on us?"

"I wasn't sneaking. I just walked right up. You two were just so engrossed in your intel, you didn't notice me. Just as well. I got to hear all the important details about our elite guests."

"It's too bad that you'll miss them," Angela said. "Won't you be off to the casino shortly? It's nearly six o'clock already. Didn't you promise the troops a full evening of poker?"

"Postponed. The stage lighting installation was moved to tonight and the crew need to be here. That must be them." A box truck branded "Show Light Specialists" was heading down the hill from the direction of Connie's property.

"Oh, so you're here to greet the truck?" Angela said. "Bea, that's nice of you to help Todd—"

Phil, the stage crew volunteer, stepped briskly out of the inn entrance and into their path. His hand was still partially wrapped with a bandage.

"Pardon me, ladies. I'm here to direct the lighting team," Phil said, stepping right in front of them. He put two fingers from his good hand into his mouth and blew a loud whistle. "Fellas! Over here!" He got the attention of the driver, then jogged lightly toward the rear entrance of the inn, waving them to follow as he went.

"Phil's fast for a guy his age," Bea chuckled. "See, Angie? Phil and the rest of the crew have the lighting all under control. I'm free to help you entertain the richies!"

"Thank you," Angela said with a gulp, "but that's really not necessary. We told them you were unavailable. And besides, don't you remember what I told you about the food?"

"You weren't kidding, either. I saw that table you set up in the ballroom. Spears of rabbit food, cucumber sandwiches, and a few lonely scallops. Oh, and cold fish eggs. Nice touch! But the little scones made a nice snack. Let the VIP woo-fest begin!"

"Yes, well that sounds good," Angela said. Anyone looking at her could see that a frantic tap dance was going on in her head. Certainly it was obvious to Bea, who had a sly little smirk forming on her face.

"Bea, there's just one problem," Angela said at last. "Todd is desperate to impress the donors, so Connie came up with a plan—"

"I don't doubt that," Bea said. "You're a bit of a fancy type yourself, Connie."

"Why thank you—I think," Connie said.

"We need to give the appearance that this is the 'right kind' of operation," Angela said. "That's why

Connie lent me this outfit. We're putting on a show—the show before the show, if you will."

"Oh, I get it. You're worried I'm not dressed right," Bea chuckled.

"We could rummage through your closet, but I'm sure you don't have any clothing this boring," Angela said with a giggle, "except maybe for a funeral!" Then she gasped with embarrassment as she looked at Connie, who mouthed, "It's OK!"

"Not to worry, ladies, I bought something special just for tonight. Close your eyes!"

With nervous looks on their faces, Angela and Connie complied.

"Ready!" Bea said. "Ta-da!"

Bea had removed her jacket to reveal a baggy t-shirt that said in huge letters,

I've been rich and I've been poor.
Rich is better.

"SEEMS like the perfect thing for the bag ladies, assuming they have a sense of humor."

"Dare I ask… *bag ladies?*" Angela said.

"The grocery bag lady and the laundry bag

lady. Get it?" Bea chuckled. "I can't wait to try that out on them. And look—that must be them. I can't see through the dark windows of that black SUV, but—"

"Yes," Angela croaked. "It's them."

CHAPTER 12

The driver opened the passenger door closest to them and Angela and Connie both inhaled deeply as they watched a thin leg clad in deep blue denim and a designer ballet flat emerge from the back seat.

The leg belonged to a refined woman in her late sixties. She was petite and slender to the point of fragility, with perfect posture. Her fine, wheat-colored hair was pulled into a simple, sleek bun at the base of her neck. Her outfit—dark designer jeans, a silk blouse, cashmere cardigan, designer scarf—looked like an old-money version of what Angela wore every day.

"I'm Victoria Hartman McGiven," the woman said, gracefully extending her manicured hand.

"And this is my friend, Elizabeth Velton," she added, as her traveling companion emerged from the car.

"Call me Tibby," Elizabeth said. "Everyone does."

Tibby was about four inches taller than Victoria. Her outfit of inky jeans, a white blouse, and a caramel-colored sweater was clearly expensive, but somehow lacked all the subtle chic of Victoria's version.

Tibby stepped forward to offer a handshake, hesitating a moment to smooth strands of her wispy hair that were untamed by her tartan headband. As she stopped to adjust her sweater on her broad shoulders, she noticed Angela gazing a bit too long.

"Victoria, I think we're under-dressed," Tibby said. Victoria looked at her friend tolerantly and shook her head in a barely perceptible way. "We just assumed there'd be set construction and other work going on around us—"

"Of course you're not under-dressed," Angela said anxiously.

"We dressed up to let you know how glad we are to meet you," Connie said smoothly. "You're the most important guests of Pinot Playhouse. We wanted to show our respect."

"Don't worry, ladies," Bea piped up, squeezing herself between Angela and Connie. "I'm here to balance things out." She'd tied her warm up jacket around her waist, ensuring no one would miss the message on her shirt.

"And you are...?" Victoria said, her eyes squinting as she stared at the message on Bea's shirt.

"I'm the innkeeper," Bea crowed, pointing at herself with her two thumbs. "Bea Sickles, also known as Betty Snickerdoodle. Shall we start the grand tour?"

Without waiting for an answer, Bea grabbed Victoria's arm and threaded hers through it. Victoria looked shocked but seemed to adapt to the situation as Bea spirited her toward the door.

"Maybe I should keep them company?" Connie said to Angela, pointing at Bea and Victoria walking away. Angela nodded enthusiastically and Connie hustled after them.

"I guess you're stuck with me, Tibby," Angela said.

"Don't worry about Victoria," Tibby said. "She can be particular, but she can handle any situation."

"That's good to know. Are you hungry? We've

prepared some light appetizers and a cocktail bar. I hope you like caviar."

"A cocktail sounds delightful, but honestly, I've been to several charity events lately and I'm so tired of that fancy stuff. Don't tell Victoria. She's trying to teach me better taste."

"I think a pizza could be arranged."

"Victoria wouldn't like that at all," Tibby laughed. "I hope you don't mind my asking, but am I right that you're the business mind behind Betty Snickerdoodle?"

"Well… I've done all the marketing for the Betty Snickerdoodle brand, but I have to say it's an easy sell."

"Marketing seems quite challenging to me. I'm interested to hear how you turned a few popular books into a media phenomenon."

"Are you sure you want to get me started? I love talking about business."

"I'm learning to love it, too. You may know that my family has a network of laundromats—"

"I've heard of it—who hasn't?" Angela said admiringly.

"My parents did well. I'm getting more involved in the business now. They've set me up with my own region. I just... I don't want to disappoint them. I've got some ideas. I've come to see the laundromats as social places. And there's been all this innovation in other kinds of vending machines—baked goods, espresso, maybe even cocktails can be sold in them."

"Sounds like a perfect social media marketing opportunity. I'd love to help you brainstorm ideas."

"That's what I was hoping you'd say. I don't—I don't even have a social media presence of my own. I don't even know how it works. That's weird, right?"

It was hard for Angela to imagine a person so close to her in age being unfamiliar with social media—especially not a wealthy young woman like Tibby. Based on what Angela regularly saw online, documenting their fabulous lives was the favorite hobby of socialites in their twenties and thirties.

"It's easy," Angela said. "To learn, I mean. If you could share more details about your business and how you see it growing, I can make some marketing suggestions."

"I'd love to talk business, and to get something to eat, too, even if it has to be caviar," Tibby laughed. "But first, could I see more of this impressive property? I understand the structures have been here for decades. I'm fascinated by the history of important properties in Northern California. Would you mind giving me a quick tour?"

"I'd be delighted. We can talk social media as we go. And Tibby—would it be wrong for me to say you're nothing like I expected?"

"I hope that's a compliment."

"WOULD ANYONE LIKE A COCKTAIL?" Bea asked Victoria and Connie.

Bea tipped her head toward the mahogany bar by the fireplace, tended by a tuxedo-clad young man. The fire Angela had built earlier roared and crackled, creating a warm ambiance (and, Angela hoped, a distraction from the disarray on the stage).

"Inviting, isn't it, Victoria?" Connie said.

But despite the allure of the bar and the fire, Victoria was barely listening to Bea and Connie. She was staring the other way at the stage, where the crew wrestled clumsily with a sagging set flat, trying to make way for the stage lights to be delivered through the back of the stage.

"Todd, I'll help!" Connie said, rushing across the ballroom to the shaky stairs the crew had attached to the left end of the stage. She barely managed to climb them in her pumps and straight skirt. "I'll take one corner," she shouted excitedly, but then one of her heels got stuck in one of the stairs. She fell forward on her hands ungracefully with an "oof" followed by "I'm OK!"

Then everyone heard the unmistakable sound of torn muslin.

"Oops! Add another task to the crew's to-do list," Bea chuckled.

"Don't they have more than enough left to do?" Victoria said sternly. "Our VIP preview is just a few days away. Perhaps I can free up that night on my calendar. I've got a good book I'd like to start."

"You should have seen where they started, though. And now it's been a couple of days without a trip to the emergency room. I'm starting to like their chances," Bea said.

Victoria's face filled with disgust. "What is that thing Connie just climbed? That pile of mismatched wood?"

"Our stage didn't have wings or side stairs, and —are you familiar with the play?" Bea said. "I don't want to spoil anything."

Victoria nodded. "I vaguely remember it."

"I won't say too much, then. Let's just say a hiding place is needed. If this were a normal theater, there would be wings and an offstage area, but Todd has to improvise."

"Look at the nails sticking out of some of those boards. Someone could get seriously hurt if they're hiding on that pile of junk. Thousands of dollars from me and Tibby and this is all it has bought?"

"Are you saying you genuinely care about the play, Victoria?" Bea said. "I thought it was all about the tax break with you big cheeses. You got a soft spot for local theater?"

"Tax breaks are nice, but I hope that my dollars are doing some good. And I hope that well-selected donations help people better understand my character."

"I get it. A little image buff-up. Write-ups in the society pages touting your good deeds."

"To put it coarsely, yes. Positive media coverage helps. It can address misconceptions the public has about people with money. Sometimes, though, a donation is just a pet project. I supported this theater because Tibby had her heart set on it. If I'm not mistaken, that's her Aunt Louisa rehearsing out on your deck. She's a poor Velton relation. Doesn't have a pot to pee in—or anything else—to show for her lifelong passion for theater."

Bea looked out at the deck through the French doors. A woman in her sixties stood next to Roberta in the center of the area they'd taped off as the stage. Like Roberta, the woman was tall—from a distance, it was hard to tell them apart. A much younger woman stood in front of the actresses. She wore jeans and a fleece and her right foot appeared to have a blue boot strapped around it. Despite the distance, Bea recognized her.

Lorelei's back. Looking pretty surefooted, too.

Lorelei was holding various pieces of clothing up against Louisa and Roberta: a tweed riding jacket, a white shirt with a bow-tie collar, beige breeches. Two pairs of tall riding boots stood on the deck next to them. As she tried out the various pieces, Lorelei conferred with Grayson. He looked displeased. His body language suggested he was barking his reaction to the costumes.

"Tibby mentioned that the title relates to the foxhunting theme of the play," Victoria said. "A 'ratcatcher' is a jacket or a shirt or some kind of garment related to foxhunting."

"Don't forget, in any murder mystery, they gotta catch the rat whodunnit," Bea cackled. "Get it? It's what they call a double entendre."

The way Bea said it, "entendre" rhymed with "laundry."

"I prefer historical fiction. As far as live performance goes, opera and ballet are my usual fare. Like I said, I'm involved with *The Ratcatcher* to support Tibby. When we started this adventure, Tibby's Aunt Louisa had her heart set on the character of Edie, but was relegated to serving as Roberta's understudy. I suggested Tibby remind Roberta that if she intends to hoard a coveted role for herself, she should fund the production with her money and return ours. Predictably, Roberta swapped spots with Louisa."

"I didn't realize Roberta had that type of money."

"Apparently, she came into a big inheritance recently. Millions left by an elderly uncle. His wealth was rather secret. He bought up hundreds of low-rent apartments as California boomed and rarely spent a cent. Lived alone in a small studio until he died at ninety-six. Pinot Playhouse is Roberta's pet project—but she's averse to opening her own checkbook to support it. Perhaps Roberta inherited her uncle's cheapness as well.

"Tibby was a logical vein to tap, once Roberta learned that Louisa was her aunt. Tibby is, unfortunately, a reliable soft touch. I'm sure Roberta was surprised when Tibby stood up for herself and for her Aunt Louisa."

"How'd you come to take Tibby under your wing, anyway?"

"It takes time to build a positive reputation—that 'buffing,' as you so colorfully described it. When the media is involved, it's usually one step forward, two steps back. Poor Tibby's had more than her share of reputational challenges."

"There's only one thing worse than being talked about," Bea cracked. "And that's not being talked about."

"I love Oscar Wilde, too, but he greatly exaggerated the benefits of unfavorable publicity. Poor Tibby. For a long time, the more she tried to correct her reputation, the uglier things got. I understood her predicament well. At first, I just offered words of encouragement. But she wanted a bit of a mentor, and I saw no reason not to help. Especially since the media was just one piece of the puzzle."

"How so?"

"Unlike other well-to-do young people, Tibby has never really gotten the hang of self-promotion. I have to say, I generally respect her for it. At the risk of mixing metaphors, though, the gossip mill abhors a vacuum. Tibby says nothing, and vicious rumors fill the gap, circulated by malignant individuals in our own echelon. Those do the most damage. It doesn't help that she's not the most confident or fashionable girl. Lies and rumors often plague anyone of our financial stature. I've been on the receiving end for decades. What Tibby faces is much worse, however."

"Heartless Grocers, purveyor of overpriced faux organic food?"

"That's one version. I know personally that just because the nasty things people say aren't true doesn't mean they don't hurt. I'm jaded now, but when I was Tibby's age, I was more sensitive. And as I said, what they say about Tibby is much worse. Because it's starting in our own circles, she's excluded from events she'd like to attend—the very places where she could make connections. Poor girl. I'd find it humiliating—she's practically begging to give her money away. There are some places I'm invited to that she isn't, so I bring her into the fold when I can."

"Those rumors haven't made it to my ears. What exactly are people saying?"

"I'd rather not risk spreading them. It's bad enough that they're gaining a foothold in our rarified world." Victoria paused, a curious look on her face. "You're rather rich. Don't you hear these sorts of things yourself?"

"Now that's funny. Me in your world. Now

that you say that, Victoria, I just noticed that Aunt Louisa and Roberta are like a matched set, and so are we. They're large and we're extra-small." Bea punched Victoria lightly in her slender forearm, prompting another raised eyebrow from Victoria. "It's fun to be with someone my own size for once. We should stick together, else we could go unnoticed."

"Oh, yes, Bea. You're quite inconspicuous," Victoria said drolly, looking Bea up and down.

"Good one, fancy pants!" Bea said, holding her bony palm up for a high five. "C'mon, girl, don't leave me hanging!"

"I don't have to worry about being invisible. People make a point of finding me. And my money."

"That's why it pays to go incognito. No one ever thinks I'm rich unless they know me. One gal even came here and was convinced I was a homeless scam artist. Unfortunately for her, she wound up murdered," Bea said, letting loose a bark of laughter and slapping her knee. "Good times."

"Charming. Speaking of handling one's money, do you have any aspirations as a donor?"

"I do all right with the ka-ching, but I'm not sure I'd fit in with you old money types. Angela's inheriting the business when I'm gone. I'll leave it to her to figure out who to donate to—she'll be great at it."

Victoria looked at Bea's t-shirt again and smiled. "The media would have a field day if you showed up at the opera in that outfit, holding a big check. You know, one of those jumbo ones—like for the lottery. Oh, that's a good one!" Victoria's smile turned into a chuckle and then hearty laughter. "They wouldn't be able either to turn you away or let you in. We might have to try it. Of course, you'd have to promise to pretend not to know me."

"Nice to see you loosening up, Vicky," Bea roared. "Oops—you sure I can't call you Vicky?"

"OK, but not in front of anyone else."

"Deal."

"By the way, I love your t-shirt. Sophie Tucker was a favorite of my grandmother's. Don't tell anyone I said that, either."

Victoria turned back toward the table full of elegant hors d'oeuvres. A primly dressed caterer stood behind it, ready to place tidbits on Connie's little bone china plates. Victoria sighed. "I'm hungry, and those petite dishes look lovely. Still, just between you and me, sometimes it would be nice to be offered pizza and beer."

Bea chortled. "That could be arranged."

"Can you put tiny discs of pizza on spoons, and serve the beer in crystal thimbles?" Victoria said. "I've got an image to uphold."

Connie rushed back over to join them.

"The crew's made so much progress! Isn't it great? They're installing the stage lights now," she said breathlessly. "It's coming together, Victoria. You'll see. So, what did I miss? Are you having fun?"

"Fun?" Victoria sniffed. "Hardly!"

When Connie looked away, Bea shot a wink and a grin in Victoria's direction. Victoria reciprocated.

"Bea, I'd like to freshen up before trying some of those morsels. Can you point me in the direction of the ladies' room?"

As Victoria walked away, Connie leaned in toward Bea's ear and whispered, "Like my granny used to say, that one has her nose so high in the air she could drown in a rainstorm!"

"So true, Connie. So true."

Angela and Tibby walked around the front of the inn, past the parking lot and toward the casitas, taking in the view of the foothills. The dusky sky created a pretty backdrop to the grade, which ran all the way around Connie's land until it connected to the mountain ridge that bounded Napa Valley.

As they walked, Tibby quizzed Angela about the history of the property. Angela confessed that she knew little about who'd owned the ranch before the people who sold it to Bea. A single family had owned it for decades before Bea bought it.

"We've added these casitas, but no other structures—at least so far. We didn't touch the bones of the main building, just moved walls around to create the guest suites and expand the ballroom.

"The realtor guessed that what's now the ball-room had once been a bunkhouse. She thought the property had been a working ranch at one point, and that perhaps the family's home had been where Connie's winery buildings now stand. The land was subdivided at some point."

"Have you looked for official maps? Historical documents, I mean? Even unofficial documents might tell a story."

"I haven't. When Bea bought the property, we were just looking for something we could convert into our Christmas inn. This place fit perfectly. We were thrilled when her bid was accepted and we got right to work customizing it."

"I'd be dying of curiosity about the history if I were you," Tibby gushed. "With these big Northern California estates, there's always a chance they were connected to successful prospectors from the Gold Rush. Or perhaps something even more intriguing—this place might have been the country home of a scandalous robber baron!"

"Why am I not surprised you're fascinated by that 'colorful' history? I've heard the real secret to your family's fortune wasn't cleaning clothes."

Angela laughed lightly but stopped when she saw the injured look on Tibby's face.

"Don't believe everything you've heard, Angela," Tibby said crossly, her voice quavering, her pale skin turning red. "People and their rumors—they don't care who they hurt!"

"Oh, Tibby, I'm sorry. I haven't heard anything I consider negative about your family at all. I'm biased, but I can't see a thing wrong with building a fortune in real estate. My mother is a realtor and I'm so proud of her. Selling real estate helped her provide for me as a single mother. I feel nothing but admiration for your family! They built a thriving business from the ground up. And I'm so impressed by your knowledge, too," Angela said, desperate to reassure Tibby.

"I must sound naive," Angela continued, "but I don't understand. Is there a different attitude toward real estate in your world? I'm just an ordinary girl—there's so much I don't know. I'm so sorry to have offended you. That wasn't my intention at all."

Tibby let out a loud sigh that sounded like a mix of surprise and laughter and relief. "I'm sorry —I overreacted. I take things too personally. I... I just feel like an outsider sometimes. It's embarrassing, but I don't have friends my own age and

I've already told you I don't even do social media. It's partly because I'm afraid of what I'll find there."

Tibby's speech grew animated, almost hyper. "The other people I meet at charity functions—the few I get asked to—most of their families got their money nearly two hundred years ago. Some of their grandparents actually *were* called robber barons. You'd never know it by how snobby and prejudiced they can be to newcomers."

A weak smile returned to Tibby's face. "My family wouldn't have a real estate business without the laundry business. Maybe laundry's not the classiest, but it pays for everything else. And people need it! That's why I want to do well with the portfolio I'm taking over. But I know I've got so much to learn."

"I'd be happy to get you up to speed on marketing. Should we head inside and talk? I'm always delighted to talk shop. Besides, it's getting dark. The days are so short in wintertime."

"Maybe just a quick peek behind the casitas first? To get a sense of the topography?"

"There's little to see, and you can come back any time. But why not? We can take a quick look and then walk back around the deck side of the inn, to catch a bit of the rehearsal."

"Oh, yes! I do want to see that! Have I told you I know one of the actors?"

BY THE TIME they approached the deck it was already quite dark. Tibby continued to surprise Angela with her interest in details of the grounds, even the plain back lawns that stretched to the foothills.

Tibby had noticed an old shovel on the ground, past a large boulder at the back edge of the lawn behind the casitas. She'd seemed oddly fascinated by it, which piqued Angela ever so slightly. It looked old and out of place and sloppy, and Angela was embarrassed that someone had failed to properly store it. The two of them also stood there long enough for Angela to notice that the light she'd replaced on Todd's landing was out again.

Maybe there's a short.

Angela frowned. A dead bulb was one thing, but she didn't know how to fix or even diagnose a short. With Aseem away for a few more days, the light might have to stay broken.

They walked past the big garage door that was used to load equipment and furnishings into the back of the ballroom. Angela noticed a living room's worth of old furniture under a large tarp, the tarp itself held up by six slender metal poles. She recognized the furniture as part of *The Rat-catcher*'s set and took it as a good sign. If they were ready to load in the furniture, then maybe, just maybe, Todd was going to pull this thing off.

As they reached the far side of the deck, Angela led Tibby off the trail and onto the grass, to avoid distracting the actors. They walked slowly and carefully, staying out of the light bathing the deck.

"That's my Aunt Louisa," Tibby said quietly. "The tall one, in the middle of the scene."

Tibby pointed to the actress who was stumbling around the stage, holding a cup and waving it about carelessly.

"The one who's playing drunk?"

"Yes, that's her," Tibby giggled. "She was *dying* to get the part of Edie. It's not tons of lines, but she says it's the most memorable role in the show. That scene is her favorite one. Can you blame her? What actor doesn't love hamming it up?"

"I'm looking forward to seeing her do it on stage."

"And besides the drunken bit, there's the scene's big finish, really the first act's big finish—oh, wait, you haven't seen the play before, have you?" Tibby said, looking like she was bursting to reveal what happens.

Angela shook her head.

"Without spoiling it, then, let's just say there's a point at the end where Edie has to do a whole lot of improvising all by herself—and in the dark! At least, that's how it was staged when Louisa did the play up in Sacramento. She says it requires a lot of skill," Tibby said, beaming.

"Anyway, it just makes me so happy to see her doing what she loves, immersed in her element. In fact—it's a little embarrassing—Victoria encouraged me to insist Louisa be given the part."

"You mean—as a condition of your donation?" Angela said neutrally.

"Yes. Maybe that sounds… inappropriate?" Tibby said, looking self-conscious. "You see, Victoria and I were Roberta's biggest donors by far. Louisa's my mother's sister, and she has no real money of her own, partly because she's chased her theater dream her entire life. My mother says theater's all Louisa has, and that we have to help her, so she doesn't get upset or… jealous."

"It must be hard when siblings' fortunes mre so different. It's kind of your mother to want to help. I bet it has to be done in just the right way, so it's not insulting—"

"Exactly! Louisa wanted us to donate, but she doesn't know the lengths we went to to make sure she got the role. People can be so emotional about money. She thinks we're the lucky ones. But isn't it just as lucky to know exactly how you want to spend your life, like she does? I'd love to have a passion like that, and the freedom to pursue it, with nothing else to worry about."

Given how Tibby described Louisa's financial situation, Angela wondered if the poor woman actually had nothing else to worry about.

"Louisa's doing great," Angela said, looking at the deck. "She seems perfectly at home as Edie. Why wouldn't Grayson have cast her in the part anyway?"

"Roberta wanted the role for herself. She'd already taken it before Grayson joined the production."

"Is that… is that typical?"

"I don't think so, but many things with Pinot Playhouse are different than other charities. I doubt I'd be a sponsor if it weren't for Aunt Louisa. Pinot Playhouse certainly wasn't on Victoria's list. I rely on Victoria to help me decide which charities are best."

"Victoria sounds like a wonderful advisor—" Angela started to say. But behind the actors, through the windows of the French doors, she saw a catastrophe unfolding. She cried out and rushed toward the deck.

"Oh, no!"

The actors turned around just in time to watch the large rig the stage-lighting contractors had been working on start to collapse. A single lighting technician held one side of the aluminum frame, a look of desperation on his face as he tried to steady the structure. Phil spotted the problem and hurried to the end of the stage. He was able to grab the other side with his good hand, but it slipped from his grip. Slowly, then all at once, it fell to the ballroom floor. The crash was loud even on the deck. It was so noisy that Angela and Tibby could even hear it from the ground.

"I need to make sure no one was hurt!" Angela said, running up the deck stairs.

"I'm coming with you!"

Angela and Tibby rushed inside, and Angela quickly scanned the crew and counted all the heads. The entire crew was rattled, but otherwise alive and well.

"Everyone's fine!" Todd shouted to the actors as he grabbed the door behind Angela and Tibby. "Go back to rehearsing!"

Grayson glared at him. "We're doing our part,

but will there even be a stage for us to perform on?"

"Not helping, Grayson!" Todd yelled, slamming the door.

"The *people* are fine, yes," the lighting tech said angrily, tugging on several of the pipes to decide if they were still sound. "Todd, you're lucky no lighting was hung yet. You'd be liable for any equipment damage. Why did you tell me I could brace the structure on these staircases when they're obviously not stable? Seriously, you're going to have people stand on these things?"

The tech was beside the stairs on the right side of the stage, pulling at a board that was dangling by a single nail. The other half of it was still strapped to a leg of the truss. The tech let go of the broken board and it squeaked as it clapped back into place. The bottom of the truss was still attached to the stairs on the other side, contorting the apparatus into a giant aluminum rhombus.

"Let's not overreact, shall we? We're not done working here," Todd said, exasperated. "Angela, thank you, but I don't need your help."

"Todd, do I need to remind you that I'm responsible for the inn property?" Angela said. "If anyone's injured, we could be liable—"

"C'mon, join us, Angie!" Bea yelled from the far

end of the ballroom, where she was standing with Connie. Even from that distance, Angela could see the worry on Connie's face. "Todd's got it under control—don't you, Todd? Let him do his job. We need you here!"

Angela frowned but escorted Tibby to the fireplace. Bea had a cheeky look on her face. Connie looked worried. She kept sneaking glances at the hubbub by the stage and at Todd.

"Thank you for joining us, Angie. We should socialize with our guests, don't you think?" Bea said, still grinning. "C'mon, Tibster, dig into some fish eggs! You know you want to."

Tibby looked at Angela with wide eyes. Angela just smiled and shrugged.

"Where's Victoria?"

"I'm right here," Victoria said, walking back into the ballroom. "I guess a lot can happen during a quick trip to the rest room."

Victoria surveyed the chaos at the other end of the room with raised eyebrows. "Tibby, I was just telling Bea we should make other plans for Thursday night. This production doesn't even have a stage to rehearse on, much less present a VIP performance."

"Victoria, you don't know Todd like I do!" Connie piped up. "I'm certain he'll have things fixed lickety-split. Try to remember the whole reason he moved the show is to protect your donations!"

"Is that so?" Victoria said.

"Of course it's so!" Connie cried. "Please excuse me. I'm going to go help Todd and the crew."

"I meant no offense," Victoria said. "It's rare to find a person selflessly protecting the interests of ultra-rich people, but I suppose it's possible."

Bea let loose a piercing laugh. Tibby's hand involuntarily shot up to her ear.

"Vicky—Vic*toria,* it seems we share some views on human nature. You ever play poker?" Bea said. "I'm hungry, and that roe is a no-go. How 'bout you and I head to the kitchen? Did I mention I own this place? There's a giant fridge in that kitchen, and if there are any chicken eggs in it, they're all mine. I cook up a mean scramble."

"Not a bad idea," Victoria said. "I prefer my scrambled eggs with caviar, however."

"That can be arranged. We've got a lot of that goo to use up. I hear some people like it with potato chips. That's a waste of a good chip in my view, but if we've got some in the kitchen, you can shovel chips and caviar down your gullet to your heart's content."

Bea threaded her arm through Victoria's once

more as if they were old friends. Bea was roaring as the pair headed off to the kitchen. Angela looked on with bemusement.

"Do you think Victoria's right?" Tibby said wistfully. "About the show not happening, I mean?"

"Honestly, I don't know," Angela said.

"I was hoping to get some good press. Victoria said that local media outlets tend to show up for these things—VIP performances, I mean. They take photos, and if any real VIPs show up, the pictures sometimes get shared on regional sites. Then again, maybe I'd look bad if the show's no good. Maybe I should just be glad if it's canceled."

Tibby tipped her chin down and shook her head.

"Don't lose heart. I think I know someone who might be able to help you—a reporter at the *Sacramento Bee*. And if I remember right, she owes me a favor," Angela said. "No guarantees, but I can call her to see what she thinks. In the meantime, shall we try some of these fancy hors d'oeuvres? We can talk about your social media a bit while we eat if you like."

Tibby sighed but smiled. "OK. If you insist."

CHAPTER 14

"You missed more drama with Todd," Angela said to her computer screen.

Or rather, she said it to her handsome fiancé. Aseem was a hundred miles away, in his part-time office in Silicon Valley.

They were both still in their pajamas, their hair mussed, their eyes sleepy. They still hadn't talked about the tension between them that had started a few days before. Angela was glad it had been swept under the rug. Hoping it would stay there, she launched into the story of the latest drama in the ballroom.

Aseem almost spilled his coffee as Angela told him about the lighting rig crashing to the ballroom floor, and how Todd's shaky stairs drew fire from the rental company—and even from Victoria.

"Victoria was a surprise in another way," she continued. "Would you believe Bea had won her over by the end of the evening?"

Aseem chuckled. "I'm not surprised by anything where Bea is concerned."

"Connie and I had to laugh. We spent hours planning and got all dressed up to court the donors and Bea wins Victoria over with a sarcastic t-shirt and a velour track suit.

"Speaking of winning people over—or, rather, not winning them over, the other donor we met last night—her name is Elizabeth Velton, but everyone calls her Tibby—seemed so sad."

"The laundry heiress? Poor little rich girl?"

Angela sighed. "I know, it's hard to overlook her millions. She's so lonely, though. She told me, 'Even as a girl I never had any friends, except for my ponies.' Her parents sent her to the poshest schools and she was bullied at all of them. She ended up being home schooled by a nanny for years. Isn't that sad?

"Now she's trying to build up the portfolio of laundromats her parents gave her to manage. She's never been on social media, though—doesn't even have the apps on her phone. She's got fun ideas for modernizing the business with all kinds of new vending machines, everything from cake to cocktails—and she wants to use social media to promote them. But she's just… lost."

"Sounds… inventive?" After a beat Aseem added, "Laundromats are gathering spots of a sort."

"The basic concept sounds smart to me. My theory is that marketing can only help, regardless of whether it grows the business. But Tibby's awfully sensitive about the family reputation."

Aseem looked thoughtful once more. "But, Angel, laundromats as social gatherings—marketed by someone who isn't very social—"

"I know. That's why I feel sorry for her—and I want to help her, at least a little. How do you learn how to socialize as an adult when you've never made a single friend? Ironically, if she knew more about social media, maybe the other socialites wouldn't be shunning her. Doesn't it seem like those rich girls are always posting selfies?"

"Some sure are. The ones you see online, anyway. But couldn't there be many more who aren't chasing internet fame?"

"You're right. You're brilliant! *Those* are the girls Tibby should try to befriend. I think she fears no one will ever like her because of these rumors about her family. Would you believe people put down her family just because they built their fortune in real estate?"

"No, not really. Lots of great fortunes were built that way, and many people who get rich in other sectors invest in real estate. Tech people sure do."

"I agree it's weird, but she got upset when I joked that her family fortune wasn't really built on laundry. I wonder if it has to do with the kinds of properties they're buying—or maybe where they buy them?"

"Are you sure she said people slam her family for real estate? Honestly, that's a puzzler. But listen, Angel, I have to go. I've got a meeting in half an hour, and I've still got to prepare."

"Oh, don't go." She paused for a moment. "Give me a moment to say that I'm sorry… I'm sorry I upset you. And that I promise we'll go ring shopping as soon as the play is over, even though I can't say I understand why it's so urgent—"

"And I really don't understand how you can say that. It's not just the ring. Maybe we shouldn't talk about this now. It will need to be a bigger conversation, Angel."

"I'm sorry. I'm getting this wrong. What I

mean is that I realize it's important to you—so I'm ready. I'm looking forward to it."

"OK. Then it's a date," Aseem said, sighing resignedly.

"I miss you. I wish you were going to be here for the play."

"I miss you, too, Angel."

He smiled and tried to lighten the mood. "Not too sad about missing the play, though. Sounds like it's shaping up to be a disaster. Why don't you give my ticket to your mom? Introduce her to Tibby. Her family might need help selling some of that mortifying real estate."

"That's a great idea," Angela said, smiling. Then tears started to well in her eyes. "I really am sorry."

"I believe you. I love you. Don't cry."

ANGELA CLOSED the lid of her laptop and wiped her eyes. She decided to shower and get dressed and go to her favorite café for coffee and a croissant. She could pick one up for Bea, too, and they could compare notes about the night before over breakfast.

She turned on the taps in her suite's oversized bathroom. As she waited for the water to warm,

Angela looked around the room. The inn's collection of wholesome, charming Christmas-themed accommodations was a far cry from where the property had started.

What had the rooms been like before Bea bought the ranch? Angela hadn't seen much of the inside of the building before the construction. They hadn't cared about the inside—it didn't have to be perfect. It didn't even have to be appealing, as long as the outside dimensions and the location were right. They were going to completely re-imagine it, anyway.

"It's got great bones, mija." Angela remembered her mother saying that over and over. "And that's what matters. With the right canvas, you can create a work of art."

So they'd focused on staying on budget and on schedule and, above all, getting the result they wanted. Now, thanks to Tibby, Angela wondered if she should have had more respect for the past—or, at least, more curiosity.

Maybe I need to learn about the lives this place—and the people in it—had lived before.

She made a mental note to look into county records, once the play was behind them. Was the county the right place to start? Her mother would know.

Clean and smelling faintly of cinnamon and ginger, Angela dried off, pinned up her hair, and wrapped herself in a fluffy robe. As she chose a white blouse from her closet and pulled a fresh pair of jeans and a sweater from the dresser, she used the internet speaker in the corner of the suite to call her mother. The code-word was 'Rebecca,' after the main character in Betty Snickerdoodle's first best-seller.

"Rebecca, call mom."

"Hola, mija," Maria said. "What a nice surprise."

"I know, it's been a while. I'm sorry—but I'm calling with an invitation. Would you like to come spend a night or two here at the inn? You could come tomorrow or Thursday."

"What's the occasion?"

Angela told her mother the outlines of the playhouse burning down, the will-they-or-won't-they saga of Connie and Todd, and the VIP preview of the show that would open in just a couple of days. And she told her how she and Connie had entertained Pinot Playhouse's major donors—and how Tibby had prompted her curiosity about the inn's history.

"The county would be a good place to start," Maria said. "Let me think about some other sources. We can talk about it when I see you. I'll try to do some research before I drive up to Napa, too."

"Sounds perfect. I'm looking forward to seeing you. Love you."

Angela finished dressing and took a quick glance at the mirror before grabbing her handbag and phone. Then she remembered one more task she wanted to take care of before heading off to the café.

She opened the address book on her phone and tapped out a text to "Lexie Greene - Sacramento Bee."

```
Hi lexie. got time for a chat
this afternoon? 3PM?
```

THE NOTIFICATION CHIME sounded as soon as Angela put the phone back in her purse.

```
maybe. what's up?
```

i need a favor.

Oh. I forgot to mention I'm on
vacation. indefinitely.

cute. it's not a big favor. it
might be kind of fun. at least
it could be a feel-good thing.
and you owe me.

if you're talking about my true
crime books w Bea, i think you
owe me the favor.

ANGELA EXHALED LOUDLY AND FROWNED. She stuck
the phone in her purse and walked out the door of
her suite toward the parking lot. Still irritated, she
plopped her purse on the passenger seat just as
her cell chimed.

just kidding ill call u at 3.
hope you haven't lost your
sense of humor.

~

"REBECCA, CALL CHARLIE CARTER," Bea shouted into the air. Her suite had a tubular internet speaker, too, just like Angela's and all the others at the inn.

Though Bea loved that speaker, that hadn't always been the case. She might once have ranked among the fiercest resisters of technology on the planet. Not because she disliked efficiency—on the contrary, Bea considered herself a creature of reason and logic. No, Bea shunned technology primarily because she believed the government used it to spy on people.

It did not matter to Bea that the risk of anyone spying on *her* appeared to be minuscule. Back then, Bea lived by herself in a little cottage, content to do nothing more intriguing than watch *The Price Is Right* and smoke cigarettes all day. Aside from occasional, brief writing sessions, this simple routine was interrupted only by meetings with Angela (who always brought life-sustaining bags of egg sandwiches or boxes of pizza) or trips to the local cardroom (when Bea felt the need to confirm she was still the best small-stakes poker player around).

If the government had actually been spying on

Bea, well, the poor grunt assigned to the task would have to have drawn the shortest straw in the history of straws!

Though she prided herself on logic, this obvious bit of it didn't intrude on her firm opinion.

Ironically, though, it was surveillance (of a sort) that ultimately changed Bea's mind. A clueless criminal named Cash had worked out Bea's pen name, tracked her down, broken into her house, stolen a manuscript, and destroyed Bea's typewriter!

Once forced to finally try using a computer, Bea found she could write books a whole lot faster—and Angela could publish them as fast as Bea could write. Ka-ching! Word processing changed Bea's life. Still, in Bea's view, it couldn't hold a candle to Rebecca.

That internet speaker could do magic tricks!

With Rebecca, Bea didn't even need to touch a keyboard. Rebecca could retrieve almost any information from the internet. That enchanted tube even alerted Bea when a new episode of *The Price Is Right* was airing.

Rebecca's ability to make hands-free phone calls was one of Bea's favorite things. It helped that Bea's newfound embrace of technology did not, and would never, include a cell phone. (Surely those devices were the easiest way for the government to monitor a person's comings and goings.)

"Rebecca, call Charlie Carter," Bea shouted.

"Hello, dear Bea," Charlie answered. "To what do I owe this pleasure?"

"It's all about your checkered past, my friend. In other words, I need a legal opinion."

Charlie was one of Bea's oldest friends and one of only a few people she trusted completely. In the early days of her author career, decades ago, she'd been the first client of Charlie's new literary agency. They'd learned the ropes together, both of them starting new careers late in mid-life.

Before that, though, Charlie had endured a too-long career as an attorney in a prestigious San Francisco firm. He was such a dear friend to Bea, she managed to forgive him for this lengthy indiscretion. Besides, she often found it handy to have a friend who knew something about the law.

"Interesting case for you, Charlie. There's a rumor about a lady who's running a nonprofit up here—a community theater group. Or maybe she owns it. The rumor signal has a lot of noise in it."

"I can see why. Owning a nonprofit would be difficult to accomplish, legally speaking."

"That's my question. Can it be done? Can a

person 'own' a nonprofit, then collect donations and hire volunteers?"

"You've identified the chief legal problems. Donors can't deduct donations that aren't made to a true nonprofit, which a business can't be if someone owns it. And a for-profit business relying primarily on volunteers is likely also illegal. But as your once and forever attorney, I hope you're not calling because you have donated to this 'charity.'"

"Only a little in kind." She explained how the fire at Pinot Playhouse had led to their production coming to the ballroom. "I love pulling off a good bluff in poker, but tricking people into 'donating' for personal profit isn't right. Not even when they're really rich people. Turns out I like richies better than I thought."

"Do I have to remind you that you are a rich person?"

"You know what I mean by *richies*," Bea said, using a nasal voice and taking a mannered sip from an invisible teacup, pinkie fully extended, which Charlie unfortunately couldn't see. "But Charlie, as a student of criminal behavior, I can't help be curious about how Roberta—that's the lady heading up the theater—is pulling this off."

"If the donors never asked for an accounting—

and for a small, local charity, they might not—they wouldn't know their deductions were illegitimate until tax time, in all likelihood."

"The two biggest donors were here last night. They said they donated for sentimental reasons. I doubt they checked anything out." Bea paused. "Angela's worried we might be liable if Roberta's cheating the donors."

"Angela's meticulous about contracts. I expect you're well protected. But what you said about the playhouse fire is interesting, especially in light of the confusing rumors. Could real estate be another angle? Is it possible Roberta bought the playhouse itself? The building, I mean—and not the organization?"

"I don't see why not."

"Mystery writing is your job, not mine, but I wonder if that suggests the possibility of another scam—one that could have a veneer of legitimacy, at least technically."

"Hot dang. I'm all ears."

Charlie explained that as the owner of the building, Roberta could rent it at whatever price she could get—including to the nonprofit she headed up. "She has no apparent oversight, right? No board of directors minding the till? And then, you say she's also in charge of all the fundraising.

One person in charge of all the money flowing in and out certainly sounds like a set-up for embezzling."

"That could explain how all those donations went up in smoke. They're trying to rebuild sets with chewing gum and rusty nails at the moment."

"Speaking of things going up in smoke, have you considered whether anyone benefits from the playhouse burning down? The value of real estate in Napa Valley has skyrocketed of late."

"So Roberta could have cleaned out the nonprofit of their donations, then burned down the theater for the insurance money? Nice theory."

"And if she charged a high rent, that might even drive up the value of the insurance payout."

"Especially since the building and the theater company were dormant until she 'rescued' them," Bea snorted. "Crime theories are fun to talk about. Maybe I can base my next mystery story on this one. You sure you don't want me to name a victim after you?"

"No, thanks. I'm superstitious," Charlie laughed.

"Speaking of murder mysteries, did I mention the play is *The Ratcatcher*—that old mystery from the sixties? Let me know if you want to come down for the VIP rehearsal. It's Thursday night."

"I don't think so. Haven't you heard? There's a huge storm coming in early Thursday morning. Atmospheric river, they're calling it. Thunder and lightning—the works. I'm not planning on driving anywhere."

"Oh, boy. Just what this production needs, another chance for people to get hurt."

CHAPTER 15

"Knock-knock," Angela said. Bea had left the door of her suite ajar for her.

"C'mon in, girlie. Just brushing my teeth."

"Be prepared to dirty them again," Angela laughed. "You've got a choice of an egg sandwich or a chocolate croissant to go with your iced coffee."

"What kind of choice is that?" Bea yelled from the bathroom. "I'll take the egg sandwich, but save the buttery goodness for my lunch. I've got a big day today and I need to tank up."

"Done. Lucky for me, I brought two croissants."

Angela took her own breakfast out of the bag and sat down on the end of Bea's bed, coffee in one hand and pastry in the other. "Ready to compare notes about the socialites?"

"Sure," Bea said, pulling up her desk chair and digging into her sandwich. "You start."

Angela explained how she'd come to feel sorry for Tibby and wanted to help her, and that she noticed Tibby had an almost "nerdy" fascination for the property.

"I guess she's got real estate in her blood, like her parents, even though she thinks it makes other heiresses she wants to mingle with uncomfortable."

"I can't say for sure, since I'm not *that* kind of rich," Bea cackled, "but that sounds very fishy. How is real estate anything to be ashamed of?"

"Aseem said the same. I find it confusing, too. Maybe it's gentrification—like, say, they buy up entire neighborhoods? Squeeze poor people with rent? That might upset rich and poor people alike."

"I dunno, Angie. Seems unlikely. You said she's kind of nerdy. Victoria thought Tibby has trouble socially because she's an oaf."

"Victoria called Tibby an oaf?!"

"That might have been my word, not Victoria's. She did say Tib's dealing with nasty rumors, and even though she's got tons of money to donate, she has trouble giving it away. Victoria's trying to help her get invited to the better events. This play wouldn't even make the cut except Tibby wanted to help out her auntie."

"Tibby told me Victoria advised her to make Roberta give her aunt the role of Edie. I didn't say so, but it seemed ethically questionable—"

"More ethically questionable than taking donations for your 'community' theater and giving yourself the pick of roles?"

"Good point. I wonder if that's why Grayson always seems annoyed with her. Could hardly blame him if he finds Roberta unprofessional."

"There's more. Victoria's got reasons for being none-too-fond of Roberta, too. Victoria says Roberta came into a big chunk of dough unexpectedly. As in, more than enough to fund *The Ratcatcher* herself if she wanted to—but, hey, why not take other rich peoples' money and hoard all your own? I got the impression Victoria wouldn't have given Roberta a nickel if she'd known."

Bea then shared Charlie's idea that Roberta's scam could be owning the playhouse and overcharging the theater group for rent, plus the suspicions he raised about the fire.

Angela put her head in her hands and moaned.

"*Charlie* said that? Kind, fair Charlie? I've done

it again, Bea. I've got us tangled up with someone who can't be trusted. Pinot Playhouse is probably ripping off donors and Roberta is probably a crook! It's just like that 'charity' poker tournament all over again. You warned me—"

"Now, now, girlie. It's not like that poker event at all. Nobody's been murdered. At least not yet!" Bea was chortling and slapping her knee with abandon. "Oh, that was good."

"Don't say things like that, Bea."

"You mean words like *muuurrrdder?* You worried about a *jinx?* Like I can cause murder by joking about it?" Bea was roaring now. She paused, grinning from ear to ear, to adopt a pose of deep thinking. "Imagine the potential for my writing…."

"Mock me all you want. Are you saying murder is a laughing matter?" Angela cried.

"OK, OK," Bea said, eventually containing her glee. "I hear you. But you worry too much, girlie. We're gossiping, for Pete's sake. It's supposed to be fun. Not to mention darn good fodder for my next murder mystery."

Angela sighed.

"Back to the matter at hand. C'mon, Angie, let's have a little fun. If you had to predict, who gets murdered? And who's the murderer? My first instinct would be Roberta as victim. She could also be a murderer if someone catches on to her game. Todd, Grayson—they probably have figured some stuff out. So are they victims or murderers? And would it be poison? Stabbing? Truck running someone over?"

"I'm not having this conversation," Angela said firmly, standing up. "Even if it's not bad luck, surely it's bad form! I'll talk to you later. Good luck with the poker tonight—not that you'll need it."

"I'm looking forward to hitting the felt. It's been a while. Plus I plan to pump the crew for information about Todd and Roberta."

"I'm going to help Todd out tonight. Connie's coming, too. Since you're stealing the crew, Todd's time's even shorter. Oh—and I forgot to mention, I'm talking to Lexie this afternoon. I thought maybe she could help with Tibby's reputation problem. Maybe help her get a little positive exposure."

"Be sure to tell Lexie we could have a new true crime book to work on once our little production concludes. Looks good for a fraud story at a minimum. If we get lucky, maybe even *murrrderrrr*," Bea said, drumming her steepled fingers together.

"Bea!"

❧

ANGELA LEFT Bea's suite and stepped outside to walk back to her own. The storms everyone had been buzzing about for a week were finally on the horizon. She seized the opportunity to enjoy the dry weather before the rains and wind rolled in.

As she looked toward the foothills, her eyes passed by Todd's casita, and she remembered noticing the light was out the night before. She decided to run back inside and grab the stepladder and another bulb. The day's emails and marketing tasks were already piling up, and she planned to knock off early to help Todd, but she could spare a few minutes. It would only take that long to test whether the trouble was just a bad bulb.

Naturally, she wanted to help the play succeed. There was probably at least a week's worth of work to do and they were already down to the wire. Todd could use every free hand. Of course, she was also looking forward to getting a close-up view of Todd's interactions with Connie.

Angela jogged back through the inn and found the stepladder and the fresh bulb, then headed out the front door. As she reached the row of casitas, she stepped off the paved walkway and onto the grass that surrounded the pretty cottages, which was now several inches long thanks to earlier rains. Todd was in the casita on the end, closest to the back of the inn, as he'd requested. Grayson's was next door.

She noticed the shades were drawn on both units. Both men must still be asleep. It was late morning, but they'd both been up past midnight. She guessed Todd might have stayed up even later, continuing the work done by his volunteers after they'd gone home.

Angela started to set up the stepladder on the landing of Todd's casita. As she did, the boulder tucked way back in the yard, and that old shovel on the ground just past it, caught her eye. She set the ladder down and walked across the grass toward the boulder.

Big rocks and boulders weren't rare in their part of the wine country, especially as close as they were to the foothills. There were loads of them on the inn property. Still, that boulder was so big, it stood out in broad daylight. But Angela was far more interested in that old, stray tool.

Angela picked the shovel up carefully, intending to stow it in the closet behind the front desk until the landscaping crew returned in a few weeks. It was old and worn and Angela inspected it cautiously, worried she might get a splinter. As she walked away, she glanced again at the boulder.

I'm not sure I remember this boulder. Am I going crazy?

She laughed to herself and made a mental note to ask the landscapers if they'd moved it there for some reason. Outdoor aesthetics weren't her specialty. She usually was happy to leave such decisions to the experts.

She walked back to Todd's landing and leaned the shovel up against the railing. Determined not to awaken Todd or Grayson, she slowly and carefully unfolded the ladder, but as she set it upright her hand slipped. The ladder fell with a clatter onto the landing. She cringed and froze and thought maybe she'd gotten away with it. Then she saw a light turn on through the door curtain and heard Todd moving around inside.

Angela cursed under her breath.

So much for not waking anyone up!

The door opened a crack, held back by the security chain, and Angela could see only one sleepy eye looking out at her. She assumed he was being careful not to show most of his face or his body, and the thought made her smile with relief.

Phew! I don't want to know what he wears to bed!

"I'm so sorry, Todd," Angela said quietly,

righting the ladder and hopping up on it. "I'll only be a moment. I saw your light out again last night and came by to try another bulb. Hopefully it's not a short. I can fix it if that bulb I put in before was a lemon."

"Um, Angela—" Todd started to say in a groggy voice.

"That's weird," Angela interrupted as she reached into the light fixture. "There's no bulb in here again."

"That's what I was starting to tell you," Todd muttered. "I took it out because it wasn't working. I meant to ask you for another one."

"Great minds think alike, I guess," Angela said, stepping down from the ladder and folding it up. "I hope this new one comes on tonight. Will you let me know?"

"Of course."

"If you give me the dead bulb, I'll take it back to recycle it."

"I'm not really dressed—" Todd said anxiously.

"Could you just slip it through the crack of the door?"

"Um—I'd like to get a little sleep—"

"Of course—I'm sorry to invade your privacy. Go back to sleep and bring the bulb back to the ballroom if you think of it. By the way, I'm coming by to volunteer this afternoon. Connie is, too. We wanted to help with your crew gone on Bea's poker field trip. I noticed the furniture stacked behind the back loading area. Does that mean you're in the home stretch?"

"That reminds me, I wanted to ask you if we can move that furniture into the ballroom temporarily. The storm that's coming is supposed to have gale-force winds. I don't trust the tarp to keep everything dry. The rental chairs for the audience will be arriving today, too—I'll get those guys to help me move the set furniture into the ballroom, if it's OK with you."

"Of course."

Todd said goodbye and shut his door. Angela snapped the stepladder shut and picked it up, along with the shovel, and was about to head back to the inn when she heard a voice from the far side of his casita.

"Miss Garcia, is that you I hear?"

Grayson! I'm batting a thousand at waking people up!

She stepped off the landing and around the front of Todd's casita to find Grayson standing in his doorway. She put the ladder on the ground, her eyes widening as she took in his ensemble: a glossy silk robe in a large black and gold baroque print, with matching slippers and boxers. Angela could see the boxers—as well as Grayson's toned and groomed torso. He'd let the robe hang open in a way that looked careless but was probably completely intentional.

"Don't be shy, Miss Garcia," Grayson said in the buttery, confident way that Angela found both irritating and hard to ignore. Standing on his landing with one hand resting on the vertical beam that held its small portico roof, his pose looked like something out of a cheesy magazine.

"It's—I'm sorry if I woke you. I was trying to be quiet—"

"I must say that you look even more lovely than usual this morning."

Angela looked down with a furrowed brow and confirmed she was wearing one of her standard, casual pairings: dark jeans and a long-sleeved white tee. Unconsciously, she reached up and verified that her simple hoop earrings and everyday ponytail were in place. Then she realized that Grayson was watching her appreciatively and caught herself. She blushed, her smile turning into a frown, and she glanced back at the inn.

Sensing he was losing her attention, Grayson got serious quickly.

"Let me brief, Miss Garcia—Angela. Is it OK for me to call you Angela?"

Angela nodded, a little impatiently.

"Miss Garcia—Angela—I'm afraid your Christmas casita, while sumptuous, has become intolerable."

"Intolerable?"

Intolerable? Really?

"Rest assured, the problem is not this extraordinary accommodation. It's the neighborhood. Or more precisely, one neighbor," Grayson said, tilting his head in the direction of Todd's casita.

"Was he shining his headlights again? I hope I've just fixed his landing light—"

"Alas, if only that were it. Todd has taken to playing loud music when he returns at night—or should I say, when he returns in the wee hours of the morning."

Angela looked dubious. Grayson read her scrunched face before she could respond.

"I'm sure it sounds preposterous, Miss Gar— Angela. You're wondering why you can't hear it, if it's so loud."

"It's nearly silent here at night. I can't imagine loud music not carrying across the property."

"I believe he aims the speakers toward my bedroom window. Deliberately. And then there's been a wind in my direction—and away from the inn—each night this week."

Angela sighed. Grayson's story wasn't completely convincing, but what was the point of arguing?

"You've been so kind to permit me an accommodation here, Angela. Is relocation to a room inside your charming inn too much to ask?"

Angela's inclination was to keep the peace, and not merely because that was her nature. The sooner she addressed Grayson's issue, the sooner she'd be done talking to him.

Still, there was another problem.

The only other room in the inn that was ready for a guest was the one she'd fluffed herself, the one right next door to hers—the one she'd planned for her mom.

My mother could stay in my room. I could take the pull-out sofa.

But then Grayson would be right next door. Ugh.

But surely Grayson won't give me any trouble with my mom around.

Then she felt a pang of guilt about a final, fleeting thought.

Aseem wouldn't like it. But he's not here....

In the end, her desire to problem-solve won

out. "I'll bring the key to you at rehearsal," she finally said.

She didn't tell Grayson the room was next to hers. If she was careful and quiet, with any luck, he'd never figure it out.

A sly, satisfied grin spread across Grayson's face. He reached his left hand out toward her right one, but Angela didn't react.

"May I?" he said smugly.

Thinking fast, Angela picked up the ladder and shrugged.

"Sorry. Hands full."

Then she turned and walked back to the inn. When she got to the supply closet, she realized she'd forgotten the shovel.

Argh! If I go back now, I'll run into Grayson again.

She decided it wouldn't hurt to leave it there until Grayson was settled in his new room—*sigh*—right next door to hers.

CHAPTER 16

Back at her desk, Angela blazed through her emails and deadlines with her usual efficiency. It felt good. Few things pleased her more than doing her job well. Today's to-dos also included reading a bunch of thank-you notes from happy guests of BettyCon. More like icing on the cake of a successful convention than work.

She looked at the clock on her computer. Fifteen more minutes until three o'clock. She stood up from her desk and stretched and lay down on her bed for a catnap, plopping her cell phone onto the pillow next to her head.

The pillows were so comfy and the yule-themed quilt so soft, she drifted off to a deeper sleep than the forty winks she'd had in mind. The phone was right next to her head when Lexie's call came in. She jumped from the bed with a yelp, rudely awakened by the blast of a locomotive's horn warning cars off the track.

That custom Lexie ring tone is less fun than I expected.

Angela shook her head and smiled a little, then tapped the screen to answer the call before the next blast of the air horn.

"Hi, Lexie. Thanks for calling."

"Sure. Your cryptic message got my attention. So what's the feel-good favor you need?"

"It's not exactly for me. You know the socialite Tibby Velton?"

Angela thought she heard Lexie chuckle softly, then cover it up with a cough.

"She's well-known up here. The Veltons are one of the richest Sacramento families."

"Tibby visited recently. She made an impression on me—I thought I'd try to help her."

"Patron saint to sad-sack heiresses? That's your new do-gooder thing?"

"OK, OK, just hear me out," Angela sighed. Then she explained about the theater group moving *The Ratcatcher* to the inn and what she'd learned from Tibby during her donor tour.

"The other society types snub Tibby. That's

why I want to help. She has everything money can buy, but nobody can get by without friends, can they? She seems so lonely."

"Where do I come in?"

"Tibby says people in her own social circle are spreading unfair rumors about how the family laundry business isn't what created all their wealth. She's getting a reputation she can't shake —she's even having trouble getting invited to the nicer charity events. Victoria McGiven has been helping her gain access."

Lexie was less successful at hiding her snickering this time. "Victoria *Hartman* McGiven? Of Heartless Grocers?"

Angela sighed. "You know, prejudices against rich people can also be wrong, Lexie."

"Really? Duly noted."

"Victoria thinks involving Tibby in more charities will get her positive press, to offset some of the meaner rumors."

"The rumors have made their way well beyond the upper crust up here. Us plebes are in on them, too. You don't have to be a reporter, either."

"So... you've heard people say Tibby's family tries to hide that their wealth comes from real estate holdings, not the dry cleaning and laundry empire? I hate to say this, but are they slumlords or something?"

"Wait, what? Are you saying Tibby claims the nasty rumors are that the Velton fortune is built on a shameful, embarrassing pile of real estate?" Lexie was laughing uproariously now. "That's a good one!"

Angela frowned. "When you're done laughing, can you let me in on the joke?"

Lexie eventually stifled her last guffaw and said, "Everyone knows they own tons of property. Everyone knows their wealth exploded far beyond the possible proceeds of the laundry business. But the rumor isn't that they're greedy landlords or whatever. It's that they built their fortune laundering something besides clothing."

Lexie couldn't contain herself and started snickering again.

"You mean…. No! Laundering *money*? As in—they're *criminals*?" Angela said, sucking in a huge lungful of air. "That… that can't be true, can it?"

Angela's face crumpled as she mentally replayed her conversation with Tibby, trying to figure out how she'd misunderstood. Her mouth dropped open as she remembered that the words never came from Tibby's lips, only her own. She hoped Lexie didn't hear her hand slap her forehead.

Laundry. Cash business. Money laundering. It adds up.

"Nothing's ever been proven," Lexie said. "They'd be quick to tell you that. It doesn't mean they're innocent, but they've never even been charged with anything."

"Then why do the rumors persist?"

"That's the beauty part. The rumors must be coming from someone who knows them very well —or should I say, knows them *intimately*."

"Someone who works for them?"

"Possibly. More likely—"

"A relative?"

"People say they've got a few jealous ones, especially on Mrs. Velton's side of the family."

"I guess… I guess this means you won't—and, I mean, we shouldn't—help Tibby with her PR problem."

"Au contraire, mon amie!" Lexie howled. "I'm much more interested now. The juicier the drama, the more clicks. The only problem is, we don't do straight-up gossip here at the *Bee*. I've got a friend who works at a gossip site, though. I bet she could be persuaded to 'help.'"

"When's this play of yours? I'll talk to my editor. No promises, OK? But I'll see if we can send a reporter down to review it—and get a few pix of poor, misunderstood Tibby. Then we share them with my gossip friend, and maybe she'll be willing to spread the nice, clean news of Tibby's generosity around."

"Thank you," Angela said after a pause. "I think."

"It'll be great. A nice article gets posted, then the comments section reveals if it turns the tide or not. Trust me, it's gonna be fun either way!"

"Lexie, maybe—"

"Listen, don't start feeling guilty now. Just because Tibby's parents are likely felons who probably treat their family like dirt doesn't mean the poor girl deserves to have no friends. Right?"

Without seeing her face, it was a complete mystery to Angela whether Lexie's last comment was serious or sarcastic. The girl was pure snark in human form.

Angela said goodbye, promising Lexie a ticket would be set aside in case a reporter made it to the VIP preview, and reminding her that the reporter should dress appropriately for the occasion, especially since she hadn't gotten anyone's approval to invite the press. The reporter should treat the gig as an undercover assignment.

"You never know," Lexie said. "A good review could kill two birds with one stone—help your new pal Tibby and bring some interest to the rest of the run."

"Don't worry about promoting the show," Angela blurted. "I'm pretty sure they're all sold out."

"Right. Sure. That bad, huh?" Lexie howled as she signed off.

"OK, everybody on the poker school bus!" Bea said to the crew and cast members who were joining her cardroom outing.

She meant it literally: with Angela's help, she'd arranged one of their friend Oliver's luxury shuttles. Oliver was one of the first Betty Bros—young men who loved Betty Snickerdoodle's wholesome Christmas romances. Oliver had been introducing new readers to Betty for years. Bea and Angela returned the favor by hiring his company regularly at the inn, helping him build his business from one car to a small fleet of vehicles.

Bea led the way from the ballroom to the parking lot, eager players walking behind her. In her green velour track suit, she looked like an odd little Pied Piper. The late-afternoon sky was gray, with ominous clouds gathering above the foothills. Stray raindrops dotted the windshield of the bus. Though the weather looked iffy, Bea's students looked excited as they climbed aboard, some ducking their heads against the drizzle.

"They're about to learn poker from a master," Angela said to Connie and Todd, as they walked behind Bea's little troop.

"Wait until they find out how much the lessons cost," Todd laughed. "I've been taught by an expert player before. Let's just say it wasn't cheap. And my guess is Bea is ten times the player he was."

"They'll have fun, no matter what," Angela said cheerfully. "And that's the point, right? A morale boost for the home stretch?"

"Thank goodness you and Connie are here to help out," Todd said. "Otherwise, my morale would be a problem."

Bea stood with Oliver by the bus door and let the others step up first.

"See you all later!" Bea said, waving to the three of them. "By the way, Todd, *lookin' good!* Have you lost weight?"

Angela's jaw dropped and her face flushed. She interpreted Bea's remark as another dig at Todd's latest uncomfortable-looking outfit. His flannel-clad belly was again severely pinched in the middle by his belt. Angela looked for signs of offense in Todd, though, and gladly found none.

"I don't think so," he laughed. He grabbed his belly by the sides and gave it a shake. "My new boss is probably going to put me on a diet. This gut could be considered an impediment to my job."

"Oh, Todd, I don't think Sergeant McGregor —" Connie started to say, then caught herself.

Angela's eyes went wide as she looked at Connie, then Todd, then turned to see if Bea had heard what Connie said. But Bea was already on the bus and Oliver had shut the door and started the engine.

"Oh, Todd," Connie fretted. "I messed up. It's supposed to be a secret. I'm so sorry. Angela can keep a secret, though, can't you, honey?"

"Of course," Angela said, lowering her voice. "But does this mean you'll be working for the police here in town? McGregor didn't mention he'd found someone."

"It's fine, Connie," Todd said. "You know better than I do that the news will be out in the *Wine Country Grapevine* this weekend, anyway. Angela, can you keep it quiet until then? McGregor wanted to control when people found out. I didn't want any favoritism or anything like that with

Pinot Playhouse, either. But yes, the news is true. That's the job that brought me to town—I'm joining McGregor's squad. I'm looking forward to wearing a badge again."

"I'm happy to keep it a secret," Angela said.

Angela hated lying, so she tucked one hand behind her back so that Todd and Connie couldn't see her crossed fingers. She was mostly being honest, anyway. There was only one person she knew she had to tell: Bea. Especially since it wasn't just the news of Todd's new job that Angela was bursting to share with Bea, it was the fact that Todd had confided in Connie!

"It's great news for our community," Angela said. "Sergeant McGregor is always looking for competent people to help him. Do you like it here so far?"

Angela couldn't miss the hopeful look on Connie's face as she waited for Todd's response.

"Of course I do," Todd said. "I like the people especially." He looked straight at Connie, who smiled and blushed and tucked her hair behind her ear.

"Have you found a place to live?" Angela asked. "If the announcement's coming out in the next couple of days—"

"Don't remind me. I've been so busy with the

play, I haven't had a chance to look for an apartment. I haven't solved that problem yet."

Connie looked back and forth between Todd and Angela, a distressed expression on her face.

"If you need to stay a few more days after the show opens, Todd, you're welcome to," Angela said. "Once you shift into performance mode, you'll have more time to look for a place, right?"

"You'll need to settle somewhere before you start work. Gosh, you'll be busy, Todd," Connie said. "The play will still be going when you're starting your job. It sounds like an awful lot—"

"It'll be fine. Sergeant McGregor says I'll be doing training sessions at first. Online stuff. I can work it all in."

Todd gestured toward the inn entrance. "Speaking of work, let's get down to it, shall we?"

"Ready to help," Angela said.

"Let's go!" Connie said brightly.

As they walked to the ballroom, Connie took Angela's arm and slowed her down.

"Isn't it exciting?" she gushed secretively. "I've been *dying* to tell you! I even wrote the *Grapevine* article myself—technically, it was just supposed to be the press release, but they're publishing it unchanged. It's been so hard not to show it to you!"

"I'm happy for you, Connie," Angela said.

· · ·

WHEN THEY ARRIVED in the ballroom, Angela was shocked—in the best way—by a transformation that seemed to have happened overnight.

The stage light structure that had crashed so dramatically was now standing tall. Larger, heavier bases had been added on each side for stability.

Forty chairs had been delivered by the rental company. They were grouped in five tall stacks. Each stack would soon form a row in front of the stage.

The ratty antique furniture that had been stored outside under the tarp was now piled haphazardly on the ballroom floor near the stage, ready to be placed in the scenery. The stage itself was outfitted with the frames and walls the crew had so quickly built and resized. Angela smiled, thinking they looked much better than she expected. The outlines of an old-money mansion library were coming into focus, though painting and decoration were yet to be done.

Even the staircases, though still ramshackle at best, looked more or less done.

Could it be that Todd is on the verge of pulling off his miracle?

But that wasn't the only surprise. As Angela started to ask Todd whether she should grab a paintbrush or a hammer, Martina and Lorelei walked in from the hallway.

"Martina!" Angela said. "What a nice surprise."

"Well, thank you," Martina said, smiling. "I knew Todd could use an extra pair of hands tonight, and I wanted to do one last check of the makeup station. Plus, I've secretly been pitching in for Lorelei, anyway. You may not have noticed me because I've been keeping a low profile."

Lorelei had an awkward expression on her face.

Angela looked down at Lorelei's feet, both clad in stylish suede booties. "It's Lorelei, right? I'm sorry, I don't think we've been officially introduced yet. I guess your foot's all healed?"

"Right on all counts. Nice to meet you. But I've heard so much about you, it feels like we've already met. From Grayson, I mean," Lorelei said. She was raising her eyebrows and grinning at the French doors behind Angela.

Her face warm, Angela turned around to see Grayson, Roberta, and Louisa walking onto the deck.

"Looks like those two needed a little quality rehearsal time with the boss," Lorelei laughed.

"Though I'm not sure why. They're already so prepared, it's hard to tell Roberta's version of Edie from Louisa's. Their 'snobby, middle-aged New England equestrian' voices are practically identical. Roberta must be the best-rehearsed understudy in the history of community theater."

"Well… that's good, right? I mean… surely there's no such thing as *excess* preparation," Angela said.

"You're right, of course," Lorelei said. "It's interesting, they look like they're the same size, but they can't share the same costumes. Roberta's very short-waisted. But then with that scene, the one with the 'blood'—" Lorelei grinned and made big air quotes.

"Don't tell me anything more," Angela said. "I haven't read the play, and I'm trying to avoid spoilers!"

"Let's just say it is good to have an extra blouse or two, anyway, in case the stains are stubborn," Lorelei laughed.

Angela looked out on the deck. "I'm glad Grayson's here. I've got a room key for him."

"He's moving out of his casita?" Todd yelled. He was on stage, taking inventory of the tasks that remained to be done. "Thank you, thank you! He was keeping me up at night!"

"Wait.. what?" Angela said, climbing onto the stage. "Grayson said you were the one making noise."

"Honestly, I think he was hearing things. Any tiny sound and he'd start yelling."

Angela bit her lip. "I guess it's better for everyone if he moves out of the casita."

"I agree. We all need our sleep tonight. It's our last chance for a good rest before the VIP preview. Speaking of our deadline, I've divided up some remaining tasks, ladies. There's painting and hanging of pictures and placing of some props, mainly."

Angela, Connie, Lorelei, and Martina carefully scaled the stairs and stood together as Todd doled out the assignments.

"Does that glass go in this window?" Angela asked, pointing to the square-framed hole in the library's main wall and a sheet of glass leaning against it. The window represented a view to the outside of the building, permitting the actors— and the audience—to occasionally see other characters approaching the mansion. "Or does it need to be left open? Does someone climb through— like in *The Mousetrap?*"

"Definitely not like *The Mousetrap!*" Lorelei blurted.

Todd looked at her askance.

"Sorry!" Lorelei said. "It's just I've done them both so many times in community theater, I'm—I guess I'm attuned to the differences. I mean, it's easy to confuse them, isn't it? Similar names, and—"

"Let's cut to the chase. No glass!" Todd barked. He was holding up four clean paintbrushes. "Now, is everyone ready to paint?"

Angela grabbed a brush and smiled, imagining Bea saying, "Good call on the glass, Todd. One less thing to break!"

CHAPTER 17

Oliver's bus was as luxurious as a shuttle gets, and he drove with great care. But the country road to the Valley Card Room was full of mounds and dips—a little uncomfortable, especially for Bea. Her feet didn't touch the floor when she sat all the way back in her seat. She had to sit on the edge of it to grab the bar on the seat in front of her for balance.

Nonetheless, Bea was secretly loving every bump and lurch. She wished Oliver would drive a little faster!

A boisterous young cast member named Melissa let out a squeal and nearly fell off her seat when the vehicle shifted unexpectedly, causing the others to chuckle and tease her. Then everyone laughed even harder at her flurry of ridiculous excuses.

Bea's little gang of pupils was loosening up, and it pleased her. Getting everyone's guard down was exactly what she wanted, and not just so they'd be relaxed enough to bet big or attempt a bluff.

Bea usually had two goals when teaching poker. First: to impart a few tips to help the newbies dominate their home games.

Second, if any of them were jerks, Bea looked for opportunities to teach them an expensive lesson while they played. (Naturally, this went double for rich jerks.) Nothing gave Bea more satisfaction than raking an arrogant jackass's entire chip stack with a well-concealed trap.

Bea couldn't expect to control everything at the table, though. Poker requires skill, which Bea had plenty of, but it's still gambling. On any given night, if Lady Luck has trouble in mind, the best-laid plans of beginners and sharks can easily go awry. Bea would have to be ready to pivot if the cards didn't cooperate. She certainly didn't intend to lose money while teaching newbies how to win it!

On top of all this, tonight Bea had a secret agenda: getting dirt on Roberta, Todd, and, if possible, the two donors she now thought of fondly as "the bag ladies."

So, the brightening mood on the bus pleased her. The jollier the gang was, the easier it would be to get their gums flapping.

Once Bea got her mind set on uncovering secrets, she'd happily go to great lengths to do so—especially if she was looking to punch holes in someone's full-of-beans story. This production of *The Ratcatcher* was full of phonies, and their stories were full of a whole lot of beans. Bea was sure of it, even if she hadn't figured out—yet—what any of them were up to. She was sure that every last one of those pretenders was up to something worth finding out about.

As the bus crunched onto the gravel parking lot of the Valley Card Room, Bea noticed confusion on her pupils' faces. Melissa half-stood in her seat and gasped, then lost her balance again. Her giggling seat-mate grabbed her jacket to keep her from falling into the aisle.

"Whoa, there, girlfriend," Bea squawked. "You haven't been hittin' the sauce, have you? Some people like to combine happy hour with cards, but as your poker teacher, I can't recommend it. Sharks flock to a table if they see someone drinking like a fish—'fish,' get it?"

"That's just Melissa, stone cold sober," laughed another actor. "You should see her when she drinks!"

The 'casino' that failed to impress Melissa—or anyone else on the bus—was a tall, shabby, single-story structure in the middle of the huge parking lot, set far back from the road. If not for the sign on the street, one might easily assume the building was an abandoned hay barn or a farmer's shed.

"I know it doesn't look like much," Bea said with a cackle. "But the action's legit. And once I train you up, you can take your skills to any fancy-pants casino you like. Tahoe, Vegas, even Monte Carlo, if you like dressing fancy."

"Monte Carlo?! I'm just hoping I leave here with a dollar or two in my pocket," Phil from the stage crew said. "I've heard stories. Apparently, you're a legend—"

"Pshaw!" Bea snorted. "I'm sure I don't have to tell a fellow golden oldie not to believe everything you hear. Besides, it's not like I enjoy taking my students' money."

Technically, this was Bea's first bluff of the evening, though she did plan to go a little easier than usual on the volunteers, provided none of them got out of line.

Bea's old pal Perry was there to greet the bus. The suit he wore was slightly worn, slightly too big, and more than slightly wrinkled. It's only purpose was to let everyone in the cardroom know he was the manager, and it was more than up to the job. His careworn face still hinted at the handsomeness of decades ago—and a bit of mischief.

"Two tables, just like you asked," Perry said to Bea, offering her his hand as she stepped down from the bus. "My best dealer is at yours. My second-best, Serena, is great at teaching the basics. She'll be at table two, bringing the newbies up to speed. Once Serena teaches them the rules, they'll be fair game for your table."

Whatever the circumstances, even if it just meant teaching a few novices, Perry was always delighted to help Bea with her poker projects. Her schemes were usually full of good card-play and always entertaining.

"Perfecto!" Bea said from the door of the bus. "Perry, you and I will lead the way! Hurry up, everyone. Try not to get rained on."

Oliver followed her with a huge umbrella that he held over the passengers as they stepped down.

"Oliver, you wanna play, too?" she said. Oliver answered with a grin and a nod.

Perry offered Bea an elbow and they walked toward the humble-looking building.

Perry pulled the wooden door's thick handle and motioned the group through to the windowless single-room casino. Their eyes went wide as they entered. It felt as though they'd been dropped out of the wine country and into the middle of a cave.

The room was lit mainly by large, fluorescent fixtures hanging over the poker tables. The lights were just bright enough to ensure that facial expressions and cards could be clearly seen by the players and the dealer. The air smelled musty and felt thick, except for occasional whiffs of fried rice and potstickers from the kitchen.

Perry showed the group which table was for players with no knowledge of poker at all. Bea frowned as Phil and his crewmate Dave headed to Serena's table with Melissa and a volunteer who worked on mending and ironing costumes.

"How much do the rest of you know about the game?" Perry asked the 'experienced' group. John from the stage crew piped up that he'd only played casually with friends and that this was his first time in a cardroom. Two male actors said nothing but nodded in agreement.

"OK, I'll play, Bea. I know you're only asking me because I'm an easy mark," Oliver chuckled.

"Don't scare them, Oliver! Your first hundred-dollar buy-in, and everyone else's is on me," Bea said.

"That's how she reels you in," Oliver joked to the others.

Perry and Bea left the group to choose their seats and went to the cage for chips.

"We've only got four experienced players and four newbies learning. You could fit one more at your table if you like," Perry said as they arrived at the cage.

As the clerk stepped away from the window to rack up their chips, Bea made a production of squawking, "Huh?" and holding her hand to her ear. Finally, Perry got the message and leaned down to whisper into it.

Once Perry was at her eye level, Bea whispered to him in a conspiratorial voice. "Be discreet when you look around. I'm pretty sure the guy in seat five at the table next to Serena's winked and mouthed something at John. Know him?"

Perry stood up straight and faced the cage window, then cautiously looked back over his left shoulder. Bea had her hands on the shelf in front of the cage window and was looking straight ahead.

"Yep. He's here pretty often. Come to think of it, John looks a little familiar, too."

"Remember my secret agenda?"

"Yep. Speaking of which, I've got something to tell you about that. I heard a couple of regulars in a tournament yesterday morning talking about your rich donor lady's auntie. I'll tell you the details later, but suffice to say you're on the right track."

"Excellent—more on that later. We gotta get these games going. Any chance you'll take a break and sit in on Serena's lesson? The people I think are most likely to blab are there. Maybe get them a round of drinks, too?"

"Haven't you given them your speech about not mixing booze and poker yet?"

Bea sighed. "Sort of. Tell 'em it's important to be a little loose so you don't play scared. Just one small drink each. Then have the bartender make it a Long Island Iced Tea, but tell 'em it's the low-octane house drink for ladies. They'll go for it. They're supposed to be having fun, right?"

"But aren't you planning to take their money?" Perry grinned.

"Sadly, not tonight. I've decided that tonight is

all about the movers and shakers of Pinot Playhouse and their dirty little secrets."

"So you're really not going to fight for every chip? That's quite a sacrifice for a little gossip."

"I know!" Bea chuckled under her breath. "Something tells me this dirt is gonna be even more entertaining. You know I'm always looking for fodder for my next mystery story. And with Todd, Roberta, and those richie-rich ladies, I bet at least one of them has the makings of a good murder victim—or even a murderer!"

CHAPTER 18

"Mija! I'm here!" Maria said loudly as she knocked repeatedly on the door of Angela's suite. She dropped her suitcase and her drenched umbrella and they clunked against the door. "Hello?"

Angela opened the door in a bathrobe, an urgent expression on her face. She held the door with her foot as she wrapped her wet hair in a terrycloth turban.

"Mamá, can you please be more quiet? It's late!"

"I'm sorry! When you didn't answer I was afraid you couldn't hear me," Maria said, smiling, without lowering her voice at all. "Besides, I thought you said the guest rooms were empty? I didn't see anyone—"

The door to the next suite opened and Grayson stepped out, wearing a smug expression and the same shiny silk robe as when Angela saw him at the casita. Thankfully, this time the robe was closed. He was rubbing his neck with a fluffy red towel that had a green Christmas tree embroidered near the hem.

"Well, well, well," he said, eyeing Maria from head to toe.

Maria had come straight from work and wore businesslike brown slacks and a short wool coat, which she unconsciously wrapped a bit tighter around her torso. Her leather boots were wet, and stray raindrops dotted the ends of her sleeves.

"You must be Miss Garcia's beautiful mother," Grayson continued. "No—of course not—you're her *sister*."

Maria giggled as Grayson picked up her hand and drew it to his lips.

"Mom, this is Grayson Gates. He's the director—"

"That name is familiar," Maria said. "Wait, aren't you an off-Broadway director?"

"Indeed. Are you a theater aficionado? Oh—*perdóname*—I mean, 'aficionada.'"

Maria smiled sweetly and looked downward with a shrug, drawing an eyeroll from her daughter.

"You know I like plays, mija," Maria stammered.

A croaky, off-key rendition of "The Gambler" floated down the hall from around the corner, diverting all of their attention.

"What do we have here?" Bea said, rounding the corner. She was soaked from head to toe, though the rain hadn't dampened her spirit. When she saw Grayson chatting up Maria, she let out a cackle. "Angie, you didn't mention your new boyfriend moved in next door. Maria, you're not flirting with Angela's new boyfriend, are you? Nice job, theater prince, two-timing your girlfriend with her mother."

Angela's face turned red and Maria's jaw dropped to the floor.

"Bea, you know that Grayson is not my boyfriend."

Grayson stepped into the hallway to face Angela. "Not yet," he said, winking lecherously.

"Grayson, *Aseem* is my boyfriend, and I love him with all my heart," Angela said.

"Probably a good thing," Bea chortled. "Grayson here is older than your mother!"

"Your *boyfriend* did not look like a man in love when he ran off without you the other day," Grayson. "You two had the look of a couple on the rocks."

"That was partly because of you—because I was worried about offending you. I've learned my lesson. I should have said right from the start that I had a boyfriend—a *serious* boyfriend—"

"Don't you mean, fiancé, mija?" Maria said.

"Right, right," Angela said. "Aseem is my *fiancé*, Grayson. Is that clear?"

Grayson looked momentarily stunned, then a smirk crept onto his face. "I don't see any ring."

"OK, that's enough, playhouse playboy," Bea said. She reached up and grabbed Grayson's bicep from below and attempted to steer him back into his suite. "Don't you need your beauty sleep? Your big VIP rehearsal thingie is tomorrow night, and you haven't even set foot on the real stage yet."

Grayson gently shook off Bea's grasp with a grin and stepped back into his suite. "You're right, I do need my beauty sleep. Angela, thank you again for providing me with this suite. At least Todd's nocturnal pursuits will not disturb me tonight. Sweet dreams, enchanting ladies," he added, blowing kisses at Angela and Maria.

"Mija, you and Aseem are fighting?" Maria

said, once Grayson closed his door. She looked down at Angela's left hand. "Wait—still no ring?"

"I'll be on my way," Bea said. "Looks like you two have some important talking to do."

"No—Bea, don't go yet," Angela sputtered. "I—I want to hear about the poker outing. And I want to tell you about my night with Todd and Connie." Then she turned to her mother. "We'll talk later, OK?"

"I do have very juicy gossip about the richie-riches from Sacramento," Bea said deviously.

Maria smiled at Bea, then looked at her daughter with concern. "Of course I'm interested in Bea's gossip," she said. "You promise we'll talk later, right, Angela?"

Angela nodded and the three of them stepped into her suite. Bea plopped down on the uphol-stered chair in the corner and Maria sat on the end of Angela's bed. Angela spun her desk chair around to face them both.

"I'll go first!" Bea said. "Out of respect for your mother—I know she'll want to hear about the bag ladies."

"Am I supposed to know what that means?" Maria chuckled.

"No one knows what she means," Angela sighed. "She's referring to heiresses."

"Victoria is the grocery bag lady and Tibby is the laundry bag lady," Bea said.

Maria laughed. "Victoria Hartman of Heartless Grocers? How's she involved with your play?"

Angela explained Victoria was hoping to help Tibby improve her position in Northern California society, so they were both sponsoring the theater. She added, cautiously, that Tibby thought the reason she'd been snubbed was because her family built their wealth via real estate.

"Poor little rich girl?" Maria laughed. "But seriously—does she really believe rich people look down on real estate investing?"

Angela frowned sheepishly. "That's what Aseem said. But she doesn't deserve to be friendless, does she? Besides… I'm not sure if Tibby actually told me she was shunned over real estate. I think maybe I assumed it and then I said it and she just ran with it. Maybe I gave her an easy way to avoid repeating the actual rumors."

"About the money laundering, right?" Maria said. "Those rumors have died down a lot, but they've been around for years up in Sac. Especially fifteen, twenty years ago, when the family went on its big buying binge. Made a few brokers rich. Many people said they were afraid to be on either side of a transaction, though—you know, because of where the money might have come from."

"Perry confirmed it, Angie," Bea said. Then she let out a cackle. "Kind of ironic that the realtors were afraid of dirty transactions when all the funds came from laundering! Get it? Laundering?" Bea gave her knee a hearty slap.

Maria laughed along with Bea, but Angela's face fell. "I did it again. When will I learn?"

"Did what again, mija?" Maria said.

"Gave someone the benefit of the doubt who didn't deserve it."

"Are you talking about Tibby?" Maria said, pausing for a moment. "You know, maybe you weren't wrong. Maybe she wasn't lying. Would her parents have told her the truth? Maybe she just doesn't know."

"Your mother's right. I don't think you're wrong at all, girlie," Bea said matter-of-factly.

"Wait—what?" Angela said.

"I suspect the snobbos *do* snipe about the Veltons making their money in real estate. After all, real estate is a classic vehicle for money laundering. It's one of the most expensive things you can buy, and you can pay cash for it."

"That's true," Maria said. "We had a training session on it in the office. Mostly, we learned about international criminals buying California real estate. But there's no reason it couldn't be a California operation. Once the funds are invested in real estate, the property can be resold to hide the source of the funds."

"Yep, so if the Veltons were working on behalf of crooked friends, they'd take their cut when the property sold. Or maybe the crooked friends buy it with cash, at an above-market price, so the Veltons get their payoff. It's like the folding and ironing stage of laundry," Bea added with a laugh. "The snotty socialites gotta know this. They probably say 'real estate' with air quotes."

Angela's face brightened a bit. "I do still feel bad for Tibby. Imagine being born into all that money and having such a hard time giving it away?"

"Speaking of Tibs, I still haven't gotten to my cardroom dish," Bea said. "It's about her so-called poor relation, Aunt Louisa. It seems it's not her unprofitable theater career that's keeping LouLou poor. Apparently, she's received quite a tidy little sum from her sister—Tibby's mother—over the years."

Bea leaned forward with a gleefully conspiratorial look on her face. "And by 'little,' I mean really, *really* large!"

"C'mon, Bea," Angela cried. "How could the people at the cardroom possibly know—oh, no. *OH, NO!*"

"You guessed it, Angie. Tibby's Auntie has a gambling problem. A little goes to poker at Perry's place, hence the chatter there. But most of Louisa's sister's largesse ends up in high-roller slot machines at the fancy Indian casinos. You can lose it a lot faster that way! And you can guess what comes next."

Angela frowned. Her mother looked perplexed.

"Just tell us," Maria said.

"No matter how much money Louisa's got, she tends to run out. Few years back, Tibby's mother set Louisa up with a trust fund meant to provide a comfy life. The money barely lasted a few months. So to help Louisa control herself, Tibby's mother switched to a monthly allowance—but, surprise surprise, before the month runs out, the money usually does. That's when the trouble starts, because it's not hard to find quick credit when word gets out you're a gambler with a rich family. The lenders come to you."

"Loan sharks?" Maria gulped.

"They prefer 'private banker,'" Bea snickered.

"No wonder Tibby is willing to pay to get

Louisa a big part in the play," Angela said. "If Louisa's busy rehearsing, she isn't in a casino."

"The trust fund she burned through—how much money are we talking about?" Maria asked.

"More than enough for Louisa to have bought some California real estate of her own."

Angela shook her head. "It's so hard to believe—"

"You'd be surprised how much inherited money turns up—and runs out—in casinos. 'Creative loan options' help people lose it a lot faster," Bea said. "I knew a guy who inherited twenty million bucks and managed to blow most of it on poker and the ponies. His mother tried the same thing as Louisa's sister—doling the money out like a salary, instead of one lump sum. Then she died and he got his hands on it all—"

"I don't even want to know what happened," Angela said. "It's too depressing."

"That story has a happier ending than most. The guy's got a big personality and the gift of gab. Got hired as a poker commentator on cable TV. That's keeping the wolf from his door for now."

"Back to the Veltons—does that mean it's Louisa who's spreading the rumors? Or her lenders?"

"No one knows for sure, but her debts must be

the connection. I'm guessing it starts when Louisa misses a payment. Someone—either a lender, a collector, or Louisa herself—revives the money-laundering rumors, then they shake the Veltons' money tree. The Veltons want to fend off hits to their reputation—or, more likely, they're worried the feds'll get interested again. So they pay off Louisa's debts to make it go away."

"It seems like there's no way the Veltons can stop the cycle," Angela said.

"Would you believe poor Tibby thought she could do it?" Bea chuckled. "She found one of the loan sharks who does business with her aunt. Tibby shows up in the grubby casino garage, innocence on a stick, and tries to convince the guy that he was picking on an addict and isn't that unethical? Perry said the guy told her he'd think about it, then came into the cardroom and told everyone who would listen how a 'rich little bunny rabbit named Bitsy' thought she could talk him out of a prime piece of business."

"That's so dangerous!" Angela moaned. "Oh, Tibby! How clueless can you be?"

"I think she sounds brave—and loyal," Maria replied. "No wonder you want to help her."

"Tibby had no idea who she was dealing with," Bea agreed. "But I think if the Veltons get tired of paying up, they'll find another solution. Even if they've gone legit, they must still have connections to some knee-breakers of their own," Bea said. "They'll probably stay on the right side of the law as long as they can, though."

"Speaking of law enforcement," Angela said. "Can I tell you my scoop? It's a deep, dark secret."

"I haven't even gotten to my news about Roberta yet, girlie!"

Maria was overcome by a huge yawn. "I'm so sorry! That was rude. I got tired all of a sudden."

"I guess we've all had a long day. And don't you two have something you need to talk about?" Bea said. Angela grimaced but didn't reply. "Angie, why don't you and I regroup in my suite in the morning? I'll have Rebecca order us breakfast."

"OK. Seven-thirty?"

MARIA PUT her suitcase on the luggage rack at the end of Angela's bed and turned down the bedspread and sheet.

"Are you sure it's OK if I take the bed?"

"Of course," Angela said, taking the cushions off the sofa and stacking them neatly. She yanked the convertible bed out and began to make it. She unfurled the fitted flannel sheet with a snap and watched it float onto the mattress.

"Mija, I'm sorry you and Aseem are fighting," Maria began gently.

"We're not—we're not fighting. Not exactly."

"Is it because of Grayson? Is there something for Aseem to worry about—"

"Of course not!"

"I'm sorry—I didn't think so, but Grayson's so persistent. And you know, it's not unusual to get cold feet—"

"I don't have cold feet!" Angela cried. She stopped talking and smoothed the top sheet methodically, collecting herself. "Aseem is just so focused on the ring. I don't see what the rush is. I just—I just don't get it. But I promised him we'll go shopping when the play's over."

"You said that you told Grayson he was your boyfriend. Not your fiancé?" Maria said. She fluffed the pillows on the bed with her back turned to her daughter. She didn't see the frustration on Angela's face, or the way her daughter put her hands on her hips.

"Mom—Mamá—I'm not sure I want to talk about this after all."

Maria turned toward her. "I understand, but

I'm worried for you. Have you talked to Aseem? Relationships need tending—"

"Oh, really?" Angela snapped. "I've never even met my father! You've never told me why you separated—why he left us. If it's OK with you, I'll take my relationship advice from people who are actually *in a relationship!*"

Maria looked stricken. She didn't respond to her daughter for a moment.

"I see now. Is this… is this what's bothering you? You can't let this make you—"

"I can't talk about this anymore." Angela turned away and pulled a white shirt and an overnight bag out of the closet. "I'm going to spend the night at the cottage." Then she stepped into the bathroom and began noisily gathering toiletries and adding them to the bag.

MARIA REACHED INTO HER PURSE. Her heart was racing and a million thoughts competed in her head. She fished for the letter she'd carried with her, transferring it from handbag to handbag, since Angela was a senior in high school.

She'd wanted to talk to her daughter, to tell her the truth she needed to know, and could never find the right time—or the right words. So she'd written her thoughts down, hoping that would make it easier. And yet she'd somehow never found the right moment—or the courage—to share what she'd written with her daughter. At least, she consoled herself, if anything happened to her, one day Angela would get to read the words.

But now she knew the time was right—or, rather, she hoped it wasn't too late.

She heard Angela zipping her tote in the bathroom and knew she needed to act fast.

Cobarde, she thought to herself. Coward. A conversation would be so much better. *But we will talk afterwards.*

Maria quickly tucked the wrinkled letter into the top of Angela's purse just before her daughter stepped out of the bathroom, her overnight bag over her shoulder.

"Bye… I'll see you tomorrow, OK?" Angela said, her voice a mix of anger and shame, tempered with love.

Maria's eyes welled with tears she hoped Angela couldn't see.

"OK, mija. Te quiero mucho."

"I know!" Angela cringed, knowing she sounded impatient. "I love you, too."

Then she opened the door and was gone.

．　．　．

ANGELA HURRIED to the parking lot. She was annoyed by the light rain and still angry—at her mother, and even more at herself.

She yanked the car door open and tossed her overnight bag and her purse on the passenger seat. The handbag bounced off the tote and landed on the floor, some of its contents spilling out. She rolled her eyes and cursed quietly.

I'll deal with it when I get to the cottage.

The night was cool and dark. The trip to the cottage was short—normally only ten or fifteen minutes—but Angela drove slowly. The roads were slick, and she was the only one driving on them.

She pulled into the driveway and the motion-sensitive light that Aseem had installed turned on. The rain came down harder. Angela got out of the car and ran to the passenger side, first grabbing the tote and slinging it over her shoulder, then reaching down on the floor for her purse. The letter—her mother's letter—had fallen out upside down. It was so thick and bedraggled, Angela at first thought it was just an old bill full of marketing slips that she'd forgotten to recycle. Then she turned it over and saw her name in her mother's handwriting.

She tucked everything into her purse and rushed to the landing in front of the front door to get out of the rain.

CHAPTER 19

Angela stepped inside the cottage and dropped her overnight bag and her purse on the floor. Wind whistled softly through the door. She slipped off her wet flats, leaving them by the door—right next to Aseem's running shoes. She felt a pang at the sight of her fiancé's sneakers.

Something was wrong. It was up to her to fix it. But how could she, when she didn't even understand what the problem was?

Pushing the question out of her mind for a moment, she cleaned up the water and mud she'd tracked in, changed for bed, then boiled water for a cup of herbal tea. It was already into the wee hours and she was tired, but not yet ready for sleep—not without knowing what was in that letter her mother had slipped into her purse.

She put the tea on the nightstand and crawled under the sheets, then slowly pulled the stack of worn pages her mother had written all those years ago from the wrinkled envelope.

Angela smiled. *Español. Por supuesto. Of course.*

Her Spanish was better than she gave herself credit for (far from the "Kindergarten Spanish" she self-deprecatingly called it), but it would have been easier for her if the letter had been written in English, especially considering how tired she was.

She understood, though, that this was a story her mother could only have told in Spanish. She would simply have to take her time reading it, making sure she understood every word.

Mija, for all these years, I know you've desperately wanted to know how I—we—came to be alone in California. How we became our little "familia de dos."

You've been so patient with me. So many times you cried when I wouldn't tell you what you wanted to know. I hope you can forgive me. I thought the answer might hurt more than not knowing.

I told you that your father left, that I didn't know why. That it was better not to think about it, to focus on the future instead. And I know I was partly right, because look at how you are growing up! I'm so proud of you, amazing niña mia.

But I also know in my heart you have a right to know the truth. And you are old enough now. Yet I still haven't found the courage to tell you.

That is why I am writing it all down—selfishly, to make it easier for me.

I was only nineteen when I met your father. Young, and as it turned out, foolish. Miguel was four years older. He was so handsome, so clever. It makes me happy to think, at least, that he passed his gifts on to you! I see them in you every day.

It was not my idea to come here. It was his idea.

His family would not accept our love—that was how he said it.

"Is it because I am alone?" I asked him. My

mother had died just months before. Now my mother and father were both gone.

"No, querida. Of course not. They simply think you are not right for me. You know how protective parents can be."

That was all Miguel ever said on the subject.

I did not think to ask why his parents thought he needed "protecting" from me. His love gave me life. So I never asked again why we always met in secret, why he concealed me from his family.

His parents were simply a roadblock for us to find a way around. As long as Miguel and I loved each other, that was all that mattered. Us against the world!

Like I said, foolish.

When Miguel said, let's make a new start in a new country... it was thrilling. He talked of a land of opportunity, a challenge we would take on together. I felt brave. Just the two of us, with only our love to build on.

We knew we would face obstacles, but they only gave the dream more meaning....

...we married as soon as we crossed the border. Just us two, a priest, and a witness. No dress. No tuxedo. Miguel made a bouquet of some wildflowers he found. To my eyes, they were more beautiful than the rarest roses....

Her mother's story was riveting, but Angela was losing the battle with exhaustion. Drowsiness made it harder to read in Spanish. She put the pages on the pillow next to her and closed her eyes for just... a moment? She shook herself awake and looked at the clock. If she went to sleep now, she could still get four or five hours, but she wanted—needed—to finish reading the letter before she saw her mother in the morning.

Just a few pages to go. I can do it!

She yawned and stretched and adjusted the pillows supporting her back. She got out of bed and went to the bathroom to splash water on her face. Then she got back into bed, swallowed a big mouthful of her tepid tea, and read on.

...we made our way to the San Joaquin Valley. A distant cousin worked at a commercial grape

farm. Miguel was hired quickly. It was summer. Harvest would start soon....

...I found work, too. I worked for a lawyer who helped immigrants from the South. Oh, mija, I know you can understand how proud I was to help support us! I was lucky, too. I didn't realize how lucky at the time. That lawyer liked me. He valued my work. That was such a blessing. Later, he helped me to stay in California. To build a life for us.

It hurts to think of it, and even more to write this, but this brief time was the happiest of my life.

Little did I know an earthquake was about to shake my world apart.

Angela was wide awake now—and afraid of what she would read next. She stroked a round spot on the paper where the texture was different. The word "earthquake" was slightly blurred. Angela felt a stab of pain in her heart. The mark must have been made by one of her mother's tears.

... I am not sure I even know how to tell you what happened next, but I will try.

It was a Sunday, hot and dry. We had come home from church to our tiny apartment. It was barely an apartment—hardly more than a room, in a tiny house divided into four apartments—but it was already home to us.

I was cooking a small feast on the stove. We had saved up a little money. Some new friends were coming to celebrate Miguel's birthday. There was a grill outside, shared by everyone in the house, and I watched through the open window as Miguel talked to our neighbors and grilled corn. I still remember the sweet, smoky aroma floating to me on the breeze....

Then a truck rumbled off the road onto our dirt driveway. I smiled as I recognized that Miguel's cousin—the one who helped him get his job— was driving. It took a moment for me to figure out who his passenger was.

He was Miguel's brother.

Could Rafa have traveled all this way to wish Miguel a happy birthday?

That was far too much to hope for, of course. Foolish me.

I saw Miguel rush to the truck. "Inside," I heard him say to his brother. "Don't say anything out here."

Miguel seemed to know his brother had anything but happy birthday wishes for him.

They rushed past me, to our bed and the small chest of drawers where we kept our clothes. Rafa looked on, his face blank, as Miguel packed his things into a bag.
Miguel moved slowly. He wouldn't look at me. His face was full of shame.

I remember how hard I fought to keep the tears from falling from my eyes.

"But we're married, Rafa. Surely your parents will see now that we belong together! We're not living in sin. We have jobs. We are making a life here," I pleaded. "You cannot make us leave!"

Rafa snorted with scorn. "You are free to stay here. You are not married, little girl. That's simply not possible."

"We can prove it!" I cried. Miguel glanced up at his brother for an instant.

Rafa exploded with laughter that felt like a punch to my stomach.

"Grow up, Miguel. This has gone too far already. It's serious now. Sofia is pregnant. It's time for you to be a proper husband."

Miguel didn't look at me again. With his head down, he told me quietly that he'd left what money he had under the mattress—and that I'd be better off here.

At first, I didn't want to believe him, but he was right.
There was nothing left for me in Mexico but pain.

Angela felt her eyes fill with tears for her mother. Between the emotion and fatigue, she struggled to read the rest of the letter. It became a jumble of words, just letters and phrases jumping out here and there.

...I didn't yet know I was pregnant.... I hoped that I was really married, but knew in my heart it wasn't true.... I tried to contact Miguel again and again, but my calls were unanswered, my letters returned....

...I knew only that I had to focus on the future. Your future—for soon I would have a child to take care of....

...I hope you can forgive me, niña mia, for giving up on Miguel... for keeping his secrets— and my own. I had to shield you from this pain.... It wasn't you that he left behind—it was me, only me....

...I vowed then that it would be just the two of us, making our way in this new world....

...because the one thing I knew for sure—that I always knew—was that I wanted to be a mom. I

wanted to be your mom. So I decided right then that I couldn't, wouldn't—won't—risk my past interfering with your future....

The impact of what her mother wrote hit Angela like an electric shock. The fatigue gave way to a desperate need to talk to her—not just about the letter. She had to apologize for the horrible things she'd said the night before.

She looked at the clock. *Five forty-five.* Her mother would be awake by seven.

She won't mind getting up a little early.

After quickly brushing her teeth and hair, Angela dressed in the outfit she'd packed in her tote, guzzled half a cup of coffee, and rushed through the pouring rain to her car.

ANGELA PARKED in the inn's lot and jogged to the nearest door, her jacket hiked up over her head to keep it dry. Rainwater rushed across the asphalt to the storm drains. Angela darted around and jumped over puddles but still was damp from head to toe when she stepped inside.

She shook the rain off her jacket and rushed down the hall to her suite. She checked the time.

Six-fifteen. Quietly, she opened the door—and found no one inside.

The bed was made. Even the convertible mattress had been stowed, the linens neatly folded on the restored sofa.

Calling her mother's name, Angela searched the bathroom—it was untouched. Her mother's suitcase was gone, too.

She must be driving back to Sacramento.

She called out "Rebecca" and commanded the tube to call her mother. The phone rang five times then went to voicemail.

I should never have stormed off like that last night!

Distraught, Angela pulled out her cell and tapped out a text to her mother.

```
I'm sorry! I was wrong. So
wrong! Please call me. <3
```

Then she lay down on the bed to wait. Was her mother's phone on silent mode? It was still early in the morning. If she stopped for gas or for coffee, surely she'd see that she'd missed a call.

I'll just rest my eyes a little. Then I'll try calling her again.

It wasn't more than a minute before exhaustion caught up with Angela, and she was sound asleep. An hour later, the clammy feeling of drool on her pillow woke her up. Groggily, she checked the time. *Seven-thirty!*

She was already late for Bea. She ran into the bathroom, ran her toothbrush over her teeth, and splashed some water on her face before heading out the door.

CHAPTER 20

"You OK, Angie?" Bea said.

"Just tired," Angela said, helping herself to one of the large lattes on Bea's desk. "Glad you got coffee delivered. I need it this morning."

"Yeah, no offense, but you look like you got run over by a truck!"

"I'll take that as a weird, Bea-style show of concern."

Angela grabbed a doughnut hole from a box of about thirty and bit into it. "And thanks for providing appropriate nutrition. Probably not what I need after an all-nighter, but I'll take it."

"An all-nighter?!" Bea squawked. "Aren't you the goody two-shoes who's always telling me that nothing good happens after midnight?"

"Another compliment—why thank you, Bea! And technically, the saying is that nothing good happens after two in the morning."

"You're a little cranky today. Who wouldn't be after an all-nighter? You're young, but not that young. I hope you weren't cavorting with our randy director—"

"That's not the least bit funny, Bea," Angela said, with an edge in her voice that Bea hadn't heard before.

"I didn't mean anything by it. How 'bout we start dishing to lighten the mood? Should you start or should I? Really, I'm... I'm.... You know, I'm...."

"You don't have to try to apologize, Bea. I know it's not your thing," Angela said, still sounding piqued. "I'm sorry. Truth is, I *am* cranky. It's just that I'm desperate to talk to my mother."

Angela pulled her cell from her pocket and tapped on it, frowned, and put it back in her pocket.

"I... I got angry with her last night and I shouldn't have. I spent the night at the cottage. I came back early to apologize, but I missed her, and now she's not answering my calls. I think she's headed home to Sacramento and doesn't want to talk with me. On top of everything else,

I'm worried about her driving. The storm's only getting worse."

"Girlie, there's got to be another explanation—"

Angela blew out a sigh. "If only. Anyway, let's get the dishing started. I'll go first. I found out about the job that brought Todd here. Care to guess who Todd's new boss is?"

Bea had just opened her mouth to answer when Angela interrupted her.

"It's McGregor."

"You didn't even give me time to guess! Nice misdirection, though, acting all matter-of-fact about it. How'd you find out?"

"I guess I'm not in the mood for guessing after all," Angela said. She checked her phone again, clucking her tongue and then shoving it back in her pocket. "Connie accidentally leaked it."

"Interesting. Todd's confiding in Connie, huh? That's a development."

"I thought it meant something at first, too. But the news is coming out in the *Grapevine* this weekend. Connie even told me she wrote the *Grapevine* piece. Maybe that's the only reason Todd confided in her, to get her to—" Angela exhaled deeply. "Let's just say Todd confiding in Connie's a data point, but it would be easy to misinterpret it. I say we shouldn't read too much into it."

Bea's furrowed brow conveyed a mix of surprise and wry amusement. She walked over to the desk and stared at the doughnut holes.

"I'm pretty sure I asked for the regular old assortment, but is there a secret ingredient in these treats that's turning you into a hyper-rational cynic?"

Angela responded with another cluck of her tongue.

Loud, giddy laughter from the hall outside Bea's suite caught them both by surprise. Angela rushed over and looked out the peephole. She gasped and hastily opened the door. Outside were her mother and Grayson, both in workout gear. They were giggling uninhibitedly, big grins on their faces.

"Good morning, cariño!" Maria said. "Are you feeling better today?"

"Angela," Grayson said with a hammy grin and half-bow.

"You two are...together?"

"Turns out we both like to work out early in the morning. Isn't that lucky?" Maria gushed. "Oh, Grayson, that was fun. Thank you for spotting me —and everything else this morning," she added with a demure smile that Angela noted with a squint and a slightly queasy expression.

"May I?" Grayson said, looking pointedly at Maria's hand. She nodded, and he picked her hand up and kissed it gallantly. Angela's jaw dropped.

"Thank you for asking first," Maria said approvingly.

"Thank you for reminding me—boundaries, right? But now, my dear, I'm afraid I must dash. Our first rehearsal starts soon, and we sorely need it." Grayson laughed lightly. "I'm heartened that I will see you for coffee later."

"I'll do the shopping we discussed. I'll come up with some options that can all be done in one day. I promise, you won't regret it," Maria said. "Shall we meet at three? You mentioned you have your rehearsal break then, right?"

"Until then," Grayson said, half-bowing again before heading down the hall.

"What was that about?"

"Oh, you mean the shopping? I suggested Grayson get some personalized gifts for the crew. He was telling me about morale problems between the cast and the volunteers, and how doing the rehearsals outdoors has made it feel like they're on the same team."

"Does he realize that a certain hotshot director's expectations are part of what's bugging the crew?" Bea snarked from behind Angela.

"He admitted he was part of the problem," Maria said. "It all started when I ran into him outside your suite this morning, Angela. I gave him a bit of a lecture about how he was treating you." Maria had a proud smile on her face.

"I don't think he'll be bothering you anymore. I was quite stern—too stern, I thought at first. I… well, you might not be surprised to hear that I didn't sleep very well last night. He didn't consider me rude, though—he even thanked me for setting him straight. As I'm sure you know, his main reason for being here in Napa is to work on himself. Ooh, is that an extra latte, Bea? Do you mind?"

"Help yourself."

Maria stepped past her daughter and grabbed the coffee off the desk, taking a minute to eye the doughnut holes. Angela looked at Bea with a perplexed expression and mouthed, "As I know? Work on himself?"

"And guess what?" Maria continued after a swig. "He invited me to the cast party on Sunday night. Isn't that exciting? Angela, do you know what people wear to those things?"

"I don't. And I'm not sure—"

"I know you and I need to talk, so maybe we can discuss everything later? I've got to take a shower and get to work on that shopping for him. Do you mind if I go first? You look like you could use a shower, too, honey."

"You go first. I could use a nap, but Mamá, did you see my texts? I've been trying to reach you. I thought you'd left."

"I just turned on my phone. Didn't you notice my suitcase in the closet? I put it there to tidy up. Anyway, I saw something about an apology—mija, you have nothing to apologize for. I was trying to help, but I see now I shouldn't have meddled in your relationship. If anything, I should apologize to you—"

"It's for more than just last night. I read your letter—"

"You still don't owe me any apology, cariño," Maria said, kissing her daughter on the cheek. "But walk with me back to your suite so we can talk a bit—about the letter, and anything else you like. I'm relieved... I'm relieved that you finally know the truth."

Maria walked out of the door full of vim.

Angela looked at Bea and shrugged. "See you in the ballroom in a few hours?"

"Sounds good. After you're done apologizing,

see if you can find out what your mother meant by Grayson 'working on himself.'"

"Oh, I'm planning on it," Angela said, hurrying after her mother.

Bea turned her attention to the overflowing supply of doughnut holes that remained on her desk.

"You're mine now," she said demonically, chuckling to herself and rubbing her hands together. "All mine!" She grabbed an alluringly glazed sphere of cake and shoved the entire thing in her little mouth.

Then Bea remembered that she hadn't yet told Angela the latest crazy rumor she'd heard about Roberta during her poker outing—or the lengths she'd had to go to get it. She opened the door and tried to call out to Angela, but only managed to spray crumbs all over the floor.

"Drat!" she tried to exclaim. It sounded more like "dwath."

She took a quick swig of her iced coffee and tried again to call Angela back, but she and Maria were already out of earshot.

"Maybe it's just as well," Bea said aloud as she poked around in the pastry box, eventually identifying one that was plump and round and bigger than a golf ball, filled with sticky jelly and coated with sugar. She took two whole bites to savor it while she considered her next move. She decided that if she wanted to do a proper job digging up dirt, it was time for professional help.

She turned toward the internet speaker in the corner and said, "Rebecca, call Pat Rogers."

Pat Rogers was a San Francisco private investigator who'd taught Bea the basics of detective work, becoming a friend in the process.

"How's my favorite amateur?" Pat said. "Staying dry? It's just light rain here in San Francisco so far. We're bracing for worse."

"Rain's not light here. I can hear plenty of it." Bea pulled open the drapes covering her suite's biggest window. "Whoa! It's worse than it sounds. There's already a small river in our parking lot."

"Good day for staying in. Makes me glad I can do most of my gumshoeing online now."

"That's exactly why I called you. I'm wondering if you can help me with a little detective project."

Bea filled Pat in on all the intriguing mysteries of Pinot Playhouse and their hapless production of *The Ratcatcher*: the fire that brought down their theater; how Todd asked to "borrow" the ballroom for their ragtag production, rankling Roberta; the rumors that Roberta somehow "owns" the nonprofit theater and could be bilking the donors; and Tibby buying a role for her auntie—who is probably blackmailing her wealthy sister.

"Are you investigating those as potential crimes?" Pat said. "And does that mean you're working with your favorite cop?"

"McGregor? Heck no. I'm not looking to solve crimes. Just satisfying my curiosity and gathering new mystery story ideas, but with this gang's bag of motives and shady connections, who knows? We could have a fresh murder any day now!" Bea said with a cackle. "I might change my mind if that happens."

"Joking about murder's bad karma," Pat said, knocking on wood hard enough for Bea to hear it. "That rumor about 'Velton's Currency Cleaners' has been around for years. Much as I'd like to take your money, I'd say it's already good as confirmed."

"You're right, I've got multiple sources on that, and on the big drama in the family, too. Turns out poor Auntie Louisa's got a one-armed bandit problem."

"The slots?"

"Yep. Among other games of chance—and after she blows her secret allowance, she borrows from the usual unsavory lenders who hang around gambling establishments. Naturally, that leads to a bigger sisterly shakedown. Rinse and repeat. And now she's got her clueless niece Tibby Velton—I mean, her unsuspecting niece—funding her acting 'career.'"

"'Unsuspecting' sounds better. So you want me to look into that?"

"Nope. That's a variation on the troubled gambler tale of woe I witnessed a thousand times during my professional poker days. No, I called you about a new rumor that wasn't on that list. It's about Roberta, our potential nonprofit racketeer. And ooh, baby, it's a doozy.

"Sources say the mega-millions she inherited from her super-rich, mostly estranged uncle Ambrose triggered a brawl with some folks who were a lot closer to the guy than she was. Now I want to know if this juicy story is credible enough to plop right into my next mystery book. As in, is it true?"

"Truth can be a lot stranger than fiction."

"If this one turns out to be true, I think it'll make some mighty fine fiction!" Bea cackled. "What I heard was that one friend in particular had known Uncle Ambrose for thirty-odd years before he died. Ambrose was this friend's college engineering professor. Over decades since those days, Ambrose encouraged this aspiring Edison to keep tinkering with his entrepreneurial ideas. He was one of the only people who'd ever been in the friend's corner. Ambrose was like the dad this friend never had. And the friend took care of Ambrose in his failing years like a loving son.

"A few years before he died, Ambrose had a scary encounter with a tax lien—as in, the tax man was ready to seize his three-million-dollar Victorian because he missed a property tax payment of a few thousand. Old Ambrose realized he needed help keeping up with his bills. So he added the friend's name onto a bank account worth half a mil or so. This meant that the friend could take care of all Ambrose's bills for him. It also meant that the friend—who'd never gotten his big break, or even a small one, with his many inventions—could keep what was left in the account when Ambrose passed.

"Ambrose dies a year or two later, leaving his dear friend with a few hundred thou. Rumor is that didn't sit too well with Roberta, who thought that money belonged in the pot with the other eighteen million she inherited."

"Eighteen *million?*"

"Yep. A one, an eight, and six gorgeous zeros."

Outside, the wind whipped up. A broken tree branch smacked into the window.

"Did you hear that? Even Mother Nature's impressed by that figure!" Bea laughed. "Ambrose was a fine real estate investor. He accumulated rental properties all over the Bay Area. Roberta got all the houses and a couple of apartment buildings, plus there was a couple mil in cash in other accounts that Roberta got outright."

"One has to wonder why Roberta cared so much about that relatively small amount. Besides, if Ambrose put the guy's name on that one account," Pat said, "what could Roberta do about it?"

"Seems you can do a lot with nearly unlimited funds and a crafty team of San Francisco attorneys. Their tactic of choice was to accuse the guy of elder abuse. Roberta didn't know her uncle well, but dementia runs in their family. She decided to claim poor Ambrose wasn't all there and was swindled by the friend."

"Holy moley!"

"I'll say. From what I hear, this poor friend drove from San Jose to Gilroy several times a week to check on Ambrose, sometimes staying over to make sure he was well. Arranged nurse visits, ordered food, took him to the doctor. Even took him to a family reunion in Oklahoma because Ambrose was too frail to go alone.

"That family reunion was the only time in two

decades that Roberta had even *seen* Ambrose. Sad thing is, out of his blood family, Roberta was the only one Ambrose even liked. The guy was a suspicious old coot. He liked that Roberta had been a teacher. But for most of his life, he was all but disconnected from his family. I guess the reunion was about making his peace."

"The friend—he sounds like a saint."

"My thoughts egg-*zactly*. Sad story. I gotta wonder how true it is."

"What does the rumor mill say happened to the money?"

"Reply hazy, like the Magic 8 Ball says. Mind you, this was all a semi-drunken conversation over poker."

"Semi-drunken? Don't you always say never mix alcohol and cards?"

"I wasn't doing the drinking," Bea chuckled. "I don't normally encourage anyone I teach to drink at the table, either."

"'Cause you want to take their money fair and square?" Pat laughed.

"Exactly! But I had one chance to get these peeps talking. I even had to go so far as to *lose* a bunch of hands to get these folks talking."

"Whoa!"

"Tell me about it. Anyway, turns out some of

the crew got the same nosy gene as you and me, so they dug into Pinot Playhouse's savior's background as soon as she came onto the scene. Boy, were they shy until I got them giddy with winning. Painful for me, but effective."

"The old chirpin' chips."

"I paid up and they chirped," Bea chuckled. "One said she'd heard the friend used up the entire account defending his case and wound up bankrupt. The other version is that dirty lawyer tricks won the case for Roberta, and the friend had to hand over the account."

"No version with the friend coming out on top, huh?"

"Not that I heard."

"I agree it's juicy. I'll start with the court documents. Depending on where probate was filed, and how far the litigation went, there could be lots of documents on the web. You'd be surprised what can be found without leaving the house if you know where to look. Don't suppose you have the friend's name, do you?"

"If it was an easy job, why would I need a professional? Nobody seemed to know the name of the friend—or maybe they didn't want to say it. If Roberta's elder abuse strategy worked, the poor guy probably has enough reputation problems.

But don't worry, I'm not going to send you on the hunt with nothing. Ambrose's last name—and Roberta's—is Newberg."

"It's a start. And if I stumble across any other dirt on Roberta—"

"You know what to do."

"Roger. I should have some results for you by the end of the day. Should I come to the wine country and deliver them in person?"

"I'd save you a seat for the play if I thought that bucket of bolts of yours would make it through the storm today. I'm sure there will be empty seats. They're expecting floods and knee-deep water on some of the roads."

"Don't worry about me and my trusty steed. If it doesn't look safe, I'll report back by phone. Otherwise, I'm looking forward to the play!"

"Lucky for you I haven't told you much about it."

CHAPTER 21

Angela rolled over and looked at the clock: eleven-fifteen. A couple of hours of sleep had improved her outlook considerably. She felt ready to face the conversation she was about to have with her mother.

She stretched and stood up from the bed, then found a short note on her desk in her mother's precise handwriting:

I am going to the café to buy us a little lunch. See you around noon.

Plenty of time to shower.

She pulled open the drapes and looked in shock at the water rushing downhill in the parking lot and the rain falling in sheets.

Sheesh! Maybe I should just go stand outside!

Standing under the hot shower longer than she normally would, Angela thought through everything she wanted to say to her mother. Her heart was full of empathy and regret and gratitude.

She turned off the water and stepped out onto the holiday-themed bath-mat, making a point of stepping directly on Santa's nose, a silly ritual that always made her smile. She dried off and wrapped herself in her robe, combed out her hair, and put on earrings and a little makeup. Just as she finished dressing, her mother showed up with a pair of Asian chicken salads and sparkling water in a plastic bag that was covered with raindrops.

"Perfect timing," she said, opening the door.

Maria shook her umbrella and leaned it up against the wall in the hallway.

"It's raining so hard! Did you hear the thunder?"

"I think that's what woke me up."

Still balancing their lunches, being careful not to drench her daughter with her wet coat, Maria leaned in and gave Angela a half-hug. "That's a reminder you have nothing to apologize for."

"I'm not sure you're right, and I want to anyway. At least… I want to talk about your letter."

A flash of lightning lit up the window. Angela and her mother looked at each other in awe.

Thunderstorms weren't common in the wine country. The two women flinched when the thunder cracked a moment later.

"They said on the radio that this storm is going to get much worse before it gets better," Maria said.

"I wonder if the play should be postponed," Angela said quietly, looking out the window.

"The weather report warned about floods."

Angela sighed and sat down on her bed, salad bowl in hand. "It's not my decision. I'll check in with Todd."

"Todd—that's Connie's new… love interest?"

"Something like that. I'm afraid he's leading her on, but Bea keeps reminding me that Connie's a grown woman."

"Bea's right, but it's OK to worry about your friend, too," Maria said. She handed her daughter a plastic fork and sat down with her own salad in the guest chair. "Connie told me she could use some help at the check-in desk tonight. I hope you don't mind."

"Not at all. If Bea were here, she'd say you're lucky you'll be sitting close to the exit," Angela laughed. She took a big bite of salad and gave her mother a thumbs-up on the selection. "Is it OK if I say what I need to say?"

Her mother nodded, and Angela started with an apology. "Not just for last night, though I had no right to say what I did. I guess… I guess you struck a nerve about me and Aseem. It's no excuse. I'm truly sorry for that, and also, for not acknowledging all you've sacrificed for me. I know now that I only ever looked at things from my point of view—"

"You were a child, mija—"

"I haven't been a child for a while now. It's past time for me to see the bigger picture." Angela started to tear up. "And it's past time for you to stop putting your life on hold for me—"

"Please don't cry, cariño—especially not for me! I have no regrets. If anything, I owe you an apology for not telling you the truth sooner."

"I see now it would have been hard for me to put all the pieces together when I was a little girl."

"That was one thing I was afraid of—it's a complicated story. And when you were very small, I was afraid to admit I wasn't even married when I was pregnant with you. It was a different time, then, mija, and I was a young Catholic girl. What if you were teased in school? What if you couldn't make friends? What if I couldn't? It seemed easier for me to have a husband who left me than for everyone to know I had never been legally married.

"Then after you went to school and saw that the other kids had fathers who loved them, I knew you probably believed that yours was cruel, and that he never wanted to know you. I didn't know how to make it better. The only thing I could think of to do was to keep trying to reach him. I kept hoping that I would hear from Miguel—that one of my messages would get through, and he would learn about his wonderful daughter. Then you could see for yourself that his leaving had nothing to do with you. I wouldn't have to explain. It took me years to accept the truth in front of my face, that he was never going to reply.

"Now that you are grown—now that you are ready to be married yourself—my worry is that you will think he left me in dishonor. Miguel did leave me—there's no denying it—but I think that, in his way, he did the honorable thing. There was no easy answer. He was already married to Sofia. He lived up to that commitment. And he didn't know you were on the way."

"But you trusted him. He didn't tell you the truth. He wasn't who he said he was."

"I saw it that way, too, when he first left. Now I see things differently—and, I think, a little more clearly. Even though we were in love, it was wrong for us to run off and get married. Miguel shouldn't have done it because he was already married to Sofia.

"But I had a part to play in our tragedy, too. I stopped asking why he kept our relationship a secret. I was blinded by love—"

"That's just it," Angela said, her voice trembling. "How do you know whether you're blinded by love or not?"

Maria laughed lightly—a sound that simultaneously stung and reassured her daughter. "I knew it. You must not let my experience cast doubt on your own. I was so immature—just a teenager! And not one who was old for her years, either. You, on the other hand," Maria chuckled again, "you were practically a grown-up when you were born. And I bet your sweet fiancé was the same way."

"You did fine on your own. And I'm ambitious, just like you. Maybe it's better to be single. Aseem and I—we're not even married yet and we're fighting. And we're fighting over something so silly, *a ring.*"

"Dios mío. It's not really about the ring though, is it? He loves you so. Anyone can see it. Is it wrong that he wants to be sure you feel the same?"

"I do love him... and he's my best friend...." Angela's voice cracked with emotion.

"Have you heard the saying, 'If you want to go fast, go alone; if you want to go far, go together'? You and Aseem both have big dreams. You can help each other achieve them. Isn't it better to have someone to share the experience with? Someone to celebrate with, someone to encourage you through the challenges? And then if you decide to expand your family, hopefully sometime soon, it will be so much easier together—"

"Mom! Where did that come from?"

"Just saying that I won't object to being called 'abuela'!"

"Aren't you too young for that?"

The two of them shared a welcome laugh as they finished their lunch. Outside, the storm worsened. The wind picked up, occasionally lashing the rain onto the windows.

Maria checked the time. "I'd better head to the ballroom to meet Connie. And don't you have a call to make to your fiancé?"

Angela nodded, then jumped involuntarily when another bolt of flashed. "I can't help but wonder if the show is still on, but I guess you'll find out if it's canceled before I will."

She hugged her mother tightly as they stood by

the door, then stepped back as if a big idea had popped into her head.

"You know, since you're not married after all, isn't it time you found someone? You're barely in your fifties—and Grayson was right, anyone would guess you were in your forties. Don't you want someone to support *you*, someone who shares *your* interests?"

"I'm surprised you haven't figured out that I already have," Maria said coyly as she walked out of the room.

Angela gulped.

No... not... Grayson?!

CHAPTER 22

Angela arrived at the ballroom and found her mother working amiably with Connie at a check-in table set by the hallway doors. Maria stood up eagerly to greet her daughter. Bea was standing nearby, observing the frantic last-minute rush in the rest of the ballroom with amusement. Despite the vast size of the room and the frantic activities of the crew, Angela noticed the sounds of rain pelting the roof and sloshing against the French doors as soon as she walked in.

"That was fast. Did you work everything out with Aseem?" Maria said.

"He has an all-day meeting," Angela sighed. "I didn't even talk to him. He texted to say he wasn't free. I sent him one back telling him it's important we talk."

"It'll be OK." Maria patted Angela's arm. "I promise it will."

"I'm not so sure everything will be OK over there," Connie said, pointing to the stage.

Todd was directing the crew as they loaded the furniture onto the stage, stumbling up the rickety stairs they'd built just days before. Phil and Dave were carrying a long, ornate side table when Phil stepped on a soft spot and cried out, "Yeow!" He and Dave dropped the table onto the stage floor with a crash. Phil walked around the stage for a moment, testing his ankle. "I'm OK," he finally said.

"Wouldn't this terrible weather be the perfect excuse to cancel the play?" Angela said. "It seems like a gift to get an extra day to prepare. Who's going to want to come out in this mess, anyway?"

"Don't be silly, girlie. It's the VIP preview. The peacocks and poseurs won't miss their chance to show off," Bea said, walking over to join them beside the table. "They're paying good money to be fawned over for their painless generosity."

"Bea, I don't think—"

"Actually, Bea's right," Connie said, smiling. "Todd and I called them all first thing this morning. We didn't reach all of them, but most of the ones we did said they're still planning to come."

A lightning bolt cast a flash of light through the French doors, and when the thunder arrived, Angela heard a familiar little yelp.

"Bijou?" she said, pulling up the table skirt of the check-in desk. "Come on out, girl." Angela picked up the little copper-colored dog, who was trailing her leash behind her. Angela coiled up the leash and gently scratched the pooch's delicate head. Bijou rewarded her by licking her face. "Aw, where are your little ones, sweetie?"

"The pups were going even crazier from the thunder than she was," Connie laughed. "Luckily, my assistant is keeping them company. She's already lost power at her house, so she decided to work at my place. And they adore her."

"Lucky we've got that generator you bought if we lose power here—right Angie?" Bea said.

"True. It's rated for a couple days' worth of power," Angela said, turning toward the scaffolding in front of the stage. "But with those stage lights, who knows? They must require a lot of electricity."

Grayson marched right past the check-in table to the middle of the ballroom.

"Todd, can you estimate how much longer

your assembly operation will require?" he shouted. "You assured me we'd have time for a run through and a full dress rehearsal. Unless you finish almost immediately, we'll scarcely have time for a single rehearsal!"

"Grayson, isn't it obvious that we're working on it?" Todd snapped back from the stage.

"It's obvious that you and your crew are in motion, but there's a difference between activity and progress," Grayson snarled. "And isn't it obvious to you that we can't rehearse outside in this raging tempest?"

Maria stepped away from the table and walked calmly toward the director. "Grayson, dear, don't forget the big picture," she said. Then she pantomimed drawing a large rectangle and mouthed "big picture" with a sweet, indulgent smile on her face. Angela stared with a look of dismay on hers.

"You're right, of course," Grayson said, turning to Maria, apparently soothed. He made a heart symbol with his fingers and mouthed "thank you." Angela averted her eyes as if she'd seen a gory accident.

"Try not to barf," Bea said, elbowing Angela gently in the ribs.

"You are *not helping*!"

"Grayson, look, we've only got the couch and a few odds and ends left to move," Todd said, with surprising evenness. "Why don't you rehearse in the back briefly while we place the last pieces? We'll scoot the remaining furnishings up here to the front to make room. You can get a quick run-through in before the sponsors show up to set up in the back."

"That sounds like a workable plan," Maria said with a smile. "Grayson, why don't I go to the breakfast room and tell the cast?"

Grayson nodded and began walking off a rectangular section of the rear of the ballroom. "I guess we could do a quick run-through in here. My God, we are lucky this play is a drawing-room affair. If we'd had to change anything between acts, we'd be doomed."

"Fun fact," Angela said informatively, "a drawing-room play is a Victorian sort of format. The action is all in a single room where people normally gather—like in *The Mousetrap.*"

Bea snorted. "Here's another fun fact: They're still doomed!" Then she slapped her knee and let loose a specimen of cackle that took full advantage of the acoustics of the near-empty ballroom.

Todd came down from the stage to assess how

to move the remaining furniture out of Grayson's way. As he hustled down the stairs, he pulled his pants up roughly over his protruding gut and adjusted the tuck of his shirt.

"Either my eyes are deceiving me or Humpty's put on weight since yesterday." Bea said. "It's like his gut has a life of its own."

"Bea!" Angela said, grateful that Todd was out of earshot.

"What? Are you denying he's got an unusual shape? Or that he's simply… unusual? I won't be surprised at all if there's less to Todd than meets the eye."

Angela's eyes narrowed in confusion. She looked anxiously at Connie.

"You know, Bea, I don't mind your wicked sense of humor," Connie said in her sweet way, "but I think Todd might be a little sensitive about his weight. He's already said he thinks McGregor might put him on a diet—oops, I… I misspoke… forget I said that!"

"Don't worry, Connie," Angela said. "I already told Bea about Todd's new job. Besides, the article will be out in the *Grapevine* tomorrow, won't it?"

"True. And I know I can trust you both to keep the secret until then, can't I?"

Bea and Angela nodded.

"In that case," Connie said, "Todd sent me a proof of the article from the editor. They didn't change my version one bit! Would you like to take a look? I admit I'm kind of proud of it."

Angela nodded enthusiastically. Connie sat back down at the check-in table and brought up a page on her laptop, then turned the screen toward Angela and Bea.

"I'm a little jealous," Angela said brightly. "I've submitted oodles of press releases and offered to write articles and they've never bitten, not once. I like to think I'm a pretty good writer, and we're one of their biggest advertisers. Good for you, Connie. This is a coup!"

Connie beamed. "Honey, I want you to know, I have no idea what—if anything—there is between me and Todd. Like you hinted, Bea, he's *compli-cated.* But at least I'm building a relationship with the local press, right? I mean, that could help my business, couldn't it?"

Angela nodded. She shifted Bijou onto her shoulder and gave Connie's arm a gentle squeeze. Bea responded with a smile, an overly enthusiastic thumbs up, and one of her hammy winks. Though she was grateful that Connie was focused on her computer and not looking in Bea's direction, Angela had to agree with Bea. If Todd's appeal was waning in Connie's eyes, that was probably a good thing.

"About McGregor," Angela said, "So what if Todd's… you know, a… a… a 'person of substance'? Anyone who's met McGregor would know he'd have a hard time claiming that a perfect physique is a job requirement."

Bea let out another needle-like bark of laughter. "I agree that McGregor won't put Todd on a slimming regimen, but I have a hunch it won't be because he's afraid of looking like a big, fat hypocrite. That's not something McGregor worries about, is it?"

Angela looked at Bea with confusion again. "What are you talking about now, Bea?"

Before Bea could answer, Maria and the actors who'd been running lines in the breakfast room arrived at the door. They were full of nervous pre-show energy—vibes that were no doubt amplified by the incomplete sets and the fact that they'd never once rehearsed on the stage.

"Everyone's here except Lorelei," Louisa said loudly to Grayson. "She disappeared more than thirty minutes ago."

"I know where she is," Todd interjected. "Sorry

—I should have mentioned that Martina needed some help with a costume issue—"

"I'll go to the costume room and find her," Louisa said.

"No need!" Todd shouted, holding up his phone. "I mean—I've just texted her."

The wind whipped up again. A large tree branch flew into one of the transom windows, landing with a crack. A sudden downpour slammed the deck. The raindrops were hitting the deepening puddles with such force, they splashed water into the air. Then a huge flash of lightning illuminated the ballroom.

"Oh my!" Angela cried. "I don't think I've ever seen lightning like that!" Bijou whined and Angela stroked her head again to try to calm her. A moment later, a thunderclap boomed.

"There's no need to see it now, is there?" Grayson said. "It's an unnecessary distraction. Angela, can you help me with the drapes?"

"If we can't see the storm, it can't hurt us?!" Bea cracked. "Is that your theory, Grayson?"

Angela put Bijou gently on the floor. Dragging her leash behind her, the dog scurried back to Connie and hid under the table. After Angela quickly explained how to find the pull cords,

Grayson hauled one side of the heavy drapes closed and Angela the other.

"Oh, look," Angela said. She stepped behind the heavy velvet drape and crouched for a closer look at one of the bottom panes, which now had a thin crack in it several inches long.

"I don't want to alarm anyone, but can a few of you try your phones?" Todd said as he walked back into the ballroom with Lorelei. His hair and shoulders looked slightly damp. "Mine's not working. When my text didn't go through I went down to find Lorelei. I tried from the business center, and even stepped outside—no signal."

"I don't have signal, either," Angela said.

"Mine's dead, too, and I think I have a different carrier than you, Todd," Lorelei said.

Todd leaned over to look at her phone screen and nodded. A few of the actors and crew murmured as they pulled out their phones and found them useless as bricks.

"Angela, I don't want to alarm you," Connie said, tapping on her laptop, "but I think the internet's out, too."

"Todd, Roberta—look, the winds have cracked one of the window panes here," Angela said, pulling back the side of the drape. "Are you sure we shouldn't cancel for tonight? We could send the cast and crew home before the storm gets worse."

"Actually, isn't it safer for everyone to stay put here?" Roberta said reasonably. "It's warm and you've still got power."

"Besides, with no phones or internet, how would we alert the VIPs?" Todd added. "If they were to show up and discover they'd made the journey for nothing, wouldn't that be worse?"

Angela looked over at Bea, who shrugged. Another lightning bolt lit the transom windows. A beat later, the lights in the ballroom all went out. There was a collective gasp—then the thunderclap arrived.

Angela peered out behind the drapes. "Connie's place is dark—"

The lights in ballroom came back to life a second later. Angela looked for the emergency light on the deck. It was out. They were no longer getting power from the grid.

"At least the generator's working," she said to the group.

"That settles it, right?" Todd said brightly. "We've got all we need here, and we'll soon have an audience of honored guests who will brave the elements to see our production."

Grayson nodded vigorously and moved to the

center of the ballroom. "As we're wont to say in the theater, the show must go on!"

The actors and crew members clapped.

"Hear hear!" shouted Todd. Even Roberta was smiling.

"I guess it's decided then," Angela said, a little bewildered. She walked across the ballroom to rejoin her mother, Connie, and Bea at the check-in table. "I wish Aseem were here. What if the generator fails?"

"Girlie, you got that generator installed in the first place," Bea said. "Why don't you have a little faith in yourself?"

"What if there's something we should try to bring the internet back up? He'd know what to do."

"It seems pretty clear there's a major cell outage, and that could be affecting internet, too," Connie said. "Todd says it could be cell tower damage. That could cut off service for a twenty-mile radius. He wasn't even able to get a signal outside."

"I know what Aseem would do!" Angela blurted. "There's one thing you always have to try first, at least with internet. I'll go restart the router."

Before anyone could react, Angela dashed out

of the ballroom to the business center to find the router. A few minutes later, she was back—looking more dejected than before. The reliable reboot trick had failed.

"The router had a code I'd never seen before," she sighed.

"Mija, we all wish Aseem were here," Maria said. "But you know you can handle anything that needs to be managed here. It would just be *nice* if Aseem were here."

"Thank you all. The truth is… I know that, I guess. I just wonder if he's trying to call me back," Angela whimpered. "With no internet, even our landlines aren't working. Who knows how long it will be until we get any phone service back?"

"But, honey," Connie said, "you know Aseem surely has internet service down in Silicon Valley. He'll be able to go online and see that we're experiencing an outage. He won't have to wonder or worry for long."

"She's right. Buck up, girlie," Bea said gently. "The worst of the storm will be done by tomorrow—maybe even later tonight. In the morning, you can drive somewhere dry and call handsome. In the meantime, why don't we just enjoy a fun evening of *theee-ah-tuh*?"

"You must be winding me up, right?" Angela

couldn't help but laugh, though her eyes were teary. "I know you're convinced the show will be a complete disaster!"

"I sure do! That's how I know it's going to be fun!"

CHAPTER 23

Bea and Angela could not believe their eyes. Less than an hour later, the set was nearly completed, with enough time left for Grayson and his cast to complete their dress rehearsal.

"No thanks to certain naysayers," Angela said, glaring facetiously in Bea's direction.

"If only I could take credit for their entertaining ineptitude," Bea chuckled. "I'd bottle it up and do three accident-prone shows a week here at the inn."

Just one last piece of furniture needed to find its way from the ballroom floor to the stage: a smelly old couch, its upholstery covered in tea stains and faded roses. It would be the centerpiece of the Helliwell Hall living room. It perfectly telegraphed the shabby-antique aesthetic of certain countrified, horsey New Englanders of the 1960s. From the moment they'd seen it, Todd, Grayson, and Roberta had all agreed it was ideal—and they'd agreed on virtually nothing else.

Most important of all, it had been obtained for free!

Almost immediately, its drawbacks became invisible. It was simply, indubitably essential to the production.

Unfortunately, like other relics of its vintage, the sofa weighed three times what anyone would have expected—and it was on the fragile side to boot. In the last few days before the VIP preview, Todd began to sour on it. When Grayson and Roberta weren't around, he began referring to it as "that lead bench on toothpicks." So virtually no one in the ballroom was surprised when the effort to hoist it up the left side stairs resulted in one crew member's foot falling through a step, two crew members face down on the stage, and the infernal object itself upside down on the ballroom floor—minus one leg.

Those stairs weren't designed for heavy lifting. As it was, they were all praying the steps were strong enough to briefly hold a cast member or two.

Of course, while no one was surprised by what happened, one person was unabashedly, inappropriately amused.

"Fellas, did someone tell you to break a leg?" Bea shouted at the crew. "Get it, guys? Break a leg? It's theater humor! You know— because you broke the sofa leg! Get it?"

Bea bent over and shook as she guffawed. No matter what anyone else thought of her quips, Bea always found them more than worthy of a hearty laugh and a slap of her knee.

Angela looked at the crew and cringed, but they hadn't even heard Bea over the wind and the thunder and all their own colorful cursing.

One man was desperately, haphazardly hammering the leg back onto the sofa. The others, huddled with Todd, were hatching a new, even crazier plan to get it onto the stage.

This time, they decided, they wouldn't bother with the stairs. Instead, they'd shove that two-ton couch directly on stage from the ballroom floor.

Dave stood near the edge of the stage, trying to grab the back of the sofa without falling onto the ballroom floor. His two teammates had tilted the sofa upright against the stage, and now were pushing from the bottom as hard as they could. Todd was shouting encouragement from the side.

Angela put her hand over her eyes and squinted through her fingers. "I can't watch. It looks dangerous!"

"I can't watch, either. At least not without laughing!" Bea's shoulders shook as she tried—and failed—to suppress a snicker. The snicker turned into guffaws. "Sorry, Angie. I have to watch. I can't wait to see where this latest genius effort leads. They've already wrecked half their set."

Angela furrowed her brow. "It's not funny. What if someone gets hurt? And they haven't 'wrecked half their set,' Bea."

"You think I should try to be nicer, but I think you of all people should get a laugh out of this circus, Angie. You're the queen of competence. And they're—"

"Unlucky. They had barely two weeks to shift gears and prepare to do their play here, with hardly any volunteers. Even the weather has turned against them."

Bea had stopped listening. She was transfixed by the crew on the floor, who huffed and puffed and hefted the far end of that sofa upwards—and, amazingly, Dave somehow managed to grab hold of one of its legs!

"Look—they're doing it!" Angela cried.

As Dave leaned backwards, now gripping two

legs of the sofa, the happy outcome of it landing safely in its proper place finally seemed possible.

The men on the floor grunted and switched their grips, pushing their half of the sofa up onto their shoulders, finding more leverage.

And then it happened: As if lifted by Hercules himself, the sofa sailed onto the stage!

And as it did, Dave hurtled backwards, unable to stop before bashing into the flimsy set wall the crew had finished installing only hours before.

Somehow, the flat was barely damaged when it fell, and Dave was unhurt. But no one, not even the people in the very back of the ballroom, missed the sounds of the accident. First, a woman's voice vainly blurting, "Careful!" Then the unmistakable crash of shattering glass.

"Oh, no! That was Clara Bowditch's portrait," Angela said. "I think Grayson was hoping to invoke her spiritual support."

Bea let loose an ear-splitting cackle. "And was that Clara herself yelling?"

"The playwright's picture smashed right before the first performance—that must be bad luck, right?" Angela said, hurrying on stage to make sure no one was injured. Todd helped Dave up and they lifted the fallen flat to find the inadvertent shouter behind it.

"All good," Martina said, picking herself up. She'd been attempting to scurry out of sight but was revealed by the large rectangular "picture window" cut into the flat.

"Martina, were you hiding?" Angela gently teased.

"Yes, shouldn't you be in the costume room?" Todd snarled.

Martina shot an irritated look in his direction. "As you know, Todd, I might need to slip back here for that, you know, that touch-up for Edie's makeup we discussed during Act Two. The blood —remember?"

"You could have picked a better time," Todd said, not backing down. If anything, his tone grew steelier.

"Why? Are you saying you and Dave were planning to knock the wall down?"

"Maybe I should just get a broom?" Angela interjected, trying to be helpful, looking down at the glass all over the stage. She picked the photo up by its frame. "What do you think? Can it be rehung?"

"Of course. No one will be able to tell there's no glass," Todd said. He rehung the picture onto the nail on the flat. "And Dave, now that you and the wall are upright again, can you clean up the glass? Angela, we've got it covered."

Angela went back down to the ballroom floor the way she came and rejoined Bea.

"Maybe that was just opening night jitters, but there seemed to be some friction between Martina and Todd."

"That's who was behind the wall? The hair and makeup person?"

"Yep. She said she had to make sure she'd fit back there for some makeup adjustment needed in the second act."

"Huh," Bea said. "I guess I don't remember *The Ratcatcher* very well at all."

It was hard to hear above the wind, the rain, and the work of the rehearsing actors and the crew, but eventually, an insistent banging on one of the French doors caught Angela's attention. She ran to it and pulled back the drape to find a drenched caterer huddling under a feeble umbrella that was not even close to a match for the storm.

"Hi, I'm from Chardonnay Café. We thought we were supposed to use the back door of the kitchen, but it was locked—"

"Oh no! I'll open it for you," Angela said.

"That would be great. There's someone from a jeweler here, also. He said he's got a table for intermission, too."

"I'll meet you there—and I'll get some towels."

A few minutes later, most of the actors had headed off to the costume room to get ready for the dress rehearsal. The set was ready—save for the staircase, which Dave was repairing with more urgency than skill. The vendors had toweled off and were setting up their tables in the back of the ballroom.

"O ye of little faith," Angela smiled at Bea. "We're going to have a play tonight after all."

"O counter of chickens before they're hatched," Bea chuckled, "this remains to be seen. However, I do acknowledge that the timely arrival of the sponsored snacks is another minor miracle."

THE DRESS REHEARSAL BEHIND THEM, Roberta asked the cast and crew to gather on stage so that she could say a few words. The cast was still mostly in costume, nearly ready for their preview performance in less than two hours. Roberta herself looked every bit old-money equestrian in riding breeches, boots, and a white shirt with a long tie collar wrapped around her neck. She was carrying a tweed riding jacket over her arm.

Bea and Angela were standing near the French doors, watching from a distance. In between checking the windows every time the wind whipped up, Angela held her phone as close as she could to the doors, hoping against hope that a cell signal would return.

"Who's playing Edie tonight?" Bea said. "You can barely tell Roberta and Louisa apart."

"Has to be Louisa. Isn't that what Tibby paid for?" Angela said. "But you can see that several of the cast are dressed as part of the hunting group. Oh yes, see? There's Louisa, looking every bit the part of Edie."

"But Roberta does, too—" Bea said.

"Roberta's carrying a jacket—she'll probably put that on and blend in as part of the hunting party."

On stage, six of the actors jammed onto the ratty sofa.

"You might want to be careful with the sofa," Phil ventured. "We just repaired that right front leg with basic first aid—"

"Now you tell me! There's a nail sticking out," Melissa shouted, reaching down and dabbing at a blot of blood on her ankle that was seeping through her nude-colored tights. A run had formed in the hose just above the cut. "They're getting ruined. Maybe I should run and take these tights off?" she added nervously.

"It's OK," Lorelei said. "There are spares in the costume room."

"Melissa, unless you're badly hurt, may I proceed?" Roberta said. Melissa nodded but kept fussing with her leg.

"I won't keep you long. I would simply like to offer a few overdue words of acknowledgment," Roberta began. Her voice trembled with surprising emotion.

"First, to Todd. I don't need to tell you I had my doubts about whether this was worth doing. As the owner—"

"Owner? Did she just say 'owner'?" Angela hissed in Bea's ear.

"Pardon me," Roberta said. "I mean, the executive director of our community theater—"

"Did you catch that? Does that mean her non-profit's fake?" Bea said.

With a nod and a gentle "shush," Angela suggested Bea keep those sorts of comments on the quiet side. "Let's discuss later."

"I thought it would only make things worse for our donors if we got their hopes up and failed. Todd, you persevered and proved me wrong," Roberta continued, fumbling a bit. "I've never been an emotional sort, but I'm afraid the destruction of the playhouse has temporarily transformed me into one. Especially when I learned that the state fire investigators suspect arson—" Roberta's voice cracked. It sounded like she might cry.

"Interesting," Bea whispered hoarsely. "Does that mean she didn't burn it down herself? Or is she just trying to throw everyone off the trail?"

Angela shrugged.

"—that's why I must also thank Grayson for joining me in pushing forward. I know you, too, were dubious, and without your skillful direction, our ragtag group of troupers would not be ready to present what I believe is a truly professional production of *The Ratcatcher*—"

Bea let out a snort so loud, the entire company on stage, including Roberta, turned and stared toward the source of the noise. Bea followed up the sound with various coughing and honking noises. "Sorry! Allergies!"

Connie looked over from the other side of the room at the pained faces on stage and then at Bea, her mannerly instincts kicking in. "Oh, Bea, I think you need some water!" Then she rushed over with a bottle and handed it to Bea.

"Nice save!" Angela whispered to Connie.

"Last, but most definitely not least, I must thank Louisa, my talented co-Edie. I want to announce to everyone here that I'm delighted you'll be taking the role for the majority of our short run, Louisa. As some of you know, I had originally intended to play the role myself. I ask forgiveness for a moment of bumptiousness when I took over the company—"

"What the hell is *bumptious* again, Angie?" Bea snickered. "It's been a few decades since I took the SATs."

"It means full of oneself."

"Of course you knew it," Bea snickered. "You really are a smartypants."

"I'll take that as a compliment," Angela smiled. "By the way, I thought you never actually took the SATs. Had they even been invented when you were a teenager?"

"Good one, girlie."

"—I had high hopes—and for once in my life, I had the money to accomplish something of real significance," Roberta said. "That turned into a certain… overeagerness to involve myself a little too fully in the first production of the Pinot Play-house. Louisa, you are a genuine professional, and I thank you for bringing your skills and talents to our production—and for your generosity in al-lowing me, your humble understudy, to take on two of our lower profile matinees. I shall learn from you and relish my chances to follow in your footsteps."

A croaky bark of laughter escaped Bea's lips. She mostly camouflaged it with another hasty cough. "Is she sincere now or sarcastic?" she whispered to Angela.

"Honestly… I'm not sure."

"Lastly, I must say the hardest bit of all." Roberta paused dramatically and looked at the ceiling, apparently hoping gravity would guide tears back into their ducts. "With the insurance money in jeopardy, and, and, whatever other consequences may come my way as a result of the investigation, I'm afraid this will, in all likelihood, be the last run of Pinot Playhouse."

The actors and crew on stage gasped.

"Bea, did you see that?" Angela whispered to Bea, who nodded. They'd both spotted Todd and Lorelei smirking at each other as the rest of the company looked shocked and saddened.

Roberta tried to rally. "But please, let us not be sad! Let's celebrate our opportunity to shine and have a marvelous preview show tonight! Break a leg, all!"

Roberta concluded with a sniff and quickly excused herself. The group applauded, full of good cheer, then dispersed to complete their last-minute preparations.

Angela looked at Bea with a crooked grin. "Well, that was… interesting. On the plus side, I told you Todd and company would pull it off. I was right for once—go on, admit it."

"We shall see, Angie. We shall see. In the meantime, should we ready ourselves for our big night of *theee-ah-tuh*? Guess what? I've got a brand new outfit for the occasion!"

"Oh, boy."

CHAPTER 24

Pat closed the lid of her laptop and smiled. She could always count on Bea to put her on the trail of something fascinating. This time, the secrets Bea's project led her to were so tantalizing, so explosive, she didn't want to wait a minute before passing them on to Bea.

She picked up her cell and dialed the number for *Betty Snickerdoodle's Christmas Inn & Ranch*. After a couple of rings, she heard an unfamiliar "boop" tone, then more rings. A woman's voice answered.

"Um, Snickerdoodles," she said, sounding flustered. "Sorry, 'Snickerdoodle Christmas Ranch.'"

"Is this *Betty Snickerdoodle's Christmas Inn—*"

"Yes, sorry. You're my first call."

"That's OK. I'm looking for Bea Sickles. Could you try her suite?"

"Yeah, so that's the problem. I guess they've got an outage? Big storm in Napa Valley? Their calls are getting transferred here. I'm in a call center in Bakersfield."

"Hmm. OK… well, thank you."

"Would you like to leave a message?"

Pat told the operator to pass along to Bea that she'd called, feeling confident that message would never be delivered. She pulled up her phone contacts again and found Angela's cell number.

The first time she tried, the phone rang a few times and then she heard a fast busy tone before the call disconnected itself. Then she tried again and heard a voicemail greeting that said no messages could be accepted at this time.

Huh. Could the storm have knocked out a cell tower?

Pat stood up and looked out her apartment window. The storm was getting worse in San Francisco, too.

It must be easing up in the wine country, though. Right?

Knowing full well it might be crazy, Pat considered the possibility of driving the forty miles or so to the inn in her trusty, rusty jalopy.

On the plus side, there probably won't be any traffic.

She opened her laptop again and pulled up a weather website. The storm would pummel Napa Valley for a good few more hours, at least. Flash flood warnings were in force in parts of the wine country.

It's not getting worse, though.

Then it occurred to her that if there was a cell tower down near the inn, the outage should be reported online. She checked all the sources she knew for that kind of information and found nothing.

That's strange. To say the least.

She tapped the address of the inn into a search engine and checked the map. The roads were all still open. Just as she'd guessed, traffic was practically nonexistent. A few yellow and orange accident markers here and there... but surely those could be easily avoided.

That settles it, I'm off to Napa. Lucky for me, I'm an excellent driver. It's just rain. California is full of careless people who have trouble with a little precipitation, but I'm not one of them.

Drive slowly, watch out for the big puddles... that's all I have to do.

Pat pulled a thick sweatshirt over her flannel

shirt and khakis, laced up her heavy boots, and slid her arms into an old-school yellow rain slicker. Then she grabbed her keys and headed out the door.

~

THE VIP PREVIEW of *The Ratcatcher* was back underway after its impromptu intermission when the ballroom door next to the check-in table slowly opened a crack. A slender young woman dressed in a hoodie, jeans, and boots, all of them black, quietly slipped through into the ballroom. She was carrying a small, dark leather backpack.

"Lexie!" Maria whispered urgently to the woman. "Nice to see you. The play's just started. I don't see you on the list, though."

Lexie bent down and spoke softly to avoid disturbing the twenty or so members of the audience. Droplets of rain fell from her head and shoulders onto the stack of papers in front of Maria and Connie. Connie hastily moved them to her side of the table and Maria dabbed at the table with a tissue.

"Sorry about the raindrops. I'm not on the list. Angela asked me to send a colleague to check out the play—it's a long story—but anyway, the other journalist backed out because of the weather. I figured, I'm not made of sugar, I won't melt in a little rain. And I've got a Tahoe-ready SUV. So here I am in her place."

Another lightning bolt lit up the transom windows, causing several in the audience to turn reflexively toward the French doors.

"A little rain?" Maria said, laughing a little. "Oh, Lexie, nothing scares you."

Lexie grinned. She pulled her cell phone out of her pocket. "Don't worry, I'll put it on silent."

"That's probably not necessary," Maria whispered. "No service. A cell tower must be out."

Lexie raised her eyebrows briefly and stuck the phone back in her pocket.

"The seats aren't assigned, and you can see there are quite a few open," Connie leaned over and whispered. "Choose whichever one suits you—"

"I will. Thanks." Lexie scanned the room. Even in the dark, she spotted socialites with coiffed hair and glinting diamond earrings. She cursed under her breath, realizing she'd forgotten what Angela said about "blending."

"Can the two of you keep my presence here under wraps, at least for now? I don't want to distract the big cheeses or the performers. Pretend I'm not here. I'll find Angela at the inter-mission."

Lexie padded to the last seat of the last row, closest to the hallway doors. She scooted down to a low slouch and pulled the ties of her hood tight, so that her face could barely be seen.

The play was definitely not Lexie's normal cup of tea. She liked her crime stories to have a tougher edge. The various foibles of the cast amused her, though. Bea's inappropriate outbursts did, too—doubly so.

She thought she recognized the two women in front of Bea and Angela as Tibby Velton and Victoria McGiven. From the back row, she had trouble figuring out what Bea meant when she shouted out "bum leg," from the back row, but seeing the blue bloods craning their necks to see who the vulgarian was made her laugh hysterically inside.

Lexie was carefully unzipping her backpack and taking out a small notebook to jot a few observations when she heard the groaning metal and the first gasps from the front rows of the audience. Then she looked up and saw what they were so afraid of: the stage light plowing straight toward the front row. She watched with a mix of horror and fascination as the huge cylinder swung and dropped.

As the lights came up and Todd announced the unplanned intermission, she stood up and quietly moved next to the closest ballroom door to watch. Then, as the audience turned around and headed for refreshments, Lexie slipped out into the hallway, still unnoticed by any of the guests.

It had been a long drive from Sacramento, but she'd already been a few minutes late for curtain time, so she hadn't stopped for the bathroom. Now she really needed to. She found the nearest one and made quick use of it. It was empty at the moment, but surely guests would be flocking to it within a few minutes.

Tibby probably wet herself when that light bore down on her face! Hmm... that gives me an idea.

Just a few steps from the bathrooms, there was a little alcove that led to one of the exit doors to the parking lot.

Not a bad spot for surveillance. Or to play amateur paparazza.

Lexie stepped into the corner to watch for Tibby and Victoria. She pulled out her phone and got ready to snap a picture—or fake some deep, innocent thoughts in the event anyone noticed her there.

～

ASEEM TURNED his wipers up to their highest speed and their thunk-thunk-thunk threatened to drown out one of his favorite Silicon-Valley themed podcasts. Rex Allen, one of the Valley's most extroverted billionaire venture capitalists, was pompously opining on cryptocurrency with the complete confidence of an oracle.

Aseem chuckled to himself. Rex Allen was the opposite of Aseem's boss, the technology legend Gary Wheaton. What Rex had in bluster Gary matched with nerdy, self-deprecating charm. Even their opinions about bitcoin were polar opposites.

Aseem didn't care much what Gary thought about crypto one way or the other, but he knew he'd be forever grateful to have lucked into such a brilliant and kind boss.

"I know you wanted me here tomorrow. It's just, I'm worried about Angela—"

"Say no more," Gary had replied. "Go, but you be careful, OK? You'd be surprised how dangerous these rains can be."

"I will."

Another drenching downpour bucketed down. Even with the wipers working their hardest, it was hard to see what was ahead of him on the freeway. Aseem shut off the podcast.

Sorry, Rex. Hard to believe, but this atmospheric river's outshouting you.

Aseem had been driving for well over an hour and was nearing the southern edge of San Francisco. The traffic had been light, but it was early evening and already almost dark. Visibility was compromised by the storm. Aseem almost welcomed the illumination the occasional lightning provided.

He could see a car far ahead of him suddenly start moving horizontally across the freeway, its front and back end waving back and forth. The driver was undoubtedly trying to correct his steering and only making things worse. Aseem gripped the wheel even harder. He breathed a brief sigh of relief when the out-of-control car somehow found its way to the shoulder and stopped, miraculously without colliding with anything or anyone.

Hydroplaning—what a nightmare! Another reason to go slowly.

But an even bigger worry than hydroplaning was the hidden puddles—especially because they were really more like small lakes. They had a frightening way of popping up out of nowhere in parts of the freeway where the drainage wasn't up to its task.

Whenever there was a big rainstorm in Northern California, the news reports would include one or more poor souls whose cars wound up stranded—or floating—in one of these invisible bodies of water. It was easy to see how it could happen, how an unsuspecting driver could cruise right into a terrible situation that could ruin their car—or much, much worse. In fact, Aseem had already passed two cars that had done just that and were now stalled out, having barely made it to the waterlogged shoulder of the road. At least the cops had shown up to help them. Their blue and red lights provided a clear warning to people behind them that hazards lay up ahead.

Stick to the center lanes. Stay well under the speed limit. Keep it simple.

Oh, and am I crazy for making this trip?

It's a little late for that.

The freeway ended and Aseem steered cautiously onto the surface roads that led from South San Francisco to the Golden Gate Bridge. It was the part of the journey he normally liked the least —six miles of city streets with stoplights, mall traffic, and light rail trains dragging the average speed down to thirty miles per hour, sometimes even less. Tonight, for once, he welcomed this section of boring, well-lit driving.

Yet even on city streets there were treacherous spots. At one point, two of three lanes of the main cross-town avenue were covered in water! Aseem was grateful that he'd stuck to the middle lane and had been able to move quickly away from the standing water.

As he reached the northern edge of San Francisco, he breathed easier. Winding through the Presidio, he was reminded once more of the awesome beauty of the California coast and the bridge that stretched nearly two miles from San Francisco to Marin County. The red lights atop its brick-colored towers twinkled against the deep indigo sky.

There was almost no traffic on the bridge, and there were no floods. The rainwater poured easily off the sides and into the Golden Gate Strait. He relaxed, noticing his hands had gone stiff from gripping the wheel. One at a time, he released and shook them to restore their circulation. But then the full force of a gale shook the bridge, and Aseem found himself pushed from the middle lane to the right.

Thank God I'm practically alone on this bridge!

He gripped the wheel again, feeling anxious—and glad his drive was more than half over.

The night grew darker and the traffic lighter as he put Sausalito and San Rafael behind him. Approaching the outskirts of the wine country, he drove past farms: Dairy farms. Chicken farms. Strawberry farms. The scenery grew more rustic and charming, but also quieter—almost deserted.

The thought of getting stuck felt more ominous.

Aseem tapped on his phone in its holder. Still plenty of signal. He decided to try Angela again, and then the inn's main number.

I guess if a cell tower's down, it must be on the other side of the inn.

He was within ten miles of the inn when he turned onto the unlit, two-lane road. It was a dividing line that meant he was now squarely in the wine country. The home stretch!

But for the rest of the way, there'd be almost no lights. Long gaps between properties. No shoulders to pull onto—just roadside ditches. And plenty of dips where standing water could be lurking.

You know this route like the back of your hand. Just keep the high beams on and stay calm and alert—

Wait—what's that?!

Up ahead, not more than thirty yards away, Aseem saw a stranded car, its tail end twisted partway into the middle of the road. It was a small car, an older model, and water had reached past its bumper. Aseem could make out the sodden miserable silhouette of the car's poor driver, who was trying to push the wreck up onto the side of the road, more securely out of the way.

Aseem slowed down and turned on his flashers. His plan was to creep around the drowned vehicle as far from it as possible, hoping not to create waves in the water and harm the car or the driver, then pull over on the drier side of the road and try to help.

The miserable driver suddenly realized headlights were coming up from behind. She turned around with a terrified look on her face.

Oh no! I think that's Pat!

CHAPTER 25

"Everyone! Listen up!" Todd shouted down at the audience, desperate to get the frantic VIPs to focus on him. Most of them had gathered in the front of the room, looking for comfort in numbers and trying to figure out what had happened to poor Edie on stage. "As I said, I'm in charge here." Bea and Angela had quietly stayed put in the second row, keeping out of the fray.

Behind Todd, the actors playing Fred and Ellen were kneeling next to their fallen fellow performer. The other actors were standing over Edie with their backs toward the ballroom, mostly blocking the audience's view. Fred periodically felt Edie's wrist for a pulse, seemingly unwilling to believe the evidence. Ellen had removed Edie's hat and cast it aside, and was making an obviously inexperienced—and futile?—attempt at resuscitation.

Fred, Ellen, and everyone else on stage appeared distraught and hopeless. No one in the audience had observed any movement by Edie in more than a minute.

Bijou was clearly distressed, too. She trotted back and forth from the set flat that represented the wall in the back of the room—the lightweight structure that Dave had knocked over—and Edie's body. Each time she returned to Edie, she sniffed her repeatedly, her tail wagging anxiously.

Unaccustomed to being treated like anything less than gentry, the attendees didn't take kindly to Todd's attempt to shut them up.

"What do you mean, 'you're in charge?'" an irate male donor shouted at the stage.

"Yeah, what do you mean?!" and "says who?" cried several others.

"Don't we need real help—like, from the *police?* And doesn't the actress—the program says that's Louisa McClure, right?—doesn't she need an *ambulance?!* Oh my goodness, that's Marian Velton's sister, isn't it?"

People pulled out their cell phones and started trying to dial nine-one-one, then crying out in renewed frustration that there was still no signal.

"Calm down, please, everyone," Todd said, flailing as he tried to soften his tone. "I promise you, I have this under control. And… and, I have… well, I have *good* news. Because even though the cell tower remains down, you don't need to worry about summoning police here. That's not necessary!"

Angry murmurs started softly, then increased.

"What do you mean?" a woman near the stage called out, above the rumble.

"I mean that the police are already here—because *I am the police!*" Todd bellowed, smiling broadly. "The announcement won't be published until tomorrow, but I've been an official member of Sergeant McGregor's unit for over a week now. So don't you see? Everything's in hand."

The murmuring started again, prompting Connie, now standing by her check-in desk, to loyally pipe up.

"It's true!" she cried. "I have the article right here on my computer, if anyone wants to see it."

Though the people in the audience were too far away to read it, Connie held the laptop up and waved it slowly from left to right, hoping they'd at least see the *Grapevine* logo at the top and the large photo of Todd's face on the right.

"Come on over and take a closer look if you want."

"Wait—I'm not finished!" Todd shouted sharply.

"I'm sorry!" Connie said. "After Todd'—I mean, Officer Jameson—after he's done, you can come over to see the article."

Grayson had been sitting next to Maria at the check-in desk. Maria had her arm on his shoulder, trying to calm him down. Earlier, he'd started to charge the stage and challenge Todd's authority. Maria had coaxed him to sit with her, but now he jumped up and angrily grabbed Connie's laptop to take a closer look for himself at the article proclaiming Todd was "the police."

"OK, but why aren't you helping Louisa?" the woman near the stage cried, turning to the rest of the audience for help. "Is there a doctor here? Is there anyone here who can help her?"

Todd turned around and bent down near Edie's body.

"I'm afraid—" he said slowly as he stood up, "I'm afraid no one can help her. I'm afraid she's... dead."

"And I'm afraid she's not Louisa," someone

whispered from behind Angela and Bea, who turned around in alarm. Lexie had slipped into the next row unnoticed, thanks to the chaos in the ballroom.

"What?" croaked Bea.

"Lexie, what are you doing here?" Angela cried.

"Long story short, that reporter I wanted to send here for you chickened out because of the storm."

"I thought you journos were supposed to be brave and stuff," Bea said.

"Tell me about it. So—care to step away a bit so I can tell you what I saw?"

"You know what?" Bea whispered hoarsely. "I have a hunch Todd's gonna lock this room down any minute. If we could find an opportunity to slip into the kitchen—"

The storm had been slowing down, but the three of them got a little lucky. A last-gasp bolt of lightning, followed by a big clap of thunder, sent poor, traumatized Bijou into a tizzy of hysterical barking.

"Connie! Come get your blasted dog!" Todd bellowed.

The dog barked and cried even louder. The audience seemed full of animal lovers who grew even angrier at Todd.

"Oh, poor Bijou!" Angela said.

"I know, but we gotta move!" Bea said.

With the audience, the actors, and Todd all completely focused on the on-stage chaos, Bea and Angela and Lexie took their shot and headed for the kitchen.

Angela camouflaged herself against the drapes, pretending to check the windows. When she reached the end of the French doors, she scooted in a flash through the swinging door to the kitchen.

Lexie went in the other direction. She tied her hood tight around her face and managed to slip out of the hallway door side like a cat burglar. Then she ran down the hall to enter the kitchen from the other side.

And just in case they'd need it, Bea provided a temporary distraction. She walked straight down the middle and stopped at the unattended champagne table to grab a drink, knowing that no one would likely question the oldest, tiniest person in the room, who happened to also own the place.

Once she reached the table, Bea took a quick look behind her to confirm that no one was paying her the slightest attention. They were all watching poor Connie, who was running around on stage trying to capture her petrified Bijou, who helped the cause by continuing to bark. Bea scurried, hunched down, to meet Angela and Lexie behind the catering door to the kitchen.

Lexie quickly explained her comment about Louisa. While Lexie talked, they kept the door cracked open and tried not to lose track of what Todd was saying.

"After the unplanned intermission, I slipped out so that I wouldn't be seen. I forgot what you told me about wearing haughty couture to blend in—"

"Ha!" Bea cackled. "Haughty couture, that's a good one." She held her fist up for a bump with Lexie's.

Angela smiled but also put her finger to her lips. No one could have noticed them now, though. Everyone in the ballroom was now clustered near the stage, far away from the kitchen, and they were fully engrossed with Todd's announcements.

"—now I'm going to ask all of you to stay put here while I start investigating. In all likelihood, this was an unfortunate heart attack or the result of an undiagnosed condition. We must rule out the unlikely case of foul play, though, which means I must secure the scene—" Todd continued, his voice booming.

"See? What did I tell you—lockdown!" Bea said. "He hasn't said it's not Louisa yet, has he? Lexie, you're sure it's not her?"

"I'm sure. Let me finish telling you what I saw," Lexie replied softly. With speed and efficiency, Lexie explained that she'd been hiding by the bathroom, hoping to catch a candid photo of Tibby on her way back to the ballroom. Instead, she wound up catching Louisa, Tibby, and a reluctant Victoria making a hasty exit.

"At first, I hid closer to the bathroom. Then I realized someone was around the corner in the business center, so I moved past that hallway to the broom closet and snuck inside. Glad it wasn't locked, Angela," Lexie said with a smirk. "Tight security around here."

"Um, if someone wants to grab a mop and clean up, I'm not going to discourage them."

"Anyway, this tall, imposing, middle-aged woman comes charging into the hall from the business center. Then I hear what sounds like Tibby calling out, 'Aunt Louisa! Where are you going? Why aren't you in costume? Won't you be on stage soon?'

"Louisa shushes her. She hisses, 'I can't be seen here! I've got to go!' Then she races past my hidey-hole to the exit."

Bea grinned and her eyes grew wide. "Someone didn't want Louisa playing Edie tonight," Bea said.

"Or maybe someone wanted *Roberta* playing Edie," Angela said. Her eyes were wide, too, but with fear rather than intrigue.

"I think you're both right," Lexie said. "Especially because Louisa was clutching a large, folded-up manila envelope. If I had to guess, it had two ten-large stacks—"

"That means twenty thou, Angie."

"I know what ten large means," Angela said irritably—though not convincingly.

"Oh, we know you do," Lexie said with an exaggerated wink that reminded Angela of someone else's mannerisms.

"Is it possible you're Bea's long-lost granddaughter?" Angela said.

"Girlie, you might want to learn where babies and grandbabies come from before you get married," Bea chuckled.

"Very funny, Bea. We're trying to be quiet, remember?" Angela hissed. "Just 'cause you never raised a child doesn't mean you never had one."

"I'm flattered by the idea of Lexie having inherited my best qualities," Bea said, "but I've never put a baby up for adoption."

"And I'm definitely not adopted," Lexie said, "but it's a fun idea. I would have loved having a granny who spoiled me with poker tips and cigarettes. Every youngster needs a role model."

"Oh, brother!" Angela said. "Wait—has Todd stopped talking?"

"He's talking softer," Lexie said. "Since everyone calmed down, he's stopped yelling."

The three of them had been bunched together near the edge of the swinging door that led from the kitchen to and from the ballroom, trying to stay hidden as they watched. They could hardly see what was going on through the tiny opening of the door, though.

"I've got an idea," Angela said, carrying a chair over to the door and hopping up on it. Now she had a clear view out the door's window without putting her face square in the frame. "Now let's try for a better view."

Angela took her phone out of her pocket and held the camera up toward the stage, keeping the phone near the bottom of the window. Then she used the camera to zoom in on the stage.

"So much better! Todd's leaning over Edie again. Fred and Ellen are still sitting by her body, but they've given up trying to revive her. They look sad and dazed. Todd's patting them on their backs. Oh, sure. He's trying to act all warm! The other actors have their arms around each other, consoling themselves.

"Oh, look—Connie's in the back of the stage, holding Bijou. I think she's crying! She's white as a sheet," Angela gasped. She had to look away for a minute. "She must have realized that's Roberta on the floor."

"I can kind of hear Todd again," Lexie said, leaning on the door. "He's speaking louder. The audience must be getting restless again—"

"Look—there are glasses over there. Why don't the two of you try to get a better listen?"

"Does that really work?" Lexie said, grabbing two tumblers. She and Bea held them against the door. "Huh. I guess it does help some."

Angela put her phone to the window once more. "Todd's back in the middle of the stage. Lorelei's next to him. She looks upset. He's putting his arm around her shoulder."

"He says he's 'deputizing' her," Bea said. "Lorelei, I mean. He called her 'Lori' again!"

"He's got another gun strapped to his leg—a little one," Angela said. "My goodness, you're right, Bea—his leg is so skinny! He's handing the small gun to Lorelei. She's holding it up but she looks scared. Her hand is shaking so hard, Todd has to keep lifting her hand. I think she's crying."

"Todd's saying again that there's probably no reason to suspect foul play, but in cases like this, he still needs to walk the perimeter and look for evidence, especially since he knows a couple of people who were here for the play who now are missing—" Lexie said.

"—and that if anyone else disappears while he's gone, that will cast suspicion on them—" Bea said.

Then together, Bea and Lexie parroted, "Remember—I have the guest list. So no sneaking out!"

"Is Todd a cop—for real—or is he… is he up to something?" Angela cried.

"I vote B. Remember what we saw before he closed his jacket?" Bea said.

"Oh, right—what was that? It looked like a piece of memory foam."

"I think ol' Humpty's wearing a Dumpty disguise."

Lexie scoffed. "Well, that points to option B. Plus, you know, the *Grapevine* may not be in line for any journalism prizes, but they have standards. Like, you know, editing. I don't buy for one minute that they let Connie write some puff piece about a new police officer and agreed to publish it word-for-word."

"I never thought I'd say this," Bea chuckled, "But we really need McGregor."

"Todd's probably not gathering evidence right now. He's probably getting rid of evidence! If only that stupid cell tower wasn't down," Angela moaned.

"Yeah, about that," Lexie said. "I'm not convinced there's a real outage. At least… I was on the phone right up until I turned into the inn parking lot. It would be quite a coincidence if the range of the tower ended just beyond the inn."

"So… some kind of signal jammer?" Angela said.

"That's exactly what I'm thinking. I can test it—slip out to the parking lot and call McGregor from my car—"

"That's dangerous. If Todd is a murderer and he catches you," Bea said, "we already know he's got a gun."

"Besides, Lexie, what if McGregor asks you for details you don't have? He might not act fast enough. We've got to get him here *now!*" Angela said. "I've got a better idea. I'll do it. I know just the place, and I think I can sneak out to it unseen."

"You just want to call Aseem, don't you?"

"Maybe—what if he's been trying to reach me? But it makes more sense for me to do this. So, quickly, let me tell you my idea."

CHAPTER 26

Bea, Angela, and Lexie stood by the service entrance of the kitchen, which looked out in the direction of Connie's property, now enveloped in complete darkness. The electricity was out everywhere except the inn. Angela's generator was powering the only lights for as far as the three of them could see. The downpours of earlier in the day had eased, giving way to lighter, steadier rain.

A paved path that vendors used to wheel in deliveries extended from the door to the right, then wended around to the main entrance of the inn. Just beyond that concrete path was grass, and then a steep downhill drop to the trail that headed upward to Connie's. On that trail was the key to Angela's plan—the old barn.

"It'll work, I'm sure of it," Angela said. "Once I get to the drop I'll just slide down—no problema. Then it's a quick sprint to the barn. If there's no signal in the barn, I'll slip behind it and keep walking up the road until I get one. Even if Todd's nosing around here—and why would he? There's nothing to see here—he's unlikely to spot me because of the drop, especially because it's dark and still raining."

"How do you know there's nothing he wants to see here? We don't know if he thinks there's evidence here," Lexie said.

"Or if he left some here," Bea added.

"Well, I'm going to be moving very fast, and like I said, it's dark. But now that you say that, I think you two should find a place to hide yourselves after I go, OK? There are lots of places to hide in here. Be safe."

"You just be quick," Bea said. "If he shows up, we'll distract him. You just hurry, OK?"

The three of them peered out of the door, triple-checking each direction that no one was around. Then, before she could change her mind, Angela bolted toward the grass and the ledge that dropped onto the trail. The grass was sodden and her feet were sinking. She slid onto her backside without even trying and slipped down the hill out of view.

"I hope she's OK!" Bea said. "It looked like she twisted her ankle!"

After a tense pause, Bea sighed with relief. She spotted the top of Angela's head—and, a second later, the rest of her. She and Lexie could just make out Angela urgently scanning the trail and racing down it and across the grass to the old red barn.

"That girl runs like a gazelle. I think she's in!" Lexie said.

"That's a relief. OK, I say now it's our turn. It's up to us to figure out where Todd's lurking, and to make sure he doesn't destroy any evidence."

"Sounds dangerous. What if Todd sees us? Angela wouldn't like to know you're doing that. Didn't we just promise to hide here?"

"That's why neither of them must know what we're doing."

~

IT DIDN'T TAKE LONG, fortunately, for Aseem to help Pat move her subcompact beater car to a safer section of the road. But by the time they were done, the two of them were soaked and grimy, and Aseem lamented that they would be sitting in the leather seats of his brand-new SUV.

"It only took a foot of water to kill your car," Aseem sighed as they settled in, their wet clothing squeaking against the leather. "What were you thinking, driving that… that car of yours up here in this weather? I mean, your car is—er, was—a bit of an antique. Have you already called a tow truck?"

"That was my second big problem. When water came into the car I panicked and dropped my phone in it. Man, am I glad you showed up—I can't thank you enough."

Aseem knew he should say "you're welcome" or "no problem," but it didn't feel particularly truthful. So instead he said, "I'll call the auto club for you."

Not surprisingly, the auto club dispatcher responded that they were overwhelmed with calls. The best thing to do was what they'd done: make sure the car was safely out of the water and out of the way.

"I might ask you why you're risking this beautiful new vehicle of yours in this terrible weather," Pat said. She squirmed in her seat and added, "Really sorry about the upholstery."

Aseem sighed. "The leather? It should be able to take a little water, right? That's why I picked it—not just luxury, durability. And this car's rated for more than two feet of water. I did loads of research—actually, Angela and I did the research together—"

"Of course you did," Pat chuckled.

"Well, you know I was starting my new job, and it would involve a lot of driving back and forth to the Peninsula."

"And this gets good mileage?"

"It does—it's a hybrid. But that's not all. Angela and I have a secret goal of seeing the whole state. We love Tahoe, the Gold Country, the entire coast—of course. We want to check out the desert. I love camping—"

"Angela loves camping?"

Aseem laughed. "Not so much. We took a trip to Yosemite a while ago, and we spent one night camping and two nights in the Ahwahnee. Anyway, the point is, we picked a car that can do it all safely. Great in snow, comfortable in heat, and it can handle up to two feet of standing water."

"I know who to ask for car-shopping advice, which I am sure I'll need soon, but I'm guessing you aren't out driving in the worst storm in decades just to test your car's wading ability."

"No. I've been trying to reach Angela for hours. I tried the inn's main line. I even tried Connie's business line."

"Me, too! I've been trying to reach Bea. At first I thought maybe the storm knocked out a cell tower, and that affected the internet. But there was nothing online about an outage—"

"I had the same thought—then it occurred to me that maybe the carriers can't even update their alerts because of the outage. The thing is, I didn't think about it too hard. I felt like I had to get to the inn."

Aseem sighed and paused for a moment. "I need to talk to Angela. We've been fighting, and I've been acting like it's all been her fault. Then it started to dawn on me that it's probably all *my* fault."

"Isn't it always the guy's fault?" Pat joked.

"When the woman is Angela, it's a good bet."

"Good news—there's the ranch. You're just moments away from apologizing."

"I've never looked forward to saying 'I'm sorry' so much."

Aseem smiled as he slowed down for the turn onto the road that led to the inn.

Pat waited a beat and then said, "You know, I've got a reason for heading out in this crazy weather. A good one, I think. I learned something about Roberta Newberg and how she got her money. And once I did, well, I hope I'm overreacting, but the dead phones made me a little nervous."

Aseem glanced at Pat curiously for a moment, but before he could say anything, a jacked-up black truck with a mismatched aftermarket cap over the cargo bed came flying out of the inn's parking lot toward them. The truck plowed through a large puddle on the side of the road, sending a wave over its own windshield, the tail end of which splashed onto driver's side of Aseem's SUV.

"Whoa! I don't like the looks of that!" Pat yelled.

"Should we follow them? We should follow them, right?"

Pat cried out "yes!" but Aseem hadn't waited for her approval before turning around in the inn driveway and racing to catch up with the speeding truck.

Hands clenching the wheel, Aseem leaned forward, his eyes trained on the truck ahead of him. The rain had slowed down, but Aseem still felt cautious. The gap between his car and the speeding truck was widening. Pat watched him anxiously.

"I know, I know. I have to drive a little faster."

"You can do it. I can tell you're a fantastic driver. And we already know this is the perfect all-weather vehicle."

Aseem took a deep breath, turned the wipers on high again, and pressed harder on the gas.

"That's it. We're gaining on them—"

The phone suddenly rang in the cradle between the two seats, startling them both. Aseem glanced at it quickly.

"It's Angel! Pat, can you—"

Pat turned the phone toward her and tapped the speaker-phone.

"Aseem?! I'm so happy I can reach you! Our phones were out. We thought it was a tower down, but now we think they might have been jammed. I just wanted to let you know—"

"Oh, Angel, I'm sorry!" Aseem exclaimed.

"No, I'm sorry!"

"But it was all—"

"Listen, Angela, Aseem, pardon the interruption, but we're in the middle of a crisis here."

"Pat? Is that you?"

"It's Pat, and she's right, Angel."

"We were approaching the inn and a pickup with big, raised tires blew past us," Pat continued.

"I had a hunch we shouldn't let them out of our sights. Am I right?"

"You're right! That's Todd's truck! Stay on it!"

"Will do!" Aseem shouted.

"Be careful. I love you," Angela said. "I gotta go. McGregor's calling me back! Whatever you do, keep up with the truck. Don't lose him!"

Angela clicked off.

They were quiet for a moment. Then Pat turned to Aseem and said, "Did she say don't lose *them* or don't lose *him?*"

BEA AND LEXIE crept down the hall from the kitchen toward the reception area. They were startled by a loud crack of thunder and both had to cover their mouths. Both of them were more nervous than either of them wanted to admit to themselves. There also were no windows in the kitchen or the hallway leading to the reception area. They assumed that was why they hadn't had the warning of a lightning flash to prepare them for the thunderclap.

They reached the reception area and scanned it from the hallway.

All clear, Bea turned and mouthed to Lexie.

They peered carefully through the glass of the main inn doors. From that angle, they could only see the end of the parking lot closest to the entrance, but it was clear of people and movement. They checked the supply closet. Locked, as usual.

They quietly huddled and agreed they'd next check the public spaces closest to the ballroom and all other areas where Todd had easy access for the play.

Next stop: the business center-cum-costume room.

They passed the ballroom and quietly hurried toward the end of the hall, hugging the wall, ready to dart into any open door if necessary. They passed the bathrooms where Lexie had hoped to capture a candid shot of Tibby, then found Lexie's hall-closet hiding spot. It was just past where the hallway they were in intersected with the one leading to the business center.

Lexie tapped Bea on the shoulder and tipped her head toward the closet. "It's a safe spot to watch for a minute."

Lexie turned the knob silently, but something prevented the door from opening more than a crack. She leaned on it with her shoulder and it budged a little further. The opening was a few inches now, enough for her to reach in and flip the light switch.

Lexie gasped, then covered her mouth with her hand.

Bea looked down and gasped, too.

Through the narrow opening of the door, on the floor of the closet, they saw the top of Grayson's lifeless head. He was bleeding from a bullet-sized hole in his temple.

"I say we skip the business center," Lexie whispered. "Ladies room?"

Through the exit door at the end of the hall, they heard the sound of a large truck starting up and driving off at high speed. Bea moved to the door and took a careful step outside.

"On the plus side, that was Todd's truck," she said. "And I think we know now what that 'thunder' we heard was."

"Should be safe for us to look for what he left behind in the business center now."

"If he left anything at all," Bea sighed.

"Exactly."

CHAPTER 27

Angela was soggy and muddy and cold, but she felt like a huge weight had been lifted from her shoulders.

She'd had to stand in the far corner of the cold barn and hold her phone against the wall, but she'd accomplished her mission: McGregor was on the way.

Todd was on the run, but with Aseem on his tail, he wouldn't get away. He was no longer a danger to anyone at the inn. McGregor had promised to alert law enforcement in neighboring towns. Once Aseem called back with Todd's location, his chances of escape would evaporate.

She couldn't wait to tell Bea and Lexie her

good news—and to start looking for that phone-jamming device.

And on top of all that, she felt overwhelmed with relief that things would soon be right again between her and Aseem.

No longer worried about hiding from Todd, Angela didn't try to climb back up the slippery, muddy grass to the kitchen. Instead, she sprinted down the trail toward the inn's front door, then onto the paved walkway that led to the kitchen service entrance.

Once inside, she expected to find Bea and Lexie and share her victorious news! But she was horrified to discover they had not stayed put as agreed.

Oh no! What did those two get up to?

She should have known they'd never have been able to resist figuring out what Todd was doing. Now she worried that whatever sleuthing they'd done might have led them right to Todd.

She pushed through the swinging door and found the ballroom eerily quiet.

Lorelei was still holding her gun but sitting on the end of the stage, her feet dangling. And unlike when Angela had peered at Lorelei through the kitchen door window, this time there was no doubt: Lorelei was crying.

The others in the room looked exhausted and stressed.

Adrenaline crash. I've been there.

Most of the guests were in chairs they'd arranged in a few small groups. The actors and crew on stage behind Lorelei looked dejected. Several had their heads in their hands.

Angela scanned the room as she hustled over to the check-in table. Her mother stood up, looking ready to burst into tears.

"Angela, I didn't know where you were—"

"It's OK now. It's all OK," Angela said, hugging her mother tightly. "Todd took off in his truck. Aseem and Pat are tailing him, and I was able to call McGregor from the barn. It'll be over soon."

"Where's Bea?" Maria said.

"And Lexie," Connie said absently. "Did she leave?"

Bijou was sitting quietly on Connie's lap. Connie was softly stroking her fur, looking completely dejected.

"That's what I was wondering. The three of us sneaked into the kitchen before Todd locked everything down. Lucky for us, Bijou's barking gave us a window. I ran outside to call McGregor. When I came back… they weren't in the kitchen," Angela said carefully, not wanting them to know that she was worried. "Give me a minute. I'll be back."

She walked toward the stage and shouted, "Lorelei—it's over! Todd's gone. Put the gun down."

Weeping louder, Lorelei gently placed the gun on the stage floor. "I don't even know how to use it. I told James—I mean, you know, Todd—I told him I didn't want to hold a gun."

"Good to know," Angela said sarcastically. She hurried to the stage and carefully picked up the diminutive weapon.

"It was an accident, I swear," Lorelei continued between sobs. "I only grabbed her—Roberta—a little harder than we'd done in rehearsal. It was play-acting, see—to make the scuffle Edie had in the dark sound more realistic.

"Sometimes, actors do those fighting and scuffling sound effects by themselves, stomping around enough for two, making self-defense noises, as you can imagine, but Grayson wanted to be sure it was realistic. I hadn't rehearsed it with Roberta much, since Louisa was supposed to play Edie. I thought I should play-choke her a little harder than usual, just to help her, but… but not hard enough to hurt her, I swear.

"Right before the show, James told me this was

an opportunity to plant a seed—to scare her—as a form of revenge, for what she did to our family. It might help her performance, too, he told me. I said things in her ear—"

"What kind of things?" Angela said sternly.

"Just… things to make her feel like her life could be at risk—that would only help her performance, right? And James suggested saying, 'What if your reputation is ruined forever, Roberta? You might be better off dead, then, wouldn't you?' I barely said any of it! Roberta just fell—she fell so hard, and so fast! I hardly tugged the necktie at all!"

"I'm sure Sergeant McGregor will want to hear the entire story of how you conspired with your boyfriend to commit murder. Oh, I mean, 'scare her.'"

"What? James—James Todd—he's not my boyfriend. He's my cousin. And what Roberta did to James's father, my uncle Paul, it was so wrong. He's dead, and the court let her get away with it! But we—at least, I—never meant for her to get hurt… and certainly not to *die*."

"Save it for the police. They'll be here any minute, Lorelei."

"It's… it's Lori. Lori Lyman. And my cousin, who you know as Todd Jameson, is James Todd."

"Did Todd—I mean, James—did your cousin do something to the cell service here?"

Lori stopped crying and seemed to smile a little. "That's a jammer. It was something my uncle, James's father, invented. He was such a clever man. A genius, really. Always tinkering with ideas, especially to protect children. His inventions were rejected—or worse, ripped off by big companies. With the jammers, he wanted to help families control kids' access to the internet. We put one here and a remote one up at Connie's place—"

"Aren't cell jammers illegal?"

Lori nodded morosely.

"Do you know how to turn it off?"

Lori stood up and walked behind the flat that represented the library wall in Helliwell Hall. She came back with a black device that looked like an old cell phone with two antennae. She pushed a little switch.

"It's off."

"Could someone check their phone for signal?" Angela said.

"It's working!"

"Mine, too!"

"It looks like the internet's coming back, too," Connie said, tapping on her laptop.

"Good," Angela said. "Now, I want you all to

know that the police will be here any minute. You've been so patient already, but I'm going to ask you to stay put until Sergeant McGregor gets here. He'll want to question each of you—at least, he'll want to be sure he knows how to get in touch. Call your families—let them know you're fine. If you have drivers waiting or coming back for you, let them know, too. But stay here until the police arrive, OK?"

The crowd nodded and murmured and Angela jogged lightly to the check-in desk.

"Can you two take care of this thing?" she said, dangling the little gun over the check-in table with all the caution of a bomb expert snipping a wire. "I'm going to find Bea and Lexie!"

"Give it to me," Connie said, grabbing the pistol. "What?" she added when she noticed Angela looking at her funny. "I grew up in a Kentucky whiskey family. Of course I know how to deal with a gun—especially a little peewee like this."

"OK, all yours," Angela said, then rushed out the door to find the other two.

~

BEA AND LEXIE didn't have to look hard for their first piece of evidence in the business center. They started with the cabinet that Roberta and Louisa used to stow their clothes when performing, where they found the dead woman's cell phone.

"Should we use gloves?" Lexie said.

"Got gloves?"

Lexie smirked. She pulled the sleeves of her hoodie down over her hands to keep her fingerprints off the device, then clicked the power button to restore the screen.

"Well would you look at that," Lexie said.

Bea peered over her shoulder. "Something to do with diabetes?"

"It's an app that controls her insulin delivery. Look—it feeds back blood sugar readings to determine how much she needs. But that's not the interesting part."

"I'm guessing those red 'override' tags means someone decided to give her a little extra."

"A lot more than a little extra. And look at the times—starting a few hours before and right up until her performance."

"And here I was thinking her drunk-and-cranky acting was improving."

"What do you think it means? I've heard some diabetics use insulin overdoses to commit suicide."

"Huh," Bea said, her brow scrunched. "Roberta

did give a mopey speech about her theater dreams going up in smoke. I suppose dying on her own stage has a certain… flair." Bea suppressed a chuckle.

Lexie smirked. "Indeed. Very operatic."

"Here's something else," Lexie said as she tapped the screen. "The last text she got was from Louisa. It says she's sorry for the short notice, but could she take over the role of Edie?"

"Oh, boy," Bea said, pulling a large kraft envelope from one of the drawers. "Drop the phone in here. We're gonna have to keep it safe until McGregor gets here."

Bea folded up the envelope and stuffed it in her largest pocket.

"Now what?" Lexie said. They'd carefully looked through the other cabinets and hadn't seen anything that looked relevant.

"Next stop, Todd's casita."

It was a short walk to the casitas from the back entrance to the inn. The rain was light now. Lexie held her hoodie over her and Bea's heads. Inside the casita, they found what appeared to be a treasure trove of evidence on the bed and on the desk.

"Hot diggity, I knew it!" Bea shouted, holding a t-shirt modified with pouches in the front on the inside and out. A few pieces of foam were still inside both pockets. Others were scattered on the floor by the bed. "No human person can look that much like Humpty Dumpty."

"Hasn't he heard of fake maternity bellies? Would've made his daily dress-up routine a lot easier."

"He could have had the same size belly every day that way, too," Bea laughed.

"His beard and hair were pretty realistic, though." Lexie held up the hairpieces, which still had traces of glue on them. "Looks like he was actually a blond. And check all this stuff out!"

In a few slightly haphazard piles were several other apparent clues. There were envelopes with the logo of a local bank ("Enough to hold twenty large?" Bea said).

In another pile, there were various printouts of internet stories about Roberta, her fortuitous windfall from Uncle Ambrose, and her rescue of Pinot Playhouse theater company. ("File under 'questionable generosity'?" Bea cackled.)

And there were a bunch of legal documents printed from the internet that referred to a probate dispute between Roberta and someone named "Paul Todd" ("Hmm. Todd Jameson, Paul Todd. Coincidence?" Bea said.)

"Oh, boy. This makes me a little sad."

Bea was looking at what appeared to be Todd's laptop on the desk. His email program was open to a long thread between him and Connie, in which he instructed her on drafting the *Grapevine* story. The last message told her that only he should communicate with the editor, but that he'd be sure she got the credit.

"Don't be sad," Lexie said. "At least we know she won't end up with that guy."

And then Lexie found what appeared to be the most useful clue of all: ransom-note-style pages that looked like early drafts of instructions to Louisa about getting Roberta onstage as Edie. The words had been cut from women's magazines. Unused ones were piled next to pasted-up versions of threatening notes.

"Follow instructions and 20 K comes your way," said one. "When you receive a text, collect your money and leave. DO NOT be seen," warned another.

"I can top that," Bea said, still poking around on Todd's laptop. "Look." Lexie peered over her shoulder at another email. This one was to 'Lori' from Todd, and it seemed to be asking her opinion about a "suicide note" he'd drafted to look like it was written by Roberta.

"Todd kept calling Lorelei 'Lori,'" Bea explained.

"So did Todd and Lori conspire to kill Roberta and make it look like suicide? How'd they get her cell phone?"

"In theory, Lori or James might have been able to do that. She helped on costumes, in addition to acting. And as the stage manager, Todd had the run of the place. So if Roberta got ready far enough in advance and stowed her phone in the locker, the timing might work for either of them to have used the phone to dose her."

"All the evidence here seems to stack up against Todd. This is his casita, right? And that's his laptop."

"True. This is all pretty darn perfect." Bea paused and grinned. "There's just one teeny, weeny problem."

Lexie picked up two of the cutouts and examined the ads on their backs. "Is it that we can't imagine Todd collecting magazines hawking mascara?"

"Count that as a second problem," Bea chuckled.

Lexie looked at Bea and then stared for a moment at all their little piles of clues.

"I get it. It's all too perfect, right?"

"Egg-zactly! I think we might have more sleuthing to do."

Angela heard the police cruiser arrive as she was rushing around the halls of the inn in search of Bea and Lexie. She ran out the rear door and found McGregor inside his car in the parking lot, scanning the scene through his open driver's side window. Then she saw Bea and Lexie standing in the doorway of the casita.

"There you two are!" she yelled with relief. "I guess you can tell I was able to reach McGregor," she added.

"Yep," Bea said. "Good job, girlie! You look pretty rough but I guess it was worth it. Why don't you both come in out of the rain and see what we found? Unless you're hoping the rain will wash some of the dirt off you?"

McGregor climbed out of his car and lumbered carefully to the door of the casita, dodging the huge puddles scattered throughout the parking lot and scanning the grounds around the rear of the inn as he walked.

"C'mon in, Sarge. We've got a lot of evidence for you, but first let me bring you up to speed.

We've got a dead body on stage in the ballroom, plus a bunch of potential witnesses—"

"That's why I'm here. Miss Garcia filled me in on that. Before you launch into anything, Miss Sickles, I assume you and Miss Greene haven't been disturbing any crime scenes?"

"Not if we can help it," Bea cackled. "But listen, this is important. There's another dead body in the housekeeping closet. It's right inside the door Angela just came out of."

"Oh, no! Who is it?" Angela said, running through the possibilities in her mind. "Who wasn't in the ballroom…?"

"I'll give you a hint," Bea said. "On the plus side, he won't be hitting on anyone anymore."

"Grayson?"

"Yep," Bea said. "Sergeant, by 'Grayson,' she means the famous off-Broadway theater director, Grayson Gates. I mean, he's famous if you follow that sort of thing."

McGregor rolled his eyes. "OK, I'll take a quick look here and head to the hall closet next. Officer Babiak will be here as soon as he finishes a safety call. This weather has—never mind," he said, pulling out his phone to direct the junior officer to the ballroom to collect contact information, and to alert the coroner to come for two bodies, not one. "What have we got here?"

"The person dead on the ballroom stage is Roberta Newberg," Bea said. "We've found her phone. It has a clue about how she might have been killed."

Lexie pulled the phone carefully from the envelope and turned it on, then quickly explained how the app on the phone would have given Roberta repeated overdoses of insulin, adding that this might have made her weaker and easier to strangle—or she might have died from the fall, or from the overdose, or a combination.

"Then there are all these documents, which seem to show Todd Jameson—I mean, James Todd—had a reason to harm Roberta. And we saw Todd's truck high-tailing it out of here—"

"Luckily, Aseem's tailing him!" Angela blurted. "The truck blew past him as he was arriving here. He turned around and started following him!"

"Miss Garcia, did you advise him to stop following the suspect—like I told you? Because that's simply not safe—"

"I know, but I knew you'd be here any minute, and you could track his cell phone or something. And I told him to hang back, just keep the truck in sight. Isn't it better that you know where Todd went?"

"Call Aseem right now and tell him to stop chasing that truck!"

Angela pulled out her phone and it started to ring before she could even tap Aseem's number.

"Angel, I need help." Aseem's voice sounded breathless as it projected through the speaker. "We're at a gas station—I was running out of gas and luckily the truck was, too. I was afraid we'd have to stop the chase—"

"Young man," bellowed McGregor, "you *do* have to stop the chase. Right now!"

McGregor tilted his head to hold his phone between his shoulder and his ear and pulled a small notebook out of his pocket.

"You're going to give me your location and we're going to have local cops intercept this driver! This suspect is likely responsible for two murders! You are to stay away!"

"OK," Aseem said, sounding chastened.

"Where is this gas station?"

McGregor took his notes and his phone and stepped onto the landing outside the door of the casita to call in the instructions. When he finished, he took the opportunity for another scan of the grounds behind the buildings.

"It's OK," Angela said softly into her cell's speaker. "McGregor stepped out to call in your location."

"There's something else I want to tell you, but I've got to hurry. Pat and I worked up a little scheme. The driver of the truck went inside to pay, so Pat decided to create a little distraction at the cashier stand. Then I was going to try to peek in the truck. Now that Pat's keeping her busy—"

"I've got an idea!" Bea said with a cackle. "Go poke a hole in one of her tires!"

"Wait—keeping *her* busy? *Her* tires?" Angela cried.

"That's another thing I wanted to tell you. The driver of the truck—it's not a man."

"Don't worry about that, handsome. I've already figured out exactly who it is," Bea said. "Go —see what you can find in the truck. And if you poke the tires—bonus!"

"Be careful!" Angela said.

"I will!" Aseem said as he clicked off.

"OK, Bea, time to fill me in on who you think the murderer is," Angela said, throwing up her hands. "And how you figured it out this time."

"I'd like to know, too," McGregor said, stomping mud off his feet on the doormat before stepping back into the little cottage.

"Here's the thing," Bea said. "This person has left piles of evidence to point the finger at Mr. Fake-cop-slash-stage-manager, and it's awfully neat and tidy. And there's a particular person I can think of who seems to have disappeared. And, what a coinkydink, she's also the person who would have had the easiest time accessing Roberta's phone and making a money drop for Louisa."

"Martina!" Angela cried.

"But doesn't that leave one big question?" Lexie said. "If Martina's in his truck, alone—"

Angela gasped. "Then where's Todd?"

Angela's phone rang—it was Aseem calling back. She quickly put him on speakerphone.

"Don't worry, Angel, I did what McGregor said. I'm not following the truck. I'm still at the gas station. But guess what? Luckily, I had a screwdriver in the glove box, so I did manage to let air out of one of her tires," Aseem laughed. "I bet a flat tire will put her out of commission soon. Wait, am I on speaker again?"

"I'm gonna pretend I didn't hear that!" McGregor roared.

"Um, yes, honey, you're on speaker again," Angela said.

Aseem sighed. "Forget what I said about the tire. Here's something you will all want to hear. I saw two things in the cab of the truck. A big, lumpy duffel full of something… and an old shovel."

"That shovel! It's rusty, right? With an old wooden handle, cracked and bleached by the sun? It was here, near the casitas."

"That's it!"

"Young man, Angela—I'm going to ask you to hang up now because we've got some evidence-gathering to do here. Like I said, you are to stay put until the local cops arrive, Aseem. Got it?"

"Got it."

"That shovel reminds me of a question I've wanted to ask since the second I walked up to this casita," McGregor said. "What's underneath that fake boulder in the back yard?"

"Fake boulder?!" Angela cried.

CHAPTER 28

"Even from a distance, I thought it had the look of a fake boulder," McGregor said, wiping stray raindrops from his thick mustache. "I took a chance at knocking on it. Sure enough, it felt hollow."

McGregor, Bea, Angela, and Lexie were standing on the mushy grass about twenty yards behind the casitas. McGregor had pulled an over-sized umbrella from the trunk of his cruiser and was holding it over all their heads, even though the rain had slowed to little more than a hearty drizzle.

The coroner's van and another cruiser were now parked in the inn lot. Officer Babiak had started interviewing witnesses and examining the scene around Roberta's body in the ballroom. The coroner had just wheeled a gurney in from the parking lot and was starting her work as well.

"How could you have guessed the boulder was fake?" Angela said.

"I've seen a lot of fake boulders. They're common up here in wine country. People use them to cover up pool filters, energy meters, anything that will ruin their landscaping," McGregor said. "If you've never used one before, I'm not surprised you were fooled, Miss Garcia. They wouldn't be worth anything if they didn't look real, would they? Mind if I do the honors?"

Bea and Angela nodded and McGregor handed Bea the umbrella. Then he bent down with a grunt to lift one edge of the boulder, but it wouldn't budge.

"Huh. This is the biggest fake I've ever seen, but I can't imagine it weighs more than sixty or seventy pounds."

"Too bad I left my cane in the ballroom," Bea said. "You could have used it like a lever."

"I can help," Angela said, grabbing an edge. Lexie pitched in, too.

With a heave, they got their side of the boulder

off the ground. Something shook loose with a *thunk* and the boulder tipped over the rest of the way easily.

The heavy object that had been wedged against the inside of boulder—Todd's foot—fell with a creepy thud, drawing a squeak from Angela. His body was bent at the waist, his butt stuffed inside a deep, narrow hole.

"How deep is that?" Lexie said, peering down the narrow gap between Todd's body and the wall of the hole. "Must be eight, ten feet? Look—I think there's something else underneath him."

"I guess you got the answer to your question about what happened to Todd," Bea said.

"That sticky gash on the top of his head sure looks like a shovel could have done it," McGregor said.

Angela squinted at the body in the hole. "How are you so sure it's him? He doesn't look much like Todd to me."

"Skinnier, blonder for sure, but the pants and the shoes match up," Bea said. "And he's about the right height. And look—there's a little piece of foam belly stuck in his belt."

"We'll verify it's him using our normal methods, but it seems pretty likely," McGregor said. "We'll check for gunshot residue, too."

"Digging that hole would have been some work, especially doing it a little at a time at night," Angela said. "That must be why Todd drove Grayson out of his casita with noise—so that he and Martina could do their digging undetected."

"And I bet he gave her his key, since he was always working late. He thought they'd be meeting up to escape," Bea said. "But she surprised him with a different plan."

"And a shovel," Angela said dryly.

A FEW HOURS LATER, the power was restored. A beautiful moon illuminated the early morning sky, and the only remaining signs of the terrible storm were fresh breezes, massive puddles, and very soggy grass, littered with stray branches.

McGregor and his junior officer sent the bleary-eyed guests, cast, and crew home. Aseem and Pat made it to the inn safely—full of excitement over their role in the capture of Martina (though they were careful not to gush too much about their chase when McGregor was listening). The coroner had completed her second errand—running Grayson's body back to the morgue—and was back to finally finish the night by ferrying James Todd to the same place.

When the police eventually pulled Todd's body from the hole, they found what he and Martina had been digging for underneath him: a tall iron strongbox with "Gold Country Express" in faded, old-fashioned stenciling. The box was empty, of course—the contents undoubtedly transferred to the duffel bag that Aseem had spotted in the front seat of Todd's truck.

"We're close to done, but we're going to have to come back tomorrow," McGregor said. He and Officer Babiak had taped off the crime scenes and McGregor had sent the junior officer home. "We need a few hours shut-eye. Everyone involved is dead or arrested, so I think it's safe to leave these scenes unguarded until morning."

"Don't worry, we know the drill," Bea said. "We won't touch anything."

"Thanks for the help today," McGregor said.

"Thanks for coming so quickly. Nice work, Beef Jerky—I mean, nice work, Sergeant McGregor," Bea said respectfully, earning a sweet smile from Angela.

"You, too, Beatrice—I mean, Bea. Or rather, Miss Sickles," McGregor said.

"Beatrice is OK—you got a one-day pass. Even Tater Tot is fine for twenty-four hours."

Bea looked away for a beat and smiled to herself. Being called Beatrice got under her skin, but she didn't mind being called Tater Tot much at all.

"OK. Nice job, Tater Tot," McGregor said with a grin. "And you, too, Angela, Aseem, and Pat."

"Don't forget Lexie," Angela said.

"You all make a good team."

"You know," Bea said, "we have a little crime-solving custom around here. Would you like to join us for my traditional sleuth summation?"

McGregor looked extremely dubious, but Angela piped up, "How about we do it in a week? The chef and staff will be back by then. We'll have a special dinner. Do you like surf and turf? You can bring Mrs. McGregor, too."

McGregor looked tempted by the prospect of a fancy dinner, compliments of the richest person in his jurisdiction.

Bea raised a finger and said, "Angie, I know, let's have the chef make a special dessert in honor of McGregor. How about a beignet and zeppole bar?" Bea guffawed, slapping her knee. "Get it, McGregor? Beignets?"

"Very funny, *Beatrice*," McGregor said. "I know beignets are doughnuts."

"Like I always say, you're not as dumb as you look."

McGregor headed home and everyone else

headed to bed—Pat, Lexie, and Maria all bunking with Bea in her suite.

Maria knew Angela and Aseem needed their space, and nobody had enough energy to drive anywhere, not even to the cottage. Angela had suggested Grayson's vacant suite next door, but her mother said the idea made her too sad. Maria and Lexie took a rollaway and the pull-out sofa and promised Pat and Bea they'd do their best not to wake them when they headed back to Sacramento in just a few hours.

Finally back in her suite, Angela felt refreshed by a much-needed shower. She was sitting at her desk in her pajamas when she said, "Honey, I know it's too late for a 'real' talk, but I have something to say that just can't wait."

Aseem was already in bed, almost asleep, mumbling and fading fast. "Angel, if you're going to apologize, please, please don't. It was my fault. I shouldn't have been so impatient. And I promise to make it right tomorrow—"

"No—it wasn't your fault. I *did* have cold feet. I just didn't realize it. It had to do with my father, and how he disappeared... I never knew why, and now I do—don't worry, I can explain all of that tomorrow.

"But listen, there's something I really want you to see tonight. Can you try to stay awake one more minute while I pull up a web page? Please?" She was giggling as she tapped frantically on her laptop.

Aseem's eyes were closed but he smiled and mumbled OK.

Angela picked up her laptop and sat down on the other side of the bed. Gently, she placed the computer on Aseem's chest.

"OK, OK, I'm awake," he laughed, opening his eyes.

"Look—I found it," Angela said. "I found it!" Her eyes were shiny with happy tears.

On the screen was an antique ring with a brilliant pink sapphire in the center. The unusual stone was surrounded by small diamonds arranged in little petal shapes, all held in a simple gold setting.

"I didn't realize it was just what I wanted until I saw it. It's Victorian. And I think it's just perfect!"

"I think so, too," Aseem said sleepily. "Oh, Angel, I'm so glad you found a ring that's just... yours."

"Good—because I arranged for us to pick it up

in San Francisco tomorrow. I hope you won't mind a little more driving."

"I don't mind. But we'd better take your car. Mine needs a professional detailing," Aseem said, smiling as he drifted off to sleep.

Ten days later, a reunion of sorts was happening in the ballroom.

Pat, Lexie, Maria, and Bea were chatting over wine and a special appetizer designed just for Bea: miniature egg sandwiches, cut into rounds the size of a quarter, served on toothpicks.

Back at the inn for the first time since Grayson's death, Maria made a beeline for the door when she saw Angela and Aseem walk in arm-in-arm. Maria didn't say a word to either of them. Instead, her gaze homed in on the sparkling ring on her daughter's left hand. Her excited *oohs* and *aahs* were everything any daughter would hope for.

The ballroom itself had been restored to its

festive self. The jury-rigged stairs on the stage had been dismantled and the center staircase put back in place. A blaze roared and crackled in the fireplace. Lights twinkled on the gargantuan wreath above the fire. And Angela had refreshed the Christmas tree in the corner with pink garlands that nearly matched the shade of her unusual ring.

"Someone's in a pink phase," Bea said.

"And you're in your mustard period?" Angela said. Bea's brand-new track suit was a dark yellow color, tinged with brown. Her bronze-colored sneakers were a perfect complement.

"I prefer 'goldenrod,'" Bea said, smoothing her jacket sleeves with her hands.

Maria laughed. "Actually, Angela has always loved pink. Right, mija?"

"It's true," Angela said. "I've never not been in a pink phase."

Connie arrived with her plus five: Bijou and her adorable, rascally dachshund puppies, Garnet, Paprika, Jonathan, and Dames. The pups were almost fully grown now but had lost little of their bouncy puppy attitude—especially Paprika and Dames, the troublemakers of the bunch. Connie unhooked the pups' leashes and gave them the run of the ballroom.

Angela and Aseem were as happy as ever. Fortunately, everyone currently in the room was one hundred percent 'Team Aseem' and had a natural immunity against sweetness overload.

"I see you two have gotten over your fight," Bea said.

"It was all my fault!" Angela and Aseem said at once.

"No, Angel—it really was—"

"Stop it, Aseem," Angela said, squeezing his arm tighter and smiling at him beatifically. "I've already explained why it was my fault."

"I'm not required to accept your unnecessary apology," Aseem said, kissing her on the cheek.

"Excellent!" Bea declared. "The balance of cringe-worthy affection and cold-blooded cynicism in our world is officially restored. Lexie, I thank you for being here to help me hold down the other side of the scale."

"Just doin' my job."

"Shall I begin my recap?" Bea said, brandishing her cane as she liked to do. Between dancing and a profound attitude adjustment, Bea had decided a year ago she didn't need the cane for walking, but it still made an excellent prop for various purposes, including punctuating her points as she strode around the ballroom.

"You wouldn't start without us, would you?" a

familiar voice shouted from the hallway. A second later, dashing Northern California FBI agent Drew Faulkner appeared in the door alongside Sergeant McGregor.

"Drew!" Angela said. "What are you doing here?"

"You know I never miss Bea's drawing room routines if I can help it."

"Technically, he's on this case," McGregor said. "Once we knew what Martina had in that duffel bag, we had to involve the FBI. But I also told him there'd be lobster."

"What was in the bag? We've been dying to know!" Angela said.

"I've got theories," Bea said. "Were there gold nuggets in the strongbox? Jewels? Doubloons?"

"Nope," Drew said. "The bag was stuffed with bearer bonds. They're dated all the way back to a railroad company in the 1800s. Oh—and besides the bonds, there was Martina's disguise. She isn't actually a blond, in case you were wondering. And her real nose is cute as a button."

"Bearer bonds?" Bea chortled. "Like in *Die Hard?*"

"Exactly—but a lot older than the ones in that movie."

"Who gets them now?" Pat said. "Do you have to track down the original owner?"

"Almost certainly not. They were left behind by the prior owner of this property, and the bonds were likely buried here while they owned it. That means—"

"Bea gets them?" Maria piped up.

"Yep."

Pat roared with laughter. "Just what Bea needs. More money!"

"Don't worry yourself over my accounting problems. Those old things are probably worthless. Does the company even exist anymore?"

"You're right, Bea. The bonds couldn't be redeemed today," McGregor chimed in.

"What a numbskull Martina is—she'll be going to prison for bonds she couldn't even cash," Bea said.

"Um, and… murder," Lexie said.

"Oh, I doubt she was planning on redeeming them," Drew said, grinning. "They're worth at least two or three times their face value as collectibles."

A group gasp, followed by peals of laughter, echoed through the ballroom.

"Like I said, Bea, just what you need—more money!" Pat said, chuckling.

"I could use some help selling them. I'll want to be sure I get the best price. How'd you like to be my agent—at, say, twenty-percent commission?"

"Deal!" Pat squealed.

Angela's brow crinkled and a grin formed on her lips.

"I know that look, girlie. Someone's got a business idea."

"I was just thinking that Lost Gold Rush Treasure could make an interesting theme for a summer event."

"Sounds like fun! We get the guests digging for loot and keep anything they find," Bea said, earning a frown from Angela.

The chef came from the kitchen with two trays of decidedly sophisticated appetizers, including asparagus in puff pastry and bacon-wrapped scallops.

"Boo," Bea said. "Got any more egg things?"

"No, not 'boo!'" Angela said to the chef. "These look absolutely beautiful."

"And delicious," McGregor said, loading up a plateful.

The chef smiled and nodded before heading back to the kitchen.

A server made the rounds and filled everyone's glasses, and Bea moved to the front of the room to begin her recap. Pat helped out by tapping her glass with a spoon.

"And so another tale of woe begins, this time with an inheritance that was epically ginormous, well into eight figures, but apparently still not enough for dearly departed Roberta," Bea said. "As Pat's eagle-eyed legal research revealed, at the start of probate, Roberta might have honestly thought her estranged uncle Ambrose was being ripped off by Paul Todd. Unfortunately, she refused to back down even when it was clear she was wrong."

"Her stubborn greed cost poor Paul Todd his life," Pat said grimly. "When you accuse someone of a terrible crime like elder abuse and financial exploitation, it can stick even when it's simply not true. That can prove devastating for a tender-hearted person."

"Clever lawyers work awful magic sometimes," Angela cried. "Of course this left Todd—James Todd—enraged. His father had been Ambrose's only friend. Roberta's show of gratitude for the millions she'd unexpectedly inherited from Ambrose was to ruin the one person he'd counted on in his dying years. No wonder poor Paul was driven to suicide!"

"Well said, Angela," Bea said grumpily. "Now may I please continue?"

"Sorry," Angela said, suppressing a giggle.

"Cousin Lori was sure James wasn't the murdering type. At least, she feels certain he didn't start out that way. Heartbroken and infuriated, sure—but Lori believes he would've been contented just to terrorize Roberta—and try to ruin her reputation.

"James Todd's scheme to inflict painful revenge on Roberta Newberg began with a plan to go undercover at Pinot Playhouse. He'd dropped out of a brief stint in the police academy, but he'd learned enough to fake his press release."

"Aided by me," Connie sighed, and Angela nodded at her sympathetically.

"Lori had performed in community theater since middle school. She knew she'd be readily accepted at Pinot Playhouse. And with her help, her cousin presented himself as an irresistible gift to a struggling company: an experienced manager who didn't care about being paid. Naturally, cheapskate Roberta fell right into that trap!"

"Surely he didn't actually have experience, did he?" Aseem said. "I mean, those sets—"

"And the scary swinging stage light!" Angela

blurted. "I mean, he wasn't trying to terrify Tibby on purpose, was he?"

"That stage light screwup could have ruined their whole plan. No, clearly, he had no experience whatsoever," Bea said. "Lucky for him, Roberta had no experience running a theater, either.

"Easy as pie, he gains the access he needs to destroy the theater, and to put Roberta under suspicion as an arsonist. It was only an itty bitty taste of the medicine Roberta had dished out to poor Paul. But maybe Lori was right—maybe it would have been enough revenge for James, if only he hadn't met that one particular person—"

"Martina!" the others shouted together.

"It's funny," Angela said. "Tibby was the one who talked about finding historical artifacts and lost fortunes, but Martina was actually treasure-hunting for real."

"By the way, her real name's Emily and she grew up in Nevada City," Drew said.

"The heart of the Gold Country," Angela said.

"Yep. That's how she caught the treasure-hunting bug. She admits to dreaming of lost Gold Rush riches since childhood. There are loads of people out there who sell unsuspecting dreamers information about buried treasure.

Emily's spent years of her life learning the difference between the few true stories and all the fakes. Of course, this wasn't her only get-rich-quick scheme. She was on the hunt for any fast scores, legal or not."

"Thank you. Now if all of you are done talking, may I continue, please?" Bea said, eyebrows raised.

The group nodded and chuckled under their breath.

"We already know that Emily met Todd Jameson, who we now know as James Todd, through Pinot Playhouse. By now, Emily's been scheming, secretly, to gain access to our backyard. She's slumming at the worst playhouse in Northern California as 'Martina,' just to be closer to our place while she figures out a plan. Then in a weak moment, Lori tells her about her poor uncle's demise and how her cousin Todd is joining the production."

"O... M... G...!" Angela said. "People literally tell their hairstylists everything!"

Bea sighed and gave Angela a side-eye, then continued.

"So Emily decides to work her abundant feminine charms on our supposed stage manager. She convinces him that Roberta will be made whole by insurance—shouldn't he be serving up a little more painful revenge?

"She suggests they team up and kill two birds with one stone: teach Roberta a lesson and split the big find—at least, that's what Emily told Todd —er, James—would happen with the treasure buried out back. He just needs to move their production of *The Ratcatcher* to our inn—"

"I was such a chump. He fooled me just like Martina—I mean, Emily—fooled him. If I hadn't introduced him to you, Angela—" Connie moaned.

"Even if you hadn't been charmed by James, he still would have come to me, I'm sure of it," Angela said. "You were just a kind of insurance. And I'm pretty sure I would have bought their story even without you involved, Connie."

"Well, if Angela hadn't mixed up my brain with all her social graces, I would've just punched him in the gut two weeks ago!" Bea snorted. "Then we all would have kicked that faker to the curb."

"I wish you had," Connie said.

"Listen, the way our wannabe Bonnie and Clyde fooled you two is nothing compared to the way they roped poor Lori in. They knew she'd be up for scaring Roberta and paying her back for what happened to Paul Todd. We still don't know if James developed an appetite for murder, but it seems likely that Lori hadn't thought that was on the table. Maybe James just wanted to scare Roberta to death and ruin her theater for good.

"Either way, Emily's insulin hacking was diabolical genius," Lexie said.

Bea nodded, rubbing her palms together. "That's *definitely* going in my next mystery story."

"The time zone on Roberta's phone was the key to the whole thing," Lexie said. "Good catch, Bea."

"Why thank you! We were trying to figure out how someone could have tampered with Roberta's phone hours before the play. The answer was obvious: they didn't!"

"Aleutian time is two hours behind us. Who knew?" Lexie said.

"So Martina—er, Emily—grabs the phone once Roberta has stored it before showtime and starts dosing her with more insulin?" Angela said.

"Yep. And she manually changes the timezone first—that makes the app timestamp the overrides as if they happened hours before, when only Roberta herself definitely had access to the phone," Lexie said.

"If she'd remembered to change it back, her

plan to make it look like suicide would have had better odds," Bea said.

"Todd lucked out with the storm knocking out the phones," Connie piped up. "I was supposed to collect the cell phones originally. I had a big basket under the check-in desk for that. He was going to say that it was convention for performances of *The Ratcatcher*."

"Oh, right—the big speech about not revealing the twist," Bea said.

"I guess now I'll never find out what the twist is," Angela said, smiling. "Don't worry, Bea—I'll live."

"We can't say the same for poor Grayson," Maria said sadly. "He took one look at that article about Todd Jameson joining the police and felt sure it was fake. That's why Grayson charged out after Todd."

Bea shook her head. "James must have run into Grayson on his way to split the booty with Martina. What an unfortunate waste. Little did James know his hot date with his new girlfriend and a shared fortune was actually a rendezvous with the wrong end of a shovel."

"We've confirmed Grayson was shot with James Todd's gun," McGregor said.

"And there we have it," Bea said, waving her

cane with a flourish and taking a deep bow. Her audience laughed and rewarded her performance with a round of applause. "And look—as usual, my timing's perfect."

The chef and two servers were setting a round table near the stage with place settings, open bottles of wine, and heaping platters of lobster, grilled steaks, and steamed vegetables. They all sat down and tucked in, wordlessly at first. Then Bea broke the silence.

"Lexie and I still haven't finished our true-crime book based on last month's murders, and now we've got fodder for another one! Roberta was a lucky bonus murder. In retrospect, though, we should have seen it coming."

"Isn't that always how it is with murder?" Lexie said.

"Bonus murder? You know it's bad karma to act like a murder is good news," Pat said. "And besides, technically, it's *murders.*"

"Even Roberta deserved better," Angela added somberly. "Almost deserved better, I guess. Grayson definitely did."

"I agree with Bea. Murder was bad news for Roberta and Grayson, good news for us," said Lexie. "We don't have to be finished with our current one to put another in the pipeline. I can work on two at a time."

"Great idea!" blurted Angela.

Whatever issues Angela had with Lexie, there was no denying that her true crime collaborations with Bea were just fine for business.

"I've never seen anyone dump her morals so fast at the doorway of commerce," Bea roared.

"I can't help myself. I love publishing best-sellers."

"We can call it *The Ratcatcher Murders: Volunteering for Vengeance*," Lexie said.

"Or *Peril at Pinot Playhouse: A Ruined Reputation, a Son's Revenge, and a Fortune in Buried Treasure*."

"We don't have to decide on a title now," Angela said, a little twinkle in her eye. "But we're off to a good start."

AFTER STUFFING THEMSELVES, the group relocated to the comfy armchairs and sofa that had been set in front of the fireplace.

The chef arrived with the promised dessert tray: house-made doughnuts from cuisines around the world. There were powdery beignets, custard-filled zeppole, and churros with chocolate.

Everyone declared they were too stuffed to eat another bite, then immediately helped themselves.

"My compliments to the chef," Drew finally said. He'd swiftly grabbed the seat next to Angela on the sofa, sandwiching her between him and Aseem.

"This chef's a star, girlie," Bea said to Angela. "You finally found yourself a keeper."

"Speaking of keepers," Drew said, "does this shiny bauble of yours mean your wedding's actually going to happen? No hope—I mean, no sign—of cold feet?"

"Absolutely on the wedding," Angela said, clenching Aseem's arm. "And no way on the cold feet."

"Actually, I thought he was talking to me. And now that you mention it...." Aseem said.

"Very funny," Angela said.

"To be fair, technically, I don't have to give up unless and until 'I do' is said," Drew teased.

"About that, we've got news," Angela squealed. "It won't be long now. Aseem and I decided we're not doing the year-long planning thing. We're going to get married in Vegas!"

"What about your parents?" Pat piped up. "Won't they be expecting the whole, you know, dog and pony show?"

"We'll have a real wedding, but we decided on Vegas to pull it all together more quickly," Angela said. "We discovered the most luxurious hotels there have great ideas for multi-cultural weddings. And they take care of everything."

"We know we'll never please everybody," Aseem said. "But at least my parents have already gotten one big to-do thanks to my brother and Preeti."

"I don't care at all about big wedding or small," Maria said. "Whatever you two decide, just send me an invitation with a plus one and I'll be thrilled."

"But… the wedding could be in just a few months," Angela said. "Are you sure you'll have a new plus one so fast after, you know…? Oh, Mamá, I'm so sorry about what happened."

Angela gazed at Maria with limitless compassion and put her hand gently on her mother's arm.

Maria looked at her daughter with obvious confusion. "What am I missing? So fast after… what? Oh! Oh, no!"

Then Maria started laughing—and she seemed to find it difficult to stop.

"You thought—did you think I was with Grayson?"

Angela turned red as a beet and Maria started chuckling again.

"You were acting awfully close to him, and then you told me I should have been able to guess about your new relationship—"

"I just met him!" Maria said, laughing again.

"It seemed like you hit it off," Angela said, frowning.

"Grayson asked me to help him stay out of trouble with Pinot Playhouse and Roberta. I guess it can't hurt now to reveal that he'd been fired from his last Off-Broadway play. He was accused of several kinds of misconduct. He was protected by a confidentiality agreement, but rumors were flying.

"Volunteering with Roberta was supposed to help rebuild his reputation, but he was having a hard time containing his temper. If Roberta fired him or the cast complained to the press, that would have just proved the rumors true. I was sort of… I guess you could call it 'coaching' him.

"I thought you would have guessed my new relationship because it's my old friend Darnell. Everyone always said we have chemistry. Didn't you think so, too? About six months ago, he said he wanted to learn Spanish. I said I'd give him a lesson over dinner, and one thing led to another—."

"Oh, I'm so happy!" Angela said, throwing her arms around her mother. "Wait—isn't Darnell about ten years younger than you?"

"Eight," Maria said with a wink. "But who's counting?"

"Good for you, Maria," Bea said. "It's a new millennium. Cradle-robbing is the new appropriate dating. Actually, maybe he's a little old for you."

"Darnell is more than welcome at our wedding," Angela said. "We'll know the date soon. I'll book the venue when I go to Las Vegas in March for a business trip. I got invited to speak at a media conference—"

"Well, well, well," Bea said, standing up and rapping her cane on the floor. "Wait just one moment, Ms. Garcia. Are you intending to represent our organization at this conference?"

"Yes," Angela laughed. "Last time I checked, I am the president of it."

"No offense—you are, obviously, our most highly rated employee—but this does *not* seem like the kind of activity you should take on without proper supervision from the top!"

"Especially because that famous million-dollar

senior poker tournament you've been talking about for a year is in March," Pat shouted from across the room, laughing.

"You don't say? That poker tournament? In Las Vegas? In March?" Bea said, tilting her head and cupping her chin in her hand. "Quite a fortunate fluke. I guess that means only one thing."

"I know exactly what it means," Angela said, giggling.

Then Angela, Bea, and Pat shouted in unison. "ROAD TRIP!"

THE END

Thank you for reading *Of Mice and Murder!* If you'd like to read a short epilogue, please visit this page on pepperfrostauthor.com. (While you're there, check out a deleted scene, too!)

BOOKS BY PEPPER FROST

The Return of Betty Snickerdoodle (A Betty Snickerdoodle Mystery #1)

A Sleuth Is Born (A Betty Snickerdoodle Mystery #2)

Bake It Like Betty (A Betty Snickerdoodle Mystery #3)

Mixed to Death (A Betty Snickerdoodle Mystery #4)

Murder Takes a Bough (A Betty Snickerdoodle Mystery #5)

Of Mice and Murder (A Betty Snickerdoodle Mystery #6)

Free for newsletter subscribers (sign up at pepperfrostauthor.com):

Betty's Big Game (a Betty Snickerdoodle short story)

READY FOR MORE BETTY?

Thank you for reading
Of Mice and Murder

Be the first to know about upcoming releases in
the *Betty Snickerdoodle* series.
Sign up for Pepper's newsletter at
pepperfrostauthor.com/newsletter

Books 1- 6 are now available.

Sign up for the newsletter or follow Pepper on
Facebook to be among the first to know when she
release new books.

Pepper's on Facebook!
Follow her at **www.facebook.com/
pepperfrostauthor**

To contact the author, email
pepper@pepperfrostauthor.com